## 'Are you truly all alone? Have you no one to protect you?'

Charles read the answer in her face. Looking into her eyes, he was conscious of an overwhelming desire to hold her close and tell her that he would care for her as long as they both lived.

No other woman had ever made him feel quite like this: his stomach clenching with a fierce desire that shocked him by its intensity. And yet it was more than desire—a feeling he had never experienced before that he did not yet understand. He reached out, touching her cheek with one finger.

'Arabella...

# AUTHOR NOTE

In the late eighteenth and early nineteenth century there was a passion for gothic novels. When huge old houses were lit by candlelight, and there were none of today's modern conveniences, it must have been gorgeously frightening for society ladies to read of young girls cruelly locked away and at the mercy of evil men. How much more terrifying would it be for a young girl stolen from the bosom of a loving family to be forced to take part in a satanic ritual? And think of how her family must have suffered when she could not be found! But in the age of Romance there were at least three brave men willing to walk through hellfire for the sake of the women they loved.

This trilogy deals with the abduction of Miss Sarah Hunter and the search for her by her brother Charles, the Earl of Cavendish and Mr John Elworthy. It began with Elizabeth Travers and the Earl of Cavendish, and continues with Charles Hunter and Lady Arabella Marshall, ending in the last book with Sarah's own story.

The element of darkness is balanced by the thrill of romance, and I hope you will love reading it as much as I enjoyed writing it for you.

Look for Sarah's story in
*A Worthy Gentleman*
Coming April 2007

# A WEALTHY WIDOW

### Anne Herries

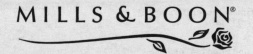

**MILLS & BOON®**

First published in Great Britain 2006
Paperback edition 2007
Harlequin Mills & Boon Limited,
Eton House, 18-24 Paradise Road, Richmond, Surrey TW9 1SR

© Anne Herries 2006

ISBN-13: 978 0 263 85159 5
ISBN-10:    0 263 85159 1

Set in Times Roman 10½ on 13½ pt.
04-0207-92344

Printed and bound in Spain
by Litografia Rosés S.A., Barcelona

**Anne Herries**, winner of the Romantic Novelists' Association ROMANCE PRIZE 2004, lives in Cambridgeshire. She is fond of watching wildlife, and spoils the birds and squirrels that are frequent visitors to her garden. Anne loves to write about the beauty of nature, and sometimes puts a little into her books, although they are mostly about love and romance. She writes for her own enjoyment, and to give pleasure to her readers.

**Recent novels by the same author:**

THE ABDUCTED BRIDE
CAPTIVE OF THE HAREM
THE SHEIKH
A DAMNABLE ROGUE*
RANSOM BRIDE

*Winner of the Romantic Novelists' Association ROMANCE PRIZE*

**and in the Regency series *The Steepwood Scandal:***

LORD RAVENSDEN'S MARRIAGE
COUNTERFEIT EARL

**and in *The Elizabethan Season:***

LADY IN WAITING
THE ADVENTURER'S WIFE

**and in *The Banewulf Dynasty:***

A PERFECT KNIGHT
A KNIGHT OF HONOUR
HER KNIGHT PROTECTOR

**and in *The Hellfire Mysteries:***

AN IMPROPER COMPANION

# Prologue

'I had begun to think you would not come today,' the girl said, smiling at her visitor. She was a pretty girl with soft fair hair that gently waved to the nape of her neck, though at the temples the wings of white testified to the suffering of a debilitating illness. Her eyes were a deep green, but there were shadows in them, and hollows in her cheekbones. She was recovering her health, but the nightmare of her past still haunted her. 'Nana has been a little better this morning, but she looks forward to your visits so much—and so do I, of course.'

'I know.' Arabella placed her basket on the table. It was filled with delicacies, the kind of thing that would tempt an invalid to eat. Her old nurse had cared for her all her life until she retired to this cottage on the estate, and Arabella was very fond of the elderly lady. She smiled at the girl, of whom she was also extremely fond, loving her as she would a sister. 'I look forward to them too, but Nana is so fortunate to have you to look after her, May. It was a lucky day for us when you came into our lives.'

For a moment the girl's face clouded. Her friends called her May because it was during that month that she had wandered into their lives more than a year earlier. She had not known where she came from or even her own name. All she knew was that she had been walking a long time. She had been cold and tired and very hungry when she arrived at the isolated cottage at the edge of the village. She hardly remembered knocking at Nana's door to beg for food, because she had collapsed on to the floor only moments after being invited inside.

May had been desperately ill, her feet torn and bleeding, almost starving and in a raging fever for days on end. Nana had nursed her devotedly, sitting by her bed and comforting her as she cried out and tossed from side to side, haunted by terrible nightmares. The doctor had held little hope of her recovery, but Nana and Arabella had cared for her, never giving up even when it seemed hopeless. Arabella had visited at least twice a day, bringing them both nourishing foods, medicines and fuel for the fire. Sometimes she sat up throughout the night so that Nana could rest. Between the two of them they had coaxed May back to life. And when she began to recover and get up, Arabella had given May pretty clothes to wear for she had only the thin silk shift she had been dressed in when she arrived. May knew that she owed her life to Nana and Belle.

'I am the lucky one,' she said now. 'You have both been so kind to me. You don't know where I came from or what kind of a person I am. I could be a thief or…anything.'

'No, you could not,' Lady Arabella Marshall said, her dark eyes bright with mischief. 'I know that you are honest, kind and loyal, May. I am so glad that you are here with Nana. Otherwise, I could not easily have gone to London, as I must next week. It is tiresome, but I am promised to my aunt—though if she imagines I shall marry to oblige her she will be disappointed. I have no intention of it!'

'Do you not wish to marry?' May looked at her, feeling a little puzzled. Belle was very beautiful with glossy hair the colour of a raven's wing and dark eyes that seemed to glow silver when she felt anything deeply. She was wealthy in her own right and had been married at eighteen to her childhood sweetheart, who had been killed fighting the French. 'Are you still grieving for your husband, Belle?'

'I am not sure,' Belle said truthfully. 'We were very much in love, May. I adored Ben all my life. Our fathers' estates were side by side and we saw each other often. He taught me to ride when I was little and I worshipped him, tagging behind him like a puppy…' Her laughter was rich and warm and wholly delightful. 'He was always so brave and he was killed being a hero. His commanding officer wrote me a charming letter about how much he was loved by all who knew him. How could any other man measure up to him? If I married, I think I should be for ever comparing my husband to Ben— and that would not be fair, would it?' Her lovely eyes were sad, haunted by regret for the husband she had lost.

'No, but perhaps you might love someone if you let yourself.'

'I love you and Nana,' Arabella said. 'And my aunt too, of course. I shall visit Aunt Hester, because, apart from Tilda, who is a distant cousin of my mother's, she is my only relation. She and, of course, her son, Cousin Ralph—whom I detest, though I do not tell her so for she is a dear and cannot help having a toad as her son. Ralph takes after his father, who made poor Hester's life a misery until he obligingly died and left her comfortably provided for.' Arabella shrugged one dainty shoulder.

'I promised my aunt I would go up to town when the Season was almost over. I do not wish to join the mad whirl of the matrimony stakes, but I dare say we shall find enough to amuse us. I enjoy the theatre and there will still be those families who do not care to decamp to the sea or the country. It will be lively enough for me.' And she avoided the Season because it gave too many opportunities for unwelcome marriage proposals, of which she had already received more than she could recall.

Her eyes rested on the girl for a moment. She had not told May, but one of her reasons for going up to town was because she intended to find an investigative agent, to search for details of the girl's past. May seemed content to stay with Nana, but she did not belong here. Somewhere she must have a family who cared for her. At least, Arabella hoped that there was someone who cared about the girl.

It was nearly sixteen months since she had come to them and Belle had hoped that her memory might return. As yet the past remained a secret to them all, but Arabella was determined to discover the truth. She had waited because May was still so vulnerable, still unable to cope with questions about the past. It was time to try to discover the truth, but whether or not she told May of her findings depended on what that truth turned out to be. The girl was safe and loved with them and Arabella would never desert her. Only if she had a loving family to welcome her back would Arabella tell her what she had discovered.

'I shall go up and see Nana now, dearest,' she said. 'If you look in the basket, you will find a book of poems I thought you might like to have. And there are some embroidery silks. I know that you like to sew. I shall bring you some material from town and you may use it to make up whatever you choose. What colour would you like for a new gown?'

'You spoil me,' May said, looking thoughtful. 'But if I could choose, I think I should like yellow…yes, that is a colour I like.'

Arabella nodded. It was a small thing to discover, but she had learned not to ask the important questions. Little by little, she was teaching May to know what she liked, and perhaps one day she would remember all the things she had forgotten.

# *Chapter One*

⸺❦⸺

Charles Hunter stared moodily at the tankard in front of him. He had been drinking heavily the previous night, drinking because of the shock of the news that Daniel had told him concerning his sister. It had thrown him into turmoil again. He had been searching for her for more than a year, torn between doubt and hope. At first he had not known what had happened to his sister. She had seemed to disappear into thin air, and he had suspected that she had been kidnapped. Daniel, Earl of Cavendish, and others of his friends had vowed to help him find Sarah. After exhaustive investigations, acting on information received from a certain Mr Palmer, they had all believed the search was over. Charles had been planning to take a young girl's body from a suicide's grave and bury her at the family vault at his home, but now Daniel had aroused fresh doubts in his mind.

'Talk to Fred yourself,' Daniel had told him just before he left on his wedding trip with Elizabeth, his new and much-loved wife. 'Fred was a footman for Sir Montague Forsythe and he says that he found a girl wandering in distress at about the time we know Sarah ran away from her captors. Palmer told us that she might have drowned herself in the lake that night, but what Fred has told me makes me doubt that. I have taken Fred into my employ as an assistant to my gamekeeper and I believe him honest. I do not think he can tell you more than I have already—but it makes me think that it was not Sarah who drowned herself in Forsythe's lake, but a village girl who had been turned out by her family because she was with child.'

'Then where is Sarah?' Charles had been repeating the question over and over again in his own mind ever since his friend's revelations.

This morning his head felt as if there were a hundred hammers working at his temples. His own fault, he readily admitted, for drinking. Feeling sorry for himself would not help him find his sister—if there was any chance of it! Sarah had been missing for so many months, more than he cared to remember—and all the agents he had employed had failed to find any trace of her. It was as if she had vanished from the face of the earth. His mother believed her dead—had always believed it, even before they had heard of the unknown girl who had drowned herself. Daniel had given him hope, kept on searching when Charles might have given way to despair. Charles had thought her dead, but now he was haunted by the idea that Sarah was alive. His worst fear was that she was trapped in a whorehouse somewhere, living in fear and misery. His sweet, innocent little sister at the mercy of evil men!

'Oh, God, no! Damn it, no!' Charles said the words aloud, anger mixing with the agony of uncertainty. He brought his fist down hard on the table in front of him, making the remnants of his meal fly from the plate. 'I cannot bear it. It shall not be!'

'I beg your pardon, sir. The landlord told me I might share the parlour with a gentleman. I am sorry if you feel it an intrusion.'

Charles blinked and looked up. Until that moment he had not realised he was no longer alone in the inn parlour. For a moment he stared at the young woman, struggling to focus his somewhat bleary eyes. She was dressed in the height of fashion, clearly a person of some wealth and consequence— and he realised, as he raised his eyes to her face, extremely beautiful, though not in the usual way. The hair peeping from beneath her elegant travelling bonnet was a glossy black and her eyes were very dark, though as he continued to stare at her, he saw a silver spark in their depths.

'If I am intruding, I can leave…'

'No, of course not.' Charles belatedly got to his feet. 'Excuse me. I was about to go myself. Please feel free to call the parlour your own, ma'am.' His words were abrupt, harsh, for his mood was bleak, tortured, and he hardly knew what he said or did. 'I have things to do…'

As he walked from the parlour he was aware that he had probably sounded rude. It was not how he would have greeted such a woman in the old days, for she was certainly a beauty, and the type of woman he most admired. He had admired Elizabeth Travers—the young woman Daniel had recently married—and he had been rude to her too at the start. He had apologised to her later for his boorish behaviour, but at the moment he was too tense, too filled with apprehension to be the gentleman he was at heart. How could he be carefree and charming, when his guilt and remorse haunted him? He ought to have found Sarah by now!

It was unlikely that Fred, the footman-turned-gamekeeper, would be able to help him find Sarah, but Daniel had put him in touch with another man who might help him. Jesiah Tobbold was a man of some resources. He had helped Daniel protect his family from Sir Montague Forsythe. There was nothing to fear from Forsythe now that he was dead. Charles had killed him in a desperate struggle when the villain had tried to escape after kidnapping Elizabeth and murdering Lady Roxborough.

Not for the first time, Charles wished that they had managed to keep Forsythe alive. He should have died at the end of a hangman's noose, as Daniel had always intended. Perhaps he could have told them where Sarah was…if he knew. Had she managed to evade her captors that fateful night? Or had Forsythe found her and imprisoned her in one of his houses of ill repute? The question haunted Charles. Until he had discovered the truth he would never rest. His mind was made up. He would speak to the assistant game-keeper and then ask Tobbold for help to continue the search.

Arabella stood for a moment staring after the man who had just left the inn parlour so abruptly. His behaviour had shocked her, not so much because he was rude, but because of the expression of near desperation on his face—and because he so obviously did not recognise her. It was several years since they had met, but she had known him despite the ravages of grief in his face. She was sure it was grief that had given him those dark shadows beneath his eyes, and wondered what had caused him such pain.

Of course they had met only once, at her wedding to Sir Benjamin Marshall. She was sure in her own mind that his name was Charles Hunter and that he had been one of several young men introduced to her that day by Ben. Charles Hunter had been very different then. She remembered that he had teased her, telling her that if she grew tired of her husband she might turn to him. She had laughed at him, for nothing could have made her grow tired of her beloved Ben. Handsome and carefree then, what could have changed Charles Hunter from the devil-may-care young man he had been to this gaunt-eyed stranger? She sensed that he had suffered—was still suffering deeply.

'Oh, Arabella, they say it will take several hours to mend the wheel of your carriage,' her companion said, coming in at that moment. 'The landlord says he can offer us a room for the night, if you wish for it.'

'We shall stay here if we are forced,' Arabella said. She glanced round the small room, which was not quite what she was used to when travelling, though clean and adequate. 'But I would prefer to go on to the White Hart outside Richmond if we are able. My aunt expects us tomorrow and we may send her a message from there to tell her that we have suffered a delay.'

'What shall I tell the landlord?'

'Leave it to me, Tilda,' Arabella said and smiled at her companion. Tilda Redmond was a distant cousin of her mother's, a spinster lady of middle years, and had come to bear her company after Ben was killed. She had been meant to stay just for a few weeks, but she had shown no sign of wanting to leave and Arabella did not have the heart to send her away. Besides, she had made up her mind not to marry again, and Tilda was always so obliging. 'I have bespoken nuncheon from our host, and we shall see how they fare with mending that wheel before we decide.'

'As you wish,' Tilda said. She went to warm her hands by the fire—although it was the middle of August she felt cold, as she invariably did. 'I thought we were to share the parlour with a gentleman?'

'Oh, he left,' Arabella said with a shrug. 'I dare say he had finished his ale and was anxious to continue his journey.'

'It must have been the gentleman I saw calling for his horse.' Tilda nodded her head. 'He was quite handsome, with dark hair and blue eyes…'

'Yes, I dare say that was him,' Arabella agreed and wrinkled her smooth brow in a frown. This was getting her nowhere! She decided to forget her brief encounter with Mr Hunter. Whatever his problem might be, it was none of her business. She turned as the landlord's wife came bustling into the parlour with her tray.

'There's some nice tomato soup, my lady, and the bread is fresh made this morning—and there's some fine ham and pickles for after if you should wish for it.'

'Thank you,' Arabella, said. 'We shall have the ham and a glass of your best wine, ma'am, if you please.' She nodded her approval of the soup, which smelled delicious. 'And you will let us know as soon as the carriage is repaired?'

'Yes, of course,' the woman promised and went off, leaving them to enjoy their soup, which tasted as good as it smelled.

It was late afternoon when Arabella came out of the inn to find her carriage repaired and waiting. She paused for a moment and then gestured to her maid, who had been attending to something in the baggage coach.

'We are almost ready to leave, Iris. Please make sure that we have my small trunk with us. If we should suffer another accident, I may need it tonight.'

'Yes, my lady, of course. I'll attend to it immediately.'

Arabella stopped to speak to her coachman and one of the grooms who was attending to the horses, discussing a change in plans for that night. Because of the delay, it was possible that they might not reach their planned destination. As she did so, a curricle drove into the inn yard and a man got down. He was dressed in the manner of a dandy—his travelling cloak had six capes, and his cravat was ridiculously high and fussy, especially for a journey into the country.

Arabella tensed as the man threw the reins to his tiger and walked towards the inn. For a moment she wished that she might avoid meeting him, for he was a gentleman she knew and did not much like, but pride came to her rescue. She had no reason to feel embarrassed. Sir Courtney Welch had asked her to marry him a year after Ben's death. Still raw with grief, she had refused him as politely as she could, but he had taken offence and had later accosted her in a drunken fit. His disgusting behaviour had been one of the reasons she had decided never to marry again. She would rather remain unwed than make the mistake of marrying someone she discovered later that she could not like.

'Madam,' he said, bowing to her in an exaggerated manner that was almost an insult. 'Alas, it seems that you are always leaving when I arrive.'

He could not have failed to notice that Arabella avoided his company whenever possible, but she had always preferred to avoid confrontation with him. She was relieved when Tilda spoke to her, unwittingly saving her from having to reply to his false gallantry.

'They were much quicker mending the wheel than the landlord thought,' Tilda observed as she touched Arabella's arm. 'But we should go, my dear, it will be dark before we reach Richmond.'

'Yes, I imagine it will,' Arabella agreed and allowed herself to be directed towards the carriage. She did not look back at the man she disliked. Had she done so, she would have seen that he was staring after her, his face stark with anger. 'I had hoped to arrive earlier, but it cannot be helped. I am not sure we shall manage to complete our journey tonight.' Because the day was overcast it was already darker than she had thought possible for the hour. 'But we are well protected, Tilda. You need not fear highwaymen. My grooms are all armed and we have several of them. I believe those that make their living from waylaying unwary travellers are more likely to attack unaccompanied carriages.'

'Yes, I am sure you are right,' Tilda said, but cast an anxious look from the window of their carriage as if she feared that they might be attacked at any moment. 'But I shall be glad when we reach London and your aunt's house. Inns are never so comfortable as one's own bed.'

Arabella smiled, for she knew that Tilda was of a nervous disposition. She believed herself more than a match for any highwayman and carried a small pistol inside her velvet muff. She did not mention this to her companion—it would only distress her more—but she was glad of it as the light began to fade and the sky grew darker.

They had been travelling for more than an hour and a half when she heard a shout from the driving box and the carriage drew to a sudden halt, shuddering as Arabella and Tilda were both thrown forward. Tilda gave a little cry of fright and looked at her in alarm.

'Oh, what is it? Do you think a highwayman…?'

Arabella shook her head, but her fingers sought and found the pistol. She would use it if need be! She turned her head as one of the grooms came to open the door of the carriage.

'What is the matter, Williams?'

'There is a man lying on the ground just ahead of us, my lady,' the groom said. 'I think he has had an accident. It looks as if his horse stumbled and he must have fallen. The horse is nearby and seems to be lame.'

'Is the man badly hurt?' Arabella asked, preparing to get down from the carriage.

'Do be careful,' Tilda warned. 'It might be a trap…'

'No, I do not think so.'

Arabella had seen the figure lying on the ground now. He was not moving at all and she thought it must have been a serious accident. The cause was obvious. A rope had been tied to a tree and then pulled tight across the road so that his horse stumbled. In the fading light the rider would not have seen the sinister device until it was too late.

'What foul deed has taken place here?' she asked of her coachman. 'This must have been deliberate.'

'The intention was to rob him, my lady. We saw a ruffian

make off through the woods as we approached. Had we not arrived so opportunely, it might have ended in murder.'

'How wicked!' Arabella shivered and looked about her. It was a lonely spot with thick woods on either side of the road. Just the kind of place that a rogue might lie in wait for the opportunity to attack a lone traveller. She moved closer to the man lying on the ground, catching her breath as she saw his face clearly for the first time. It was Charles Hunter! 'Is he dead?' she asked the groom, suddenly anxious.

Williams dropped to his knees, making a swift assessment. He looked up at her, shaking his head. 'He has been knocked senseless, my lady. There is a nasty blow to the side of his head, but he still has a pulse.'

'We must take him up with us,' Arabella said, making her decision at once. 'If we leave him here, he will almost certainly die, of his injury if not further attack. Be very careful as you lift him, Williams. We shall go immediately to the nearest inn and summon a doctor. He must be examined and treated as soon as possible.'

She watched anxiously as three of her servants combined to lift the unconscious man into the carriage. Climbing in herself unaided, she instructed them to lay his head on her lap so that she might support him.

'Should you be taking up a stranger like this?' Tilda asked, giving her a doubtful look. 'You do not know who he may be. He could be anyone—a thief or a murderer.'

Arabella bit back the sharp retort that leapt to mind. For some reason she was reluctant to tell her cousin that she believed she knew the gentleman's identity.

'I do not imagine we are in any danger from him at the

moment. It is surely our Christian duty to help him, Tilda. If we left him lying there, we should be heartless creatures indeed.'

'Yes, that is very true,' Tilda said, looking slightly ashamed. 'You are always such a charitable person, Arabella. You put me to the blush.'

'I know you were only thinking of me,' Arabella replied. 'But he is obviously a gentleman and we must help him. Instead of trying for Richmond this evening, we shall go to the nearest inn and take rooms there. A doctor must examine this poor man as quickly as possible.'

'Yes, of course you are right,' Tilda agreed, but still looked doubtful. She had not yet become reconciled to her cousin's habit of taking life in her stride. To her way of thinking, Arabella seemed reckless, a very confident young woman who had no one to guide her. She was still young and, being both beautiful and wealthy, might fall prey to fortune hunters, for she had no male relative to guard or protect her—other than her cousin Ralph, whom she disliked.

'Do not look so anxious,' Arabella said, guessing at a part of what Tilda was thinking. Her cousin was of a timid, nervous disposition, but she had tried hard to be a comfort to Arabella during her period of mourning, and it would be unkind to find her constant anxiety a little tedious. 'I assure you there is no need. This poor man cannot harm us. He is far too ill.'

Tilda sighed deeply. However, she knew that she could not turn Arabella once her mind was set. 'I am perhaps being foolish, as I so often am, my dear. You will do as you think right, Arabella.'

Arabella sensed that her companion was slightly peeved. She normally made a show of listening to Tilda's advice out of politeness, though she rarely followed it, but in this instance she found it irritating.

'Ben always told me to throw my heart over the fences,' she said. 'He would have done exactly as I have.'

'Dear Ben, such a gentle, kind man,' Tilda said and took a kerchief from her reticule. 'Such a pity…' She faltered as she saw the look in Arabella's eyes, knowing that she was treading on thin ice. 'Forgive me. I did not mean to distress you, my dear.'

'You have not. Ben was strong and fearless—but, yes, he was also kind and gentle at times.' Arabella smiled a little sadly. Sometimes now she was able to think of her husband without feeling the terrible sweeping grief that had almost destroyed her immediately after the news of Ben's death. She had wanted to die then, had stood by the edge of the deep lake on her husband's estate, contemplating suicide. She did not know to this day what had made her turn away, for she had found no joy in living. 'If we do not speak of him, he is lost, as if he had never been.'

Arabella felt a sharp pang of regret. How often she had wished that she had conceived during their brief honeymoon. Just one precious week to remember for the rest of her life, before Ben left to join his regiment. His child would have been a tiny piece of him to love, to fill her life and keep her from feeling lonely, as she sometimes did, but that joy had been denied her.

'You are so brave, Arabella.' Tilda dabbed at her eyes. 'I am sure you are a shining example for any young woman. To have suffered so much so young.'

Arabella was able to ignore her remarks and the pity in her tone, for she saw they were approaching an inn. It had a low sloping thatched roof, white, limewashed walls and small windows. At first glance, it looked respectable for a small country inn, and she was pleased because they had reached it much sooner than she had expected.

The next several minutes were taken up by securing rooms and overseeing the transfer of their patient to one of the host's best chambers. A doctor was duly sent for, arriving within a short time. Arabella spoke to him a little later as he came downstairs after examining his patient.

'How is he?' she asked. 'Please tell me that he is not going to die, sir.'

'It is much too soon to be sure, ma'am,' he replied gravely. 'The wound to his head does not seem severe, but one can never tell with these causes. I believe much will depend upon his being nursed by a woman of sense. Your husband should recover in time, ma'am, but at the moment I cannot say it is certain.'

It was on the tip of Arabella's tongue to reply that his patient was not her husband, but something held her silent. Since it seemed that she must care for him herself it might be better to allow both him and the landlord to believe that she was Mr Hunter's wife.

'Thank you. What must I do to help him, sir?'

'Just watch over him carefully in these first hours. He may be violent or startled when he comes to his senses and you may need to restrain him from harming himself or others. I have seen men fight those that have cared for them in a kind of madness that comes from brain fever—but these cases are all different and you must use your own good sense. If you need me, please do not hesitate to send word.'

'You think he should remain here for the time being?'

Arabella frowned she knew that her aunt was expecting her in Hanover Square the following day.

'Oh, yes, certainly. It would be most harmful to move him until he has recovered his senses. He needs rest and care, ma'am—rest and care.'

'I see. Thank you,' Arabella said. She was thoughtful as the doctor left the inn parlour, looking about her. It was a comfortable room; quite small, but clean and respectable. She could have fared worse in an unknown inn. If her stay here were to be extended for a few days, she would need to speak to the landlord's wife—and to Tilda. Firstly, she would reserve the rooms she needed and then break the news to her companion.

'You cannot mean it,' Tilda said and looked at her in horror. 'I do not understand, Arabella—why should you allow anyone to believe you are married to that man?'

'I am determined to nurse him,' Arabella told her. 'I cannot abandon him to his fate, and it is better that others should believe him my husband.'

'But why should you run such a risk for a stranger? You could leave your maid here to care for him if you must do something, and to my mind you have already done more than necessary. Iris is a sensible girl. She could nurse him and then join us in town. It is quite impossible for us to stay here, Arabella. There simply aren't enough rooms for all of us. I have been told that I must either share a bedchamber with Iris or you, my dear.'

'You will share my room for one night, of course,' Arabella said. 'That is why I propose that you should go on to London in the morning, Tilda. You may explain that I have been delayed—though you may not tell Aunt Hester why. Just say that I have been called to the bedside of a sick friend and will come to her in a few days.'

'No! Certainly not! You cannot think that I would desert you? If you are determined to stay, I shall remain to assist you in whatever you intend.' Tilda's feathers were seriously ruffled and she looked indignant, though prepared to do her duty.

'I knew that you would wish to help me,' Arabella said and bestowed a warm smile on her. 'But Iris will be here to keep me company. Aunt Hester will worry if I do not arrive on time. Please oblige me in this, Tilda, for I am quite determined on it.' The expression in her eyes belied the smile and warned that she would not be thwarted.

Tilda opened her mouth to protest and then closed it. She was well aware that she could not dictate to Arabella. She was dependent on her charity and did not wish to risk a breach with her.

'But think of your reputation, my dear.' The cry was plaintive, for she had little hope of being listened to. 'If people should hear of you staying at an inn alone…and nursing a gentleman you do not know. And that you masqueraded as his wife!'

Arabella smiled in amusement. 'Remember that I am four and twenty, Tilda. I am not an innocent girl—I have been married. Besides, this inn is so quiet that it is not likely to be patronised by the *ton*. No one who knows me will visit—so no one need ever know. I suppose I may rely on your discretion?'

'You must know I would never betray you! But why do you wish to do this for a stranger? Why take on this responsibility, Arabella?'

Arabella was silent for a moment. She did not know why she was prepared to abandon her plans for a man she did not know—for, even if he truly was Charles Hunter, she could not claim to know him. Yet he had been one of Ben's friends and perhaps she was doing this because she had been unable to nurse her husband as he lay dying in a foreign land. She had been haunted by the thought of his dying alone, in pain and calling for her, praying that a kind woman had stooped to comfort in him in his last hours. She could do at least as much for this man.

'I am not sure that he is a stranger,' Arabella said, still pensive. 'I believe we may have met—at my wedding, if memory serves me right. I think he was a friend of Ben's.' She was certain of it in her own mind, even though he had not seemed to recognise her at the inn.

'You did not say earlier.' Tilda looked at her suspiciously.

'No, for it was not important. We met only once—and I may be mistaken, but I am willing to take that chance. For Ben's sake, I cannot abandon him.' Tears stood in her eyes. 'I have often prayed that there was someone to care for Ben…' Her throat was tight and she shook her head. The thought that her husband might have died alone was too painful.

'I see…' Tilda did not understand such sentimentality. The expression on her face was plainly one of disbelief and disagreement, but there was really very little she could do to dissuade Arabella. 'If you are set on this madness, I suppose you must do as you think fit.'

'Oh, I do not think it so very foolish,' Arabella reassured her. 'It will only be for a day or so. Aunt Hester will be happy to see you, Tilda, and I shall join you both quite soon.'

Tilda's mouth pursed, but she gave up her efforts to change Arabella's mind. However, when she reached the house in Hanover Square, she would consider whether it was right to confide in Lady Tate.

Her silent disapproval became almost oppressive when Arabella left her three times during the evening to visit the patient's bedchamber. Iris had taken it upon herself to sit with him at her mistress's request, but to Tilda's mind it seemed that nothing would do for Arabella but to sit with him herself while Iris ate her supper. Had Tilda known that Arabella crept out from the bedchamber they shared that night to relieve Iris from her vigil, she would have been most distressed. Fortunately, she was a heavy sleeper and remained in ignorance.

However, Iris looked relieved when her mistress entered the sick room. It was now the early hours of the morning and Iris had been finding it hard to keep awake.

'Has there been any change, Iris?'

'No, my lady,' the maid replied, yawning. She was a plump girl, plain faced but agreeable and devoted to her mistress. 'He muttered something a while ago—a girl's name, I think—but he hasn't woken.'

'Go and rest now,' Arabella told her. 'We may have to nurse him for some days and nights. We shall both need our sleep.'

'Are you sure, my lady? Mrs Blackstone said that she would help us and she seems a good woman.'

'I imagine she has enough to do looking after her customers, Iris. I shall sit with the gentleman for the time being. You may return in the morning.'

'Poor gentleman,' Iris said. 'He has a handsome face, my lady, but he looks gaunt, as though he has been ill—before this, I mean. When the doctor undressed him, he discovered that he had a wound to his thigh. It seemed to have recovered, but the scarring was fresh. There were other wounds on his body, and the doctor thought he might have been a soldier.'

'Yes, I dare say he may have been. I thought that he had suffered recently,' Arabella said. Her thoughtful eyes moved to the man in the bed. 'I believe he may have suffered a great deal, Iris. I saw him briefly earlier today and remarked it. You see, I think I may know him. He was a friend of my husband's.'

'Did he come for your wedding, my lady? I did wonder if I had seen him before, though I do not know his name.'

'Mr Charles Hunter, if I am right. For the moment it is best if we do not speak of him by his name. It will be easier if Mrs Blackstone continues to believe him my husband.'

'Yes, my lady.' Iris bobbed a curtsy and went out, leaving Arabella alone with her patient.

Arabella crossed to the bed, bending over him to lay a gentle hand on his brow. He seemed hot and his forehead was damp. Noticing that Iris had left a bowl of water and a cloth by the bed, she wrung the cloth out, laying it on his brow for a moment before gently wiping away the perspiration. However, in a moment or two he was sweating again, and Arabella thought that he seemed feverish.

'Poor Charles,' she murmured, feeling strangely drawn to him. She felt that he had experienced some terrible grief quite recently. She had seen it in his face earlier and it touched her, arousing her sympathy. 'You have suffered much already and it is unkind of Fate to offer you this further blow,' she said and stroked the damp hair back from his forehead. 'Rest now, Charles. We shall take care of you.'

He was so hot! She must do something to cool him.

Arabella removed one of the heavy quilts, and then, on impulse, pulled back the sheets. His body was damp with sweat and she could feel the heat coming from him. She took the cloth Iris had been using to bathe his forehead, wringing it out in the water again and beginning to sponge his arms, chest and then his legs. She would have bathed his back, but was not sure she could turn him alone. But perhaps it would not be necessary, for at last he seemed easier. He sighed and murmured something that might have been a name, but too softly for her to hear.

For a while after she had bathed his heated body he seemed to rest more comfortably, but after an hour or so he became hot again, throwing his arms and legs about as if he were in distress. His head moved restlessly on the pillow and Arabella soothed him as best she could, whispering words of reassurance and stroking his hair. Pity wrenched at her heart, and she felt a flicker of tenderness stir inside her. He looked so vulnerable, so needy as he lay there tossing in his fever, that she longed to comfort him. Suddenly, his eyes opened wide and he stared at her.

'Sarah,' he croaked. 'Thank God I have found you, my dear one. Forgive me, I beg you. Forgive me…'

'Charles…' Arabella said, but his eyes had closed and she knew that he had fallen back into the unconscious state in which she had found him. 'Please do not die. I do not want you to die.'

Arabella did not know why his survival was so important to her. It could only be that she was transferring her longing to help Ben to his friend, almost as though by saving Charles Hunter she could atone for not being able to save her beloved husband.

'You must get well,' she whispered and stroked his forehead. 'I shall stay with you until you are able to fend for yourself, Charles. I promise that I shall not desert you.'

'Are you sure you will not give up this nonsense and come with me?' Tilda asked the next morning. 'I do not like to leave you here like this, Arabella—and without your carriage. I could travel in the baggage coach…'

'No, indeed, I shall not put you to such torture,' Arabella said, a smile on her lips. Her companion was not the best of travellers at any time. 'Both vehicles may travel with you— I need only my small trunk here. My baggage may as well go with you, and the coachman will come back for me in a day or so after the horses are rested. There is no reason for you to worry at all, Tilda. I shall be quite comfortable.'

Tilda was doubtful and had to be coaxed into the carriage, but at last it was accomplished and Arabella sighed her relief. She tried not to think it, for she did not wish to be unkind, but she would be much happier here alone. Her companion's fretting had begun to seem tedious after two days' travelling. She felt relieved that for a short time she need not consider anyone but her patient and herself.

Going upstairs to her own chamber, she tidied her hair and smoothed the skirts of her serviceable gown. She had chosen one of her oldest, which was normally kept for working in her stillroom. She preferred not to dress too richly while staying at the inn, for she had now realised that she and Mr Hunter were not the only guests. She had seen another gentleman as she came downstairs that morning. By his dress he was a countryman, perhaps a merchant or a farmer of ample means, for though well turned out he did not aspire to fashion. Arabella was glad that she had allowed her hosts to believe Charles was her husband. She would not care to be thought fast in any way, which she might have had they known that she was regularly visiting the bedchamber of a stranger.

Entering Charles's room a little later, she saw that Iris was bending over him, trying to give him a little water from a pewter cup, and he seemed to be fighting her. When she went closer, Arabella realised that he was once again in the grip of a fever.

'What are you giving him?' she asked because she could see now that the cup contained more than water.

'The doctor has been again and he left a powder to be mixed with water and administered every few hours. As you can see, my lady, the gentleman is much worse this morning than he was last night.'

'Yes, he is,' Arabella said and laid a hand on his forehead. 'He is burning up, Iris. We must do something to help him. I think we should bathe him. Strip back the bedcovers while I bring fresh water.'

She went over to the washstand and poured water from the jug into a bowl, bringing it back to the bedside as Iris folded back the heavy cover. Charles was naked and the girl blushed—she had only ever seen one naked man before and that was her young brother. She placed a towel over his private parts, turning to wring out her cloth and recover her composure. Arabella came to join her, a little amused that the girl had thought fit to protect his modesty. She had felt no shame in looking at his body, finding it beautiful. He had strong firm legs, and was well formed without the slightest hint of anything to spoil the perfection.

'We shall do it together, Iris. You bathe that arm and I shall do this one. That way we can hold him more easily if he fights us.'

'He seems quieter now,' Iris pointed out. 'I think it was the sound of your voice. He kept trying to push me away, but he settled when you touched him.'

'Yes, he has,' Arabella agreed. 'I think he mistook me for someone he cares for last night. He woke for a moment, though I do not think he knew what he said, because in seconds he had gone back into his unconscious state. The fever had not gripped him so much then, but we shall do what we can ourselves to care for him; then, if he is no better in an hour or so, I shall send for the doctor again.'

They carefully bathed most of his body in the cool water, turning him one way and then the other. Arabella stroked the red marks on his thigh where he had been wounded previously, thinking that the flesh still looked sore. She had some healing creams in her baggage, and instructed Iris to fetch the pots for her once they had dried his skin. While the girl was gone, Arabella stroked his forehead, speaking him to him tenderly. It was true that the sound of her voice did soothe him. He was not quite as hot now, and, when Iris returned, she smoothed a little cream into his thigh, massaging it for some minutes before drawing the covers over him again. Then she applied the ointment to the wound at the side of his head. He had received a nasty cut, but it was not deep and she thought it would soon heal.

'There, I think he will do for the time being,' she said. 'I shall go and have my breakfast now, and you can have yours in half an hour. I shall order it made ready for you, Iris.'

Glancing at the man in the bed once more before she left, Arabella was aware of a warm glow inside her. He was resting now. Their nursing had certainly helped him. It might be only a temporary respite, but it could be a turning point. She prayed that it might be so.

When Iris came down to partake of her meal, Arabella went back to the sick room. She sat by the bedside for more than an hour and then went to fetch a book from her own room. Charles Hunter was sleeping peacefully and she would be better with something to do for a while.

After another hour, Iris came to take her place as they had agreed. Arabella went out for a walk, feeling the need for a little air. The inn was quite warm and rather stuffy as it had only small windows. She felt pleased with their patient's progress, for he seemed to be throwing the fever off. However, when she returned, Iris told her that he had begun to sweat heavily and throw the bedcovers off once more.

Arabella resorted to the same remedy as before, and once again he quietened under her hand. She was a little concerned and sent Iris to ask the landlord to send for the doctor again.

When he visited later that morning, the doctor declared himself satisfied with the patient's progress.

'You must expect a little fever,' he said. 'I warned you that he might be violent, for brain fever can be dangerous, though you seem to be nursing him very well, Lady Arabella. I had expected your husband to be in a worse case than this. Continue to give him the powders I left you and I am sure all will be well.'

Arabella thanked him, forbearing to tell him that her patient had not taken much of the doctor's remedy. She walked downstairs with him to the parlour where she took her midday meal alone. There was no sign of the country gentleman she had seen earlier and she was pleased that the inn seemed not to get too many visitors. It was as she was preparing to go back upstairs once more that Mrs Blackstone came up to her with a smile.

'Your husband is much better, Lady Arabella. He woke a few moments ago when I went in with some more water. He asked me where he was and I told him that he was staying at the Fox and Hounds in Thornborough, and that his wife was caring for him. He seemed a little mazed, my lady, but I am sure that is only to be expected in the circumstances. The poor man said he had no wife, but he will remember when he sees you.'

'Yes, of course,' Arabella said and went hastily up the stairs. It was little wonder if Charles Hunter felt confused by being told his wife was caring for him!

She entered the bedchamber and found Iris wrestling with him as she tried to keep him from leaving his bed.

'You must not, sir,' Arabella said and crossed to the bedside. 'You have been ill and I think you should stay in bed for a little longer.'

'And who the hell are you?' he demanded, looking angry. 'Are you the designing wench who has been masquerading as my wife? I have no wife and if you hope to force me into proposing because you have compromised yourself, let me tell you that you are much mistaken. I have no intention of taking a wife—and certainly not a female I have never met before in my life!'

'Thank you, Iris, you may go,' Arabella said. She fixed a

cool stare on Charles, lifting her head proudly. Now she became the lady of the manor, wealth and power at her back. 'You are the one who is mistaken, sir. I found you lying on the road and in a parlous state. Had I not taken you up in my carriage, you might have died. Indeed, the rogue who attacked you might have returned to finish his work.'

'Was I attacked?' Charles stared at her, his eyes narrowing. Something about her voice was very attractive. He found it soothing, despite his shock at the discovery that he was supposed to have a wife. 'Who are you, ma'am—and why does the innkeeper's wife imagine I am your husband?'

'Because I was determined to nurse you,' Arabella told him calmly. 'It seemed easier to allow that good lady to think us married, but I assure you that you stand in no danger of being coerced into offering for me. I have no intention of marrying again—and, I assure you, nothing would make me marry you, sir.'

Charles stared at her for a few seconds, a frown on his face. 'You are a widow?'

'Yes, that is so,' she replied. 'I had thought you might know me, Mr Hunter, but it seems that you have forgot me.'

'Have we met?'

'Once—at my wedding. I am Lady Arabella Marshall. My late husband was then your good friend. It was for his sake that I have done what I have. I always prayed that someone nursed Ben when he was dying and thought it my duty to help you.'

'Good grief,' Charles said and gave a little moan of anguish. He lay back against the pillows, closing his eyes for a moment. 'Forgive me. My head aches like the very devil and I thought… I have been damnably rude!'

'Yes, you have,' she said and smiled a little wryly. 'However, the doctor told me that you might be violent or abusive. Indeed, I was prepared for much worse. Forgive me for taking a liberty concerning my relationship with yourself, Mr Hunter—but it did seem the best way at the time. I could hardly have cared for you as I have if I'd confessed that you were a stranger to me. I am four and twenty, no longer a green girl, but I do not think it would have been thought proper even so.'

He opened his eyes and looked at her again, a wry expression on his lips. 'I am a fool. I tend to think the worst of people these days. Of course I remember Ben's wife. I am sorry for not having known you—and even more sorry that Ben died. It was a terrible thing to happen so soon after you were wed.'

'Yes, it was,' Arabella agreed, her eyes shadowed with sadness. 'Now, sir, may I have something brought for you? A little nourishing broth or some wine?'

'I detest nourishing broth,' Charles said with a grimace. 'I will eat some bread and cold meat—and a glass of wine if you please.'

'I think a little brandy might be restorative,' Arabella said. 'But not the meat and bread just yet. I shall ask Mrs Blackstone if she will cook a coddled egg for you.' She laughed as he pulled a face. 'Yes, I know what you will think of that, sir—but red meat might not suit you for the moment.'

'Do you think it might make me violent? I promise I shall not attack you, ma'am.'

'I have no fear of it,' Arabella laughed huskily. Her eyes lit up and in that moment she was very beautiful. 'You may have a little chicken this evening if you do not relapse into the fever again. Please, for my peace of mind, be sensible, sir.'

'Only if you call me Charles,' he said, looking rueful. 'We should be friends—if Ben had lived we would have known each other well. Besides, it would look odd if you called me sir in front of our good hostess. She will think me quite mad for not knowing I had a wife.'

'Just a little mazed, understandably so after the blow to your head,' Arabella told him. 'Lie still and rest, Charles. I shall order your meal and then perhaps you will sleep again.'

Smiling at him, she went out, leaving Charles to rest against the pillows and remember the soft voice and hands that had soothed him in his fever…had done things for him, intimate things that he could not possibly have expected of her. Yet perhaps it had been her maid. He had thought she was Sarah…a swift slash of pain cut through him as he remembered that his sister was still lost.

As soon as he was able he must continue his search for her, but he would say nothing to Lady Arabella. She had been generous to him despite her own troubles. It would not do to lay his burdens on her when she could know nothing of the matter.

# Chapter Two

'I think I shall get up this morning,' Charles said, smiling as Arabella entered his room the following day. She had brought his breakfast tray and he felt a new hunger as he saw that he was at last being allowed cold beef, bread and butter as well as a tankard of ale. 'Thank you. I shall enjoy this food, ma'am.'

'You asked me to call you Charles,' she reminded him. 'It would please me if you were to call me by my name.'

'You have been both generous and kind,' Charles said, a strange wintry expression in his eyes. 'I am grateful for all your attentions, Lady Arabella—but I believe you should cease to wait on me in this manner. I am much recovered now and it is not fitting that an unmarried lady should visit the bed-chamber of a man she scarcely knows.'

'I have been married, sir. I am not a stranger to such things.'

'Married for a week, I understand?' Charles saw her flinch and immediately cursed himself for his clumsiness. 'Forgive me. I should not have said that, Arabella—but I am concerned for your reputation.'

'You shall not be asked to rescue it,' Arabella replied in a sharp tone—she was hurt that he should speak to her in that way. She had thought they were well on the way to becoming friends. She lifted her head proudly, becoming the lady of consequence she truly was as the mistress of a large manor. 'But if you feel able to care for yourself now I shall not press my attentions on you, sir. My carriage has returned for me this morning and I shall continue my journey to London. I have already been delayed and I dare say my friends are anxious for me by now.'

'I have offended you,' Charles said, regretting that he had spoken harshly. 'That was not my intention. I am truly grateful for all you have done. Indeed, I may owe my life to you.'

'Think nothing of it,' she replied, her manner becoming even more reserved, cool to the point of iciness. 'I would do the same for any man—and you *were* a friend of Ben's. I shall bid you good morning, sir. I trust you may complete your journey without further accident. I should take care if I were you. It was only good fortune that you were not killed. I do not know if you have an enemy, but that rope across the road was meant to bring you down.'

'Me or any unwary traveller, I dare say,' Charles said, frowning. 'But I shall heed your warning, Lady Arabella. I should not have been so easily caught had I been less wrapped up in my own thoughts.'

Arabella nodded, but made no further reply. He seemed to be a man of moods for he was never the same twice, swinging from a smiling, good-natured gentleman to a harsh, reserved stranger. She left him to his breakfast and went downstairs, seeking out the landlady to pay the reckoning for their rooms and to tell her that they were leaving. Her grooms had informed her that Charles had been robbed and he obviously could not pay for anything himself. Arabella gave the landlady a few coins extra to pay for his keep should he need to stay on a little longer.

'I have an appointment in London,' she said to excuse the odd circumstance of her leaving alone. 'Charles will follow at his convenience. I have to thank you for taking us in. I hope we have not been too much of a nuisance.'

'Oh, no, my lady,' the woman said and bobbed a curtsy. 'It was a pleasure to have you.'

Within an hour Arabella was sitting in her carriage and ready to leave for her aunt's house in town. Glancing from the window, she saw that Charles Hunter had come out from the inn as they were about to drive off. He stood for a moment in the sunshine and appeared to be looking for someone, but Arabella told her driver to move on. They could have nothing to say to one another. Should they meet in town, she would greet him as a stranger. She had already decided to put this interlude from her mind. She had helped a man who had been her husband's friend and that was an end to it—and yet she had an odd feeling of having lost something as she was driven away.

Charles saw the carriage leaving. Had he come down a few minutes earlier he might have spoken to her again, apologised for his coolness that morning. He was aware that he had much to thank her for and she did not deserve to be treated so harshly. Yet he could not allow himself to like her too much. His life must be dedicated to finding Sarah. The guilt and fear nagged at him, mingling with the anger. Sarah was all that mattered now. Besides, he knew that he was incapable of loving a woman—especially one as beautiful and warm as Lady Arabella. She deserved passion and spirit, not the broken shell of the man he had become.

It was better that she had gone without time for another meeting between them. The memory of soft hands and sweet words soothing him would pass. He would not allow himself to remember how comforted she had made him feel—or the hurt look in her eyes when he had told her that he no longer needed her help.

'Arabella dearest! I was beginning to worry about you,' Lady Hester Tate said as her niece walked into the elegant parlour of her London house that afternoon. 'Tilda has been fretting—she did not like to leave you alone with only your maid to protect you.'

Arabella's laughter was warm and delightful. 'I do hope she did not upset you, Aunt Hester? I assure you I was perfectly safe.'

'She seemed to think you were in some mortal danger, though she would not tell me exactly what,' Lady Tate said and frowned. 'I do not know how you put up with her, my dear. She is such a fusspot.'

'Yes, she is rather,' Arabella said, smothering a sigh. 'But she has so little to live on, Aunt. I should feel awful if I told her I did not need her any longer—though I must admit that she tries my patience at times. Where is she at this moment?'

'Oh, I sent her on an errand,' Lady Tate said, pulling a little face. 'She is useful in many ways, Arabella. I had some packages that needed to be delivered to a friend—and my library book had to be returned. I could have sent a servant with the packages, of course, but Tilda likes to feel helpful.'

'Yes, she does,' Arabella said. She bent to kiss her aunt's cheek. Lady Tate was a small, slightly plump lady who had once been considered a great beauty but was now showing signs of fragility, her skin papery soft. 'How are you? When you wrote to me last, you had had a chill, I think?'

'Oh, I am much recovered,' her aunt said, her eyes avoiding looking directly at Arabella. 'I am well enough in myself— but Ralph worries me. He has been behaving oddly recently and I think he may be in debt again. He is such a terrible gambler. Takes after his father, of course, and never listens to anything I say.' Lady Tate's expression was a mixture of anxiety and annoyance. 'Goodness knows what he does with his own money!'

'I am sorry to hear that he has made you anxious,' Arabella said. 'He really should learn to stay away from the card tables. He cannot expect you to rescue him from his folly again.'

'No, indeed, I have told him that I can give him no more than a hundred guineas,' Lady Tate said. 'He says it is not enough, but I cannot spare more, Arabella. I have my jointure and a few jewels my father bought me—but he has sold the Tate heirlooms himself.'

'Oh, no, has he?' Arabella felt a slight unease. 'That was not well done of Ralph, Aunt. Do you know if he has run up claims on the Northampton estate?'

'I would not care if he has,' her aunt replied. 'I hate Tatton Court. It is an awful old place and would cost a fortune to make it comfortable. So he may gamble that away if he pleases—but I have told him that Haverhill House is not his to hazard. It belonged to my family and remains mine until I die. I have made a will passing it to my grandchildren, Arabella. Failing them, it will come to you, my dear. Ralph does not know that, but I have instructed my lawyers that he is not to have the right to sell it. He would not like it if he knew, but he would lose everything we have if I did not take some precautions.'

'Yes, I see.' Arabella thought that her cousin would be furious if he knew what his mother had done, but kept her own counsel. Aunt Hester might complain of her son sometimes, but she thought the world of him and would not like to be told the harsh truth, which was that Sir Ralph Tate cared for nothing but himself. 'Well, you must do as you think best, dearest. Now tell me, do we dine alone this evening?'

'As it happens we have an engagement. I left your first two evenings free, Arabella, so that we might be comfortable together, but you did not come when I expected you, and we are engaged this evening to a great friend of mine—Lady Samson. She is to give a little musical affair, my dear. Nothing exciting, but you know how it is. Most of the *ton* have gone to the country or Brighton for the summer.' She glanced at her niece. 'I could go alone this evening if you are too tired?'

'I am not in the least tired,' Arabella said. 'A musical evening will be very pleasant. I shall enjoy it, I am sure.'

'Yes, well, I think you will. Lady Samson's niece Melinda is in town for a visit and I seem to recall that you rather like her?'

'Yes, I do. It will be pleasant to see Melinda again. I have not seen her since her wedding last year.'

'When dear Sammy told me she was here I thought it was the very thing. It was kind of you to visit me, Arabella, but I shan't keep you tied to my apron strings. You are still young and you need young company. I believe Melinda's brother-in-law is in town too. Captain Hernshaw is a very pleasant gentleman. I believe he has just resigned his commission in favour of a political position. Do you happen to know him at all?'

Arabella glanced at her aunt suspiciously. She was wearing an innocent face, but she was well aware that Lady Tate thought that it was time Arabella married again. Indeed, most of her friends had hinted as much, but Arabella had ignored the subtle pressure from those she believed meant well. She had known true love and would not settle for less. Since she thought it unlikely that she would ever find another man who would make her thrill to his smiles as Ben had, she had put all thought of marriage from her mind. Besides, loving made one vulnerable and she had suffered dreadfully after Ben was killed. She did not wish to be hurt that way ever again.

'I believe we may have met at Melinda's wedding,' she said in answer to her aunt's question. 'But I cannot say that I know him.'

'I imagine he may put in an appearance this evening,' Lady Tate said and wrinkled her brow. 'Though you can never be sure what a gentleman will do—they are such inconstant creatures, are they not?'

'Perhaps,' Arabella agreed. 'Some gentlemen are changeable, I believe.' For a moment her thoughts returned to the man she had left behind at the inn earlier that day. Charles Hunter was a man of moods, but she believed that he had some secret sorrow that preyed upon his mind. Something about him had touched her from the moment when he had seemed rude in the first inn's parlour, and caring for him while he lay ill had made her very aware of tenderness towards him. Not that it was more than she would feel for any man in extremity! But she had been drawn to him. However, he had made his feelings plain and she must put all thought of him aside. Mr Hunter had shown her that he did not wish for her attentions! Should they meet again, he would deserve it if she gave him the cut direct.

Arabella was wearing a deep emerald-green silk gown when she walked into Lady Samson's large drawing room that evening. It was fashioned in such a way that it seemed to swathe her slender figure in soft folds, causing more than one head to turn and admire it—and her. Around her throat she had clasped a magnificent collar of pearls and diamonds, one of the heirlooms that had come to her as Ben's widow. He had been the last of his family, and as his estate no longer suffered an entail, his will had left everything to her. Arabella was therefore exceptionally wealthy, having also inherited a small fortune from her father.

Because she was uninterested in what others thought of her, she was quite unaware of causing a stir or of the many admiring looks sent in her direction. The expression in some female eyes was distinctly envious, but in others approval and even warmth was the main emotion roused, particularly in the gentlemen. She was generally liked, but thought to be a little reserved, even cool at times, and though several of the gentlemen had considered making an offer for a woman who was both beautiful and rich, some had hesitated to approach her. It was known that those who had so dared had been summarily rejected. Lady Arabella was a wealthy widow, an independent lady who had no need to take another husband unless she wished. Indeed, because of the marriage laws that would hand everything she owned over to her husband, some of the ladies secretly applauded her and wished that they had the good fortune to be in her shoes.

'It's a crying shame,' Captain Hernshaw murmured naughtily to his young and pretty sister-in-law. 'So beautiful and all that money. It is surely her duty to marry again—preferably me. I am in need of instant repair to my fortune after my ill luck at the tables last night.'

'You are a wicked tease, Richard,' Melinda Hernshaw told him, tapping his arm playfully with her fan. She knew it was all nonsense—he was his maternal uncle's heir and would inherit a large estate one day. 'But I wish Belle would fall in love with you. I hate it that she is a widow and unhappy.'

'Do you think she is terribly unhappy?' Captain Hernshaw asked, looking at Arabella's face. 'She seems to smile quite a lot and is looking very lovely this evening. She put off her blacks for your wedding, didn't she, Mel?'

'Yes, she did,' Melinda said and shot a look of speculation at him. 'She can't go on grieving for ever, Richard. Why don't you try your luck?'

'Oh, I would if I thought she might listen,' he replied and grinned. 'But I don't want to be frozen out, Mel. Some of the gallants who tried their luck last year say that she is an iceberg, and that one look from her could turn a man into a pillar of salt. Though considering they hadn't a bean to spare between them, I do not blame her for turning them down. Personally, I admire her for herself, but I shall take things very slowly.'

'You really like her, don't you?'

'She knocked me for six the first time I saw her,' he admitted with a rueful look. 'But I dare say I am not the only one. Look at her cousin. Now that I do not like to see. He is a rum cove by all accounts. She ought to be careful of him!'

'Ralph Tate rarely escorts his mother to affairs of this kind,' Melinda replied and frowned. 'Yes, I see what you mean, Richard. He's like a dog guarding its bone. The way he looks at her—that possessive manner, as if he thinks she belongs to him!'

'She wouldn't have him, would she?'

'I shouldn't think so. I don't believe she likes him. Look at the way she shrugged off his hand then. I think she is in some distress, Richard. Pray let us go and rescue her from his attentions.'

'By Jove, yes,' Captain Hernshaw agreed eagerly. 'Can't have that toad monopolising the most beautiful woman in the room—present company excepted, Mel.'

'I know Arabella is more beautiful,' Melinda told him with a smile. 'Harry says I'm pretty and I am—but Belle is special.'

Captain Hernshaw held his tongue. He was in perfect agreement with his sister-in-law's summation, and more than a little smitten with the widow, but he did not hold out much hope of her feeling the same. He was not truly in desperate need of a rich wife, for he had expectations. However, he thought it might still be too soon to offer for her and he did not wish to cause her distress. He had seen the deep grief in her eyes when she thought she was unobserved, even though her smile came bursting through like a ray of sunlight when something pleased or amused her. He frowned as he noticed the look on her face when her cousin leaned forward to whisper in her ear. She did not care for such intimacy, that was clear, but she was finding it difficult to keep him at bay.

She raised her head as he and Melinda approached, a smile of welcome on her lips. Hernshaw felt a sudden pounding in his breast, for she was truly lovely and he wished that her smile had been for him rather than his sister-in-law.

'Melinda dearest,' Arabella said and moved forward to kiss her friend's cheek. 'How are you? You look wonderful.'

'So do you,' Melinda replied. 'Please, Belle, you must come and sit with me. Sir Ralph will spare you to me, will you not, sir?'

'Arabella was going to sit with me…' Ralph's sullen look made him appear even more unattractive. Although tall and well made, he was fleshy of face and his sandy hair was already thinning at the temples. More than that, though, were the marks of indulgence in his complexion, the beads of sweat on his forehead and the faint odour of perspiration that enamated from his person.

'No, I believe I have not agreed,' Arabella said. 'Besides, I do not think you would care for Madame Casciano's recital, cousin.'

'Nor I,' Captain Hernshaw said for he had seen the flash of temper in the other man's eyes. He was motivated to self-sacrifice for Arabella's sake. 'Come and give me a game of billiards, sir. I think we may leave the ladies to themselves until supper.'

Reluctantly, Ralph gave way to the firm pressure on his arm, though he threw a dark look at Arabella as she went off with her friend. He had been trying to force his company on her ever since they left the house, but he could not insist when she had said publicly that she wished to sit with Lady Hernshaw.

'Very well,' he said rudely, 'though I am not much in the

mood for it. I shall take myself off in an hour or so. I have better things to do than dance attendance on my mother.'

Captain Hernshaw restrained himself. He would have liked to land a facer on the other man and could have done it easily enough, but was too polite to cause a scene in the house of his sister-in-law's aunt. However, should the chance arise at a more suitable venue, he would be quite happy to wipe the floor with Ralph Tate!

'I have been so looking forward to this evening,' Melinda said, hugging Arabella's arm. 'I was not well enough to come up for the Season, but I am here now and I was so pleased to learn that you had decided to visit Lady Tate. We shall be able to shop together and I dare say we shall meet everywhere for my aunt and yours share the same circle of friends.'

'Yes, I am sure we shall,' Arabella agreed. 'I was very pleased when Aunt Hester told me you would be here—and I want to thank you for rescuing me from my cousin.'

'I thought he was making a nuisance of himself,' Melinda said with a little smile of amusement. 'He is a horrid little man, isn't he? He asked me to marry him once, before Harry proposed, and was most offended when I told him that I would not—as if I would!' She shuddered. 'He is awful. I do not know how you can bear him, Belle.'

'I have to tread carefully,' Arabella said with a little frown. 'He is my cousin, after all. I do not wish to offend Aunt Hester, even though I find him difficult at times.'

Melinda smothered her retort. In her opinion it would be much better if Lady Tate knew her son for the odious creature he was. She might then be strong enough to refuse his frequent requests for money.

'Oh, well,' she said. 'I dare say you know how to manage him, Belle. After all, no one can force you to marry him, can they?'

'I would resist with my last breath,' Arabella said. 'I do not believe either he or my aunt can hope for it. I have made it clear that I do not wish to marry again.'

'Oh, but you should,' Melinda said, objecting to this instantly. 'There are lots of nice gentlemen you could choose, Belle. You don't have to marry Ralph.'

'I certainly shall not,' Arabella said and laughed. 'Enough of me, Mel. Tell me, why are you in town? Is it just to buy some new clothes? I have decided to visit my seamstress while I am here. I do not need so very much, but I think I shall buy some new gowns for the winter.'

'Oh…' Melinda looked at her, a faint blush in her cheeks. She lowered her voice to a whisper. 'I came to see a doctor…a special one. I miscarried in the summer, you see, and my dear Harry wants to make sure I am quite well again.'

'I am so sorry,' Arabella said, instantly sympathetic. She too spoke in hushed tones—it was not something to be discussed too openly in public. 'What a disappointment for you. I fear it does happen and it may be best to consult a really good doctor. He will be able to advise you concerning the future.'

'Yes, well, I have, and he says there is no reason I shouldn't go ahead and try again, so I shall.' Melinda dimpled mischievously, a note of laughter in her voice now. 'I wrote to Harry to tell him the news. He is quite pleased with the doctor's advice, as you may imagine.'

'Yes, I dare say.'

Melinda hesitated, glancing at her friend curiously. 'If you do not marry, you will not have children, Belle. Have you thought about that?'

'Yes. It is a sorrow to me that I did not conceive Ben's child.' Her eyes darkened with emotion, her voice low and throbbing.

'Oh, I am so sorry. I shouldn't have said anything.'

'Do not apologise, Mel. I have decided that I must speak about these things. It is true that it still hurts me, but I do not want Ben's memory to die and sometimes—' She broke off, shaking her head. There were times now when she could not recall Ben's face and that frightened her. She had lost him once; she did not want to lose her precious memories.

Their hostess was asking everyone to take their seats. Small sofas and elegant elbow chairs had been arranged about the room to give a clear view of the dais that had been set up for the convenience of the musicians. The evening was to begin with the soprano Madame Casciano's recital and would continue with pieces from Handel's *Water Music* and then everyone's favourite, Mozart.

Arabella and Melinda settled down on a small sofa, quickly becoming engrossed in the music. Because she seldom attended an evening such as this in the country, Arabella was particularly enjoying herself and it was not until the interval that she sensed someone was staring at her. Looking up, she saw it was her cousin and he was staring in a way that made her feel decidedly uncomfortable. She turned away. She did not care for the calculating expression in his eyes. He had been behaving in an irritating manner from the moment he arrived to escort them here this evening.

'Shall we go in to supper?' she asked of her companion as they stood up.

'Yes, of course.' Melinda glanced at Sir Ralph and frowned. 'Oh yes, I see. Poor Belle! If you are not careful, he will spoil your visit. Odious man!'

'I shall not allow him to spoil anything,' Arabella said, lifting her head proudly. She linked arms elegantly with her friend and they walked towards the dining room, where a cold supper awaited the guests. 'I believe I am hungry.' She gave Ralph a cool nod in passing, determined not to let his presence throw a cloud over her. 'What shall we do tomorrow, Mel? I have no engagements yet.'

'Harry is coming up to join me, but he will not arrive until the evening,' Melinda said and looked happy. 'I think I should like to go shopping.'

'Yes, that would be most enjoyable,' Arabella agreed and gave her arm a squeeze. 'Oh, look, here is Captain Hernshaw coming to join us.'

He greeted them both warmly and offered to help choose their supper from amongst the array of delicious foods on offer. When he had selected the choicest titbits, he asked one of the circling waiters to carry it all to the table they had found by a window overlooking the gardens. It was a pretty view—small lanterns twinkled amongst the trees, giving them a magical atmosphere.

Arabella was relieved that her cousin made no attempt to join them at supper and even more so when her aunt came to sit with them, telling her that Ralph had taken himself off to meet some friends. She thought that perhaps he had realised that she did not care for his company and would have more pride than to persist with his pursuit of her. She had discovered in the past that a certain reserve of manner was usually enough to deter any but the most thick-skinned fortune hunter.

* * *

The remainder of the evening had passed very pleasantly and Arabella was smiling as she prepared for bed that night. She had enjoyed herself a great deal; though she suspected that Melinda would try to promote the interests of her brother-in-law when she could, it did not matter. She found him excellent company, but was not in the least interested in becoming his wife. However, Captain Hernshaw was not the kind of man to push himself forward without encouragement, and, although prepared to be friendly, she had given him no cause to hope.

Getting into bed, Arabella snuffed out her candle. She was tired and thought that she would soon sleep, but as she closed her eyes she found herself thinking of Charles Hunter. It was odd the way he had shut her out so suddenly that morning at the inn. Perhaps there was a secret heartache that made him wish to keep his distance from others—something that had caused those dark shadows beneath his eyes.

'Well sir, I dunno as there's much more I can tell you,' Fred Lightfoot said and looked into his half-empty tankard thoughtfully. 'As I said to his lordship, I knew there was summat going on in the woods that night. It had happened afore, see—but there were summat different about it that time. Sir Montague were a rum cove, if you ask me. A lot of them girls what they had up there were whores and it were just a bit of a lark, no real harm done—but the girl I found wandering mazed was gentlefolk. I knew it as soon as I saw her and that's why I took her to a safe place I knew of. She didn't seem to understand what was happening to her and I couldn't look after a girl like that, sir. Like a frightened child she was, whimpering and shrinking from my touch, even though I told her I would not hurt her. So I went off to fetch my Mary and—'

'When you returned she had disappeared.' Charles frowned at him. He seemed honest and clearly Daniel trusted him. 'Could Forsythe have come and taken her away?'

'I doubt it, sir,' Fred said and shook his head. 'That cottage belongs to me now my grandfather's dead and Sir Montague knew nothing of it. I intended to do it up for me and Mary when I got the time, but I'm going to sell it now we've got this place with the Earl of Cavendish.' He scratched his head. 'I'm afraid that's all I can tell you. It ain't much, I know— but that girl what drowned herself, she were a village lass. And that's all I know, sir.'

'I was hoping for more,' Charles said and frowned. 'Can you recall what she looked like—the girl you helped?'

'Yes, sir. Lingered in my mind she has, because I felt I should have done more. A pretty girl, sir, with soft fair hair hanging halfway down her back and eyes that were more green than blue…and I noticed a little mark on her left temple. It might have been a scar or a birthmark, I can't rightly be sure.'

Charles sat forward, touching his left temple with his forefinger. 'Sarah had a scar there. She hit her head when playing in the nursery once. My mother dismissed the nurse who allowed it, though it was not truly the woman's fault.' He took a shuddering breath. 'I believe it must have been her— the description fits her perfectly. My poor sister! What can have happened to her? I have been searching for months and this is the first time I have heard anything positive. Where could she have gone after you left her?'

'I wish as I could help you find her, sir,' Fred said. 'She wandered off that night alone, but I doubt she could have gone far. It might be a good idea to start a search in the surrounding district, sir. I've got an aunt lives in the village of St Tydyll, not more than eighteen miles distant from Sir Montague's estate. Not much Madge Lightfoot doesn't know about what goes on for miles around. I could send her a letter, sir, see if she has heard anything of a girl being found.'

'Thank you, I shall be grateful for any information Mrs Lightfoot can give me, but now that I know where to concentrate my efforts I shall set my agents on the case.' Charles signalled to the innkeeper. He was suddenly filled with new hope. Sarah had somehow escaped from the rogues who had thought to use her in their evil rites and he could not think that God would have been so merciful only to let her perish in some other way. 'If Sarah is still alive, I shall find her. Someone must know where she is.'

'If she found someone kind hearted enough to take her in, she may be safe, sir—though 'tis a wonder that she has not let you know where to find her.'

'Perhaps she cannot,' Charles said. 'You said that she seemed confused—' He broke off to order more ale for them both as the landlord approached. 'It might be that she has lost her memory.' Or more likely that she was afraid to contact her family because she felt that she had shamed them.

'Thank you, sir.' Fred accepted the ale, though he had refused payment in money. 'I'll get my Mary to send that letter off today to my aunt. I can't write more than my name, sir, but Mary is a clever girl. If we hear anything, she will write to you if you give me an address.'

'You may write to my house in London,' Charles said. 'I

am grateful for your help, Mr Lightfoot, and would willingly pay for your trouble.'

'I don't want money for that, sir. I feel bad enough about what happened as it is. It would be a relief to me to know that she had been found safe and sound, sir—and to her poor mother, I dare say.'

'I dare not tell my mother anything yet,' Charles said. 'She has been ill since Sarah's disappearance, and if I should disappoint her it might kill her. No, I shall keep all this close to my chest, Mr Lightfoot. If we find Sarah, only her true friends will know what has happened to her. We have not talked of it outside our family and the people I trust.'

Fred nodded his understanding. Until the girl was found, the circumstances of that terrible night and the months succeeding it could not be known. It might be that she was ruined and would never be able to take her proper place in society.

'You can trust me not to let my aunt know your sister's name, sir. I shall just ask if she has heard of a young lady turning up out of the blue. If she is anywhere near St Tydyll, Madge will know of it.'

'I pray God she does,' Charles said, though he had little hope. Were it that easy to find Sarah, his agents would have done it before now. 'As for me, I shall return to London tomorrow and set my agents in the right direction…'

'May I speak with you, Cousin Arabella?' Ralph asked when she returned from an outing one morning later that week. She had been in town for four days now and had done her best to avoid him as much as possible. 'I have something particular I wish to say to you—in private, if you please?'

Arabella hesitated. It was on the tip of her tongue to refuse and make some excuse, but she knew that he would continue to pester her unless she acceded to his request. It might be as well to have it out now.

'Very well, Ralph,' she said in a crisp, cold tone that she hoped would deter him. 'If you wish, we shall go into the parlour—but I must not delay long. I have to change for tea.'

He nodded, his eyes narrowing as she preceded him into the front parlour. Arabella took up a position near the pretty marble mantelpiece, turning to greet him, her head high. She looked proud and unapproachable, which made him frown.

'Will you not be seated, cousin?' he asked. They were of a similar height and yet he felt at a loss while she remained standing.

'I prefer to stand,' Arabella said, her dark eyes flashing silver. 'Please say what you must, Ralph. I do not wish to not keep Aunt Hester waiting.'

'You can surely spare a few minutes,' Ralph said, looking sulky. 'You have been here four days and I have hardly seen you. You are always out when I call. I waited purposely today to see you.'

'I did not come to London to sit in the house, Ralph. I have been walking in the park with friends this morning and yesterday I went shopping.'

'As you did the previous day—but we digress. I know that Mama feels it is time you remarried, Arabella. She is very fond of you, as I am. It seems to me very sensible that we should grant her wish to see you happily settled as my wife.'

'Does it indeed?' If Arabella's manner had been cool before, it was positively frosty now. 'I am afraid that I have no plans to marry again, but if I did it would be for my own sake and not to please Aunt Hester—much as I love her.'

He frowned, looking annoyed. 'You know I did not mean it that way. I have always had a high regard for you, Arabella. I am sure we should suit very well. Besides, you have not had any other offers, have you? You can't wish to live out your life as an old maid.'

'It is very kind of you to concern yourself on my behalf, but I do not believe it would suit me to marry you,' Arabella replied with dignity. How dare he say such things to her? She would have liked to be sharper, but struggled to control her anger at his insensitive behaviour for the sake of her aunt. She could see the gleam of resentment in his eyes, but was determined to continue. 'It is hardly your business whether I have had offers of marriage or not, sir. You are my cousin, Ralph, and I wish you well for my aunt's sake, but we have never truly been friends. Please put the idea of a marriage between us from your mind at once. The answer is and always will be no.'

'Mama thought you might want to make her happy in her last years, but I told her you were too selfish.' His mouth pulled back in a snarl. 'I suppose you do not care what becomes of her if we are ruined?'

'Aunt Hester would always have a home with me if she needed it,' Arabella replied calmly. 'You cannot blame me for your misfortunes, Ralph. My aunt has told me that she has helped you time and again. I have no intention of allowing you to run through my fortune at the card tables.'

'Damn you!' Ralph glared at her. 'No wonder they call you the ice queen. You always were above yourself! Well, you will live to regret this, cousin.'

'I do not understand you.' She raised her brows at him. 'Why should I regret something that would give me no pleasure?'

'You leave me no choice,' Ralph muttered. 'I did as Mama wanted, but I would as lief go to the devil as marry a shrew!'

Arabella made no answer as he stormed from the room. She felt a little sick inside—for the look on his face had been one of hatred and she knew that she had made an enemy. Perhaps she ought not to have said as much, but she had wanted to make it clear that she would never accept an offer from him.

Going upstairs to change out of her green-striped walking gown into a pretty peach muslin, Arabella was reflective. She did not believe that her aunt had put Ralph up to it. She might wish to see her niece married, but Lady Tate could not hold out much hope of a match between Arabella and her son. She must be aware that they had never truly liked each other.

What had Ralph meant when he'd said she would live to repent turning him down? He was sometimes of a surly nature, but she did not think him capable of violence towards her. Yet he had said that her rejection had left him no choice—as if the course he now intended to follow would be her fault.

Arabella was aware of a feeling of unease as she went down to the back parlour to join her aunt for tea. Just what was her cousin hinting at?

Aunt Hester was reading a letter when Arabella entered the sunny room. She looked up and smiled, laying her letter to one side.

'Here you are, my dear. Ralph called on us earlier—did you see him before he left?'

'Yes…' Arabella hesitated and then made up her mind.

'He asked me to marry him. I refused. I am sorry if that upsets you, Aunt.'

'I was afraid he meant to do it,' Lady Tate said. 'I am sorry, Arabella. I told him not to make a fool of himself. I knew you would see through him, my dear. He is more deeply in debt than I guessed. I have promised to sell a diamond necklace that my grandmother left me, but I have told him that I can do no more. He will simply have to sell what assets he has left.'

Arabella hesitated, then, 'Perhaps I could spare a thousand or two, Aunt. For your sake I would help him this once.'

'Oh, no, my dear,' her aunt said, looking distressed at the idea. 'Please do not offer. It would be a big mistake. He would only abuse your generosity and you would never be free of him. No, no, Ralph must learn to live within his means. He should look for some form of employment. I suggested that he go into the army or the church, but he was angry. He thinks that I shall sell this house for him, but I shall not.'

'I do not see my cousin in the army, Aunt.' Arabella could not picture Ralph as a vicar either, but refrained from saying so. Her cousin had been indulged too much as a boy and had never learned self-discipline. Selfish and thoughtless, he would not heed anyone's advice. 'But perhaps if he is driven to it, the church may serve.'

'It is not to his liking,' Lady Tate said, 'but if he has ruined himself he must save what he can. While he continues to live in London and run with those friends of his... Mind you, Sir Montague Forsythe met with a fatal accident recently. I do not know the details but I think his sins had found him out, though Ralph will not say much concerning him. I believe they gambled together and Ralph was hoping that his friend would make him a loan to tide him over, but now it is out of the question.'

Arabella nodded. She had never met Sir Montague Forsythe and did not know what kind of a man he might be, but perhaps he might have been of help to Ralph.

'Yes, well, perhaps he has other friends that might help him.'

'I doubt it,' Lady Tate said. 'Another of his friends killed himself just before Sir Montague's accident—possibly he had debt problems too. It has all been kept very quiet so I cannot say.' She frowned and looked thoughtful. 'I cannot pretend I am sorry they are gone, for they were a bad influence on Ralph. He had only been involved with them for a few months and I blame them for his excessive gambling. I think there is another—Sir Courtney Welch—but I do not think Ralph truly likes him. He does not speak of him, though I have seen them together.'

'Well, I dare say my cousin may sell a part of the estate and recover,' Arabella said. She reached out to touch her aunt's hand. 'Do not worry about it for the moment, dearest. I shall tell you what I have already told Ralph—if you should need it, there is always a home with me.'

'You are such a sweet generous girl,' her aunt said. 'But I am determined not to give in to him, Arabella. This house and my jewels are all I have besides my jointure—and I do not intend to let Ralph's foolishness ruin me completely.'

Arabella nodded, but she could not help recalling the ugly look on her cousin's face when he'd told her that she had left him no choice… Just what had he meant by that?

# Chapter Three

'Haven't seen you here for a while,' Captain Hernshaw said as Charles Hunter walked into White's that afternoon. 'Good grief, man, you look awful—what happened to you?'

'I had a slight accident,' Charles admitted wryly. His injury had left him with a persistent headache. 'I ought perhaps to have rested longer, but I had things to do. To be honest, I can't stand being an invalid. Besides, Mama has decided that she will come up to town for a short visit next week and I have promised to be on hand to escort her to evening affairs.'

'How is your mama?' Captain Hernshaw frowned. He knew that Mrs Hunter had been ill for some months but was uncertain as to the cause, though he thought it might be something to do with her daughter, who was, he had heard, staying with cousins somewhere in Scotland.

'She says she feels a little better,' Charles said. 'I think she might have been more sensible to take the air at Brighton or even Bath, but she wants to visit a friend of hers and also her seamstress.'

'Ah, well, I dare say she knows best. The ladies usually do,' Captain Hernshaw said and smiled. 'Harry and Melinda are in town, you know.'

'I remember your brother's wife,' Charles said, his stern features relaxing into a smile. 'A sweet pretty girl…' Very like his own sister! The thought struck like the blade of a knife. Melinda reminded him of Sarah, as she had been when he last saw her.

'Yes, she is,' Captain Hernshaw agreed. 'She is enjoying herself very much this visit. A friend of hers is staying with Lady Tate and they go everywhere together.'

'Ah, I see,' Charles nodded. 'Do you care for a game of cards?'

'I was about to visit my fencing master. I feel in need of some exercise. If you don't mind my saying so, Hunter, you look as if it would do you good. Why don't you come along?' He glanced across the room as a gentleman entered. 'Besides, the air here has just become somewhat tainted. It is a pity that *he* cannot be blackballed.'

Charles glanced in the direction of the other's gaze, seeing the reason for Hernshaw's distaste. Sir Courtney Welch had just entered the club and was standing looking in their direction, his eyes narrowed in concentration.

'I couldn't agree more,' he said. 'The man is a devil—let us go. Did you say your fencing club?'

'I have been taking lessons from a new master recently—it is amusing to discover one's own failings at the very least. And better than being invited to join Welch in a hand of whist.'

'Well, yes, anything must be. A lesson in swordplay from a master is perhaps just what I need,' Charles agreed with a grin. He had been labouring beneath a dark cloud for too long and a good fight with the swords might put him right. 'I'm grateful, Hernshaw. I was at a loss to know what to do with myself.' He nodded distantly to Sir Courtney as they passed.

'Come to Melinda's affair this evening,' Hernshaw said as they went out into the street. 'It's only a buffet supper, music and cards, but I am sure she and Harry would be delighted to see you.'

'Thank you, I shall,' Charles said. He was feeling better for having met a friend. He had already sent three agents up to Yorkshire to search for his sister and there was no point in moping. Had his mother not decided that she would visit London the following week he would probably have posted off to Yorkshire himself in the morning, which would quite likely have been a wasted journey. His agents had far more chance of discovering news of Sarah than he had. 'Yes, I would enjoy that, Hernshaw. I need a bit of light relief to blow the megrims away…'

'I think I shall give a dinner at the end of next week,' Lady Tate said as they were taking tea that afternoon. 'A great friend of mine is coming up for a short visit. She will stay at her own house, of course, but I want to do something for her. She has been quite ill, you know. I think there was some kind of bother with her daughter, though she didn't say quite what… Sarah was ill of a fever, I believe, and went to stay with cousins in Scotland. Selina was rather vague about it all, but she had a severe chill herself and was unwell for months.'

'Poor lady,' Arabella said. 'It will be nice for you to see her, Aunt. We shall, of course, arrange a dinner party in her honour, but I dare say you will want to be private with her one afternoon. If you let me know, I shall take Tilda out so that you are not disturbed.'

'Ah, yes, dear Tilda,' Lady Tate said, smiling absently. 'Always such a help to me, but rather inclined to come in when one doesn't want her.' She shook her head. 'Being a companion is not an easy life, my dear. We must always remember that.'

'Yes, of course I do,' Arabella replied. 'Tell me when your friend is coming to tea and I shall take Tilda shopping. It is quite time she had a new dress and a bonnet too.'

'Such a generous girl,' Lady Tate said, giving her a look of approval. 'I was thinking about this evening, my dear—' She broke off as the door opened and Tilda entered a little hesitantly. 'Ah, there you are. I was about to send for you again. I shall have some more hot water brought in.'

'Oh, have I kept you waiting? I am so sorry. Only I went to the library and changed your books and I happened to meet someone—' She was about to blurt out her news, but then checked. 'It was just a friend…no one important.' Tilda blushed and turned away, for she had almost embarrassed Arabella by telling her that she had seen Mr Hunter in front of her aunt. 'Oh, yes—and I spoke to Captain Hernshaw, such a pleasant gentleman! We passed in the street and he went out of his way to be polite to me, Arabella. He asked if you were going to Melinda's musical evening, and I assured him that we all would be there.'

'Yes, of course,' Arabella said. 'I am looking forward to it.'

'That is what I was about to say when Tilda came in,' Lady Tate said, glancing at Arabella. 'I wondered if you would mind if I didn't join you this evening, dearest?'

'Are you feeling unwell, Aunt?'

Lady Tate shook her head. 'Not really, my dear.' She placed a hand to the centre of her chest. 'Just a little discomfort. I suspect I have been eating too much rich food lately. It might be as well if I stayed home and had an early night. I think I shall have a light supper and go to bed with a book—if you do not mind?'

'Would you like me to send for the doctor?'

'No, indeed not,' Lady Tate said. 'It is nothing very much. I shall be better by the morning.'

'Shall I stay with you this evening? I do not mind.'

'Certainly not. I should not hear of it,' Lady Tate said. 'You must go, Arabella. You have Tilda to bear you company. I know Melinda would be very disappointed if you did not go.'

'Yes, she would,' Arabella agreed. 'But she would understand if you needed me. However, if you feel that spending the evening in bed will suit you, I shall go as we agreed. If you are no better tomorrow, we shall have the doctor.'

'It was perhaps those dates that Ralph bought me,' Lady Tate said glancing at the small box of sweetmeats on the table beside her. 'Some are stuffed with nuts and others with marzipan. He knows they are a favourite with me and I have eaten too many. I believe I shall tell the maids to throw them out, for I cannot resist them.' She glanced at Tilda. 'Unless you would like them? I shall not eat any more, for I cannot stop at one and I really should not have them.'

'Oh, may I have them?' Tilda looked pleased. 'I am very partial to them, Lady Tate—but only if you are sure?'

'Yes, perfectly sure. Take them up to your room—if they stay here I shall continue to eat them,' Lady Tate pulled a face.

'Foolish, I know, but as I said, they have always been a favourite with me.'

'I found all the books you asked for,' Tilda said, wanting to show herself deserving of the gift. 'And I brought a book of poems that I thought you might like, Arabella.'

The conversation turned and they talked of their favourite books, poetry and music until it was time for them all to go up and change for the evening, Tilda carrying the precious box of sweetmeats that she had been given.

At the top of the stairs they parted, each going to her own room. Arabella said that she would pop in to say goodbye before she left and received a kiss on the cheek from her aunt. She was thoughtful as she went to her own room. It was unusual for Lady Tate to complain of feeling unwell—but she must not jump to conclusions. Just because Ralph had given his mother a box of sweetmeats and she was feeling ill after eating some of them, it did not follow that there was anything wrong with them.

Arabella saw Charles Hunter almost as soon as she entered the large, elegantly appointed drawing room. It came as a complete surprise, making her heart jerk with shock and then race on. For a moment she was stunned. What was she to do? She had imagined that she would simply ignore him if they met in passing, but that was obviously going to be impossible, because he was standing with Melinda and her husband. She hesitated, taking a deep breath as she steadied her nerves. Lifting her head proudly, she walked towards her friend, determined to behave as though nothing was wrong.

It looked as though both he and Captain Hernshaw were preparing to leave the small group, but as she approached

Charles Hunter turned and saw her. His gaze narrowed, a little nerve flicking at his temple.

'Belle!' Melinda cried and darted forward to kiss her cheek. 'How lovely you look! You know Captain Hernshaw, of course—but I do not think you are acquainted with Mr Hunter?'

A picture of Charles lying naked in his bed, his very masculine body damp with sweat, flashed into her mind, almost slaying her confidence. However, she smiled politely and nodded her head.

'I believe we have met before, Mr Hunter, though I am not sure where.'

A flicker of appreciation showed in his eyes as he followed her lead. 'I am sure it must have been at the house of a mutual friend, Lady Arabella. I hope you are quite well?'

'Oh, yes, very well, thank you.'

Just behind her, Tilda gasped, but prudently said nothing.

Arabella's heart was racing as she lifted her gaze to meet his eyes. She saw that he was smiling and for some reason her nervousness vanished as if it had never been. She was quite sure that he would neither say nor do anything that might damage her reputation.

'I am glad to hear that, ma'am,' Charles said and turned to his companion.

'We had better take our places, Hernshaw, or we shall be missed.'

'Yes, I believe you are right,' Captain Hernshaw replied and smiled at Arabella. 'Will you excuse us, ladies? No doubt we shall meet again before the evening is out.' The two gentlemen crossed the room to where others had begun taking their seats at one of the tables set up for cards.

'Belle, love,' Melinda said. 'I am so glad you are here.'

'You saw me only yesterday,' Arabella reminded her with a little smile. 'But I am equally glad to see you, Mel—and you, Harry.'

Sir Harry nodded his head. 'The same, I'm sure, Belle,' he said with the easy confidence of old friends. 'You must come and stay with us in the country this autumn. Mel would love to have you.'

'Yes, I should,' Melinda agreed at once. 'We are here until the end of next week and then we must go home—but I should be so pleased if you would come to us after you leave your aunt.'

'Perhaps,' Arabella agreed. 'Though I may stay in London a little longer than I had first thought. It depends how my aunt is feeling.'

'She is not with you this evening?'

'A little indisposed,' Arabella said. 'It may be nothing, but I shall see how she goes on.'

Melinda nodded, tucking her arm through Arabella's. 'Do you wish to play cards or simply listen to the music?'

'If you will excuse me, my love,' Sir Harry said. 'I must join my table. I shall see you at supper, ladies.' He nodded his head to them and walked off to join his brother, Charles Hunter and another gentleman at the card tables.

'Oh, I think I shall be content to listen to the music,' Arabella said. 'I may not stay long after supper, Mel. I am a little concerned about Aunt Hester, even though she would not hear of my staying at home this evening.'

They settled themselves on a convenient sofa, though Tilda found herself being borne away to play cards with three elderly ladies who refused to take no for an answer. Glancing her way a little later, Arabella thought that she was enjoying herself. Since she had remarked on how delicious the dates were on their way here, it had clearly been misguided of Arabella to suspect Ralph of having deliberately given his mother something intended to make her ill. She must put such an idea from her mind at once. She decided to enjoy the music and put her doubts aside, at least for the moment. However, she could not prevent herself from occasionally glancing in the direction of the card table at which Charles Hunter was seated, and it was with a little shock that she discovered his gaze was directed at her more often than not.

It was not until the supper interval that Arabella had a chance to speak with Charles more privately. She was standing at the long table, which was loaded with platters of delicious meats and side dishes, when she sensed someone beside her and looked to her left to see him standing there.

'Lady Arabella.' He inclined his head, a faint smile on his mouth.

'Mr Hunter. I did not ask you earlier, but how are you now?'

'Much recovered, thank you,' Charles replied, his eyes moving over her intently. After that morning at the inn, he had intended to put her completely from his mind, but seeing her so suddenly that evening had made him very aware of her and he had found his thoughts wandering too often at the card table. She was a beautiful woman and seemed universally popular—a woman who would attract attention wherever she went. Until this moment he had not realised just how much she had risked by helping him in the way she had. 'May I be of service to you? Fetch you a glass of champagne, perhaps?'

'That would be kind of you,' Arabella said. 'I am sitting with my companion over there by the window. Perhaps you would be kind enough to bring a glass for Tilda too?'

'Yes, certainly,' he said. 'Are you enjoying your visit to town, ma'am?'

'Yes, I think so,' Arabella said. She frowned slightly, for she could not quite shake off her feeling of foreboding. 'Yes, thank you, sir.'

'Is anything bothering you?' Charles narrowed his gaze, for he sensed that she was anxious about something. 'If I may be of assistance, I should be only too pleased. You were there when I needed help. I should be happy to return the favour if I could. And, of course, I must repay the money you spent on my behalf.'

'That is not necessary, sir. But perhaps…' Arabella hesitated. They were strangers and yet she felt that she knew him intimately, having nursed him through his fever. There was little that she had not discovered about his person—save for what had caused that deep sadness in his eyes sometimes. But how could she confess to a man that she hardly knew that she was concerned for her aunt's safety? It was a delicate subject and not one she could speak of at an affair like this. As it happened, Captain Hernshaw hailed them at that moment and the opportunity was lost. 'No, no, there is nothing, thank you.'

Returning to her table with the food she had selected, Arabella waited for the gentlemen to join them. She noticed that Tilda was merely picking at the plate of cold chicken and green beans she had chosen.

'Are you not hungry?'

'Oh, no, I do not think I want very much this evening,' Tilda replied. 'I had two scones for tea and some of those delicious dates Lady Tate was good enough to give me.'

'You do not feel ill, do you?'

'Not exactly ill,' Tilda said and pulled a face. 'Just a little unsettled in my stomach. It is strange for I do not often suffer from dyspepsia, you know.'

Arabella nodded. It had often amazed her in the past that her companion could eat as much as she did without feeling discomfort. Once again she felt a pang of unease for her aunt. She kept remembering the look of menace in her cousin's eyes when he had told her that she had left him no choice. Was he saying that, because Arabella would not marry him, he meant to dispose of his mother to gain what remained of her fortune?

'No!' she said aloud and shook her head just as the two gentlemen approached with the champagne.

'I am sorry,' Charles said, brows rising. 'I believed you wished for a glass of champagne.'

'Yes, I do,' Arabella replied and accepted the glass with a rueful look. 'My remark was not directed at either of you gentlemen, but at my own thoughts. I am not sure that Tilda wishes for anything. I believe she feels a little under the weather. If one of you would be kind enough to call for my carriage, I think we shall go home shortly.'

'Yes, of course,' Captain Hernshaw said. He looked kindly at the companion. 'I hope you are not ill, ma'am?'

'Oh, no, just a little discomfort,' Tilda said, but she had gone quite pale. 'If you will excuse me, Arabella, I must go to the retiring room for a moment.'

She got up rather quickly and went off as Captain Hernshaw departed in another direction. Charles sat down at the table, his eyes dwelling on Arabella's face as she took a sip of her champagne.

'I believe you *are* troubled in some way,' he said. 'I am sincere in my offer of help, Lady Arabella. You may call on me if you wish at any time and I shall do whatever I may.' He took a card with his town address from his waistcoat pocket and handed it to her.

'Thank you.' Arabella accepted it, slipping it into her reticule. 'It is true that I do have something on my mind. I cannot yet quite come to terms with it, sir, for it is unpleasant—but it may be that I shall ask for your advice.' A faint blush came to her cheeks. 'In saying that, I do not mean to presume on our somewhat unusual acquaintance.'

'Believe me when I say that you could not,' Charles said and smiled at her in a way that made her catch her breath. 'I must beg your forgiveness for my manners that last morning at the inn. It was very foolish of me. There are reasons why I am not free to pursue my own life—but friendship is another matter. I hope that we may be friends and that, should you need it, I may be permitted to perform a service for you.'

'You are very kind,' Arabella said and her heart skipped a beat. It was ridiculous to feel so happy because of this brief meeting, but she did. His brusque words had lingered at the back of her mind, leaving her feeling oddly hurt, but now that had eased. She knew that she liked him, perhaps more than most gentlemen of her acquaintance, and, strangely, felt that she could confide in him if her fears proved to have some truth in them. Perhaps it was because, in nursing him so intimately, she had stepped over the barriers that usually prevailed with a new acquaintance. 'I am not sure enough of my suspicions to speak of them just yet, sir—but another day I may be more certain of my facts.'

Charles nodded. He had sensed that something was worrying her and was glad that he had spoken as he had. It was true that he had nothing more to give other than friendship, even though she stirred forgotten feelings in him, but there was nothing to stop him offering the little he could.

Their chance for private conversation was at an end, for at that moment Melinda came up to them, concerned that Arabella was leaving early.

'I hear that Tilda is feeling unwell—and you said that Lady Tate too was a little indisposed. Do you imagine that they have taken some kind of a fever?'

'I believe they may both have eaten something that disagreed with them earlier today,' Arabella said. 'I think it may be just a touch of dyspepsia, Mel. Please do not worry. Hopefully, they will both be better soon.'

'Oh, I see,' Melinda said, looking relieved. 'Shall I see you tomorrow as we planned?'

'Yes—unless my aunt's illness is more serious than I fear. If something occurs to prevent me, I shall let you know,' Arabella said. She stood up as she saw that Captain Hernshaw had returned to the room and was looking her way. 'I think I must go. Goodnight, Mel—goodnight, Mr Hunter.'

'Goodnight, Lady Arabella.' Charles looked at her thoughtfully as she walked away. There was more here than she was yet prepared to say unless he was mistaken. He did not know why that should concern him, but it did. Of course he owed her a debt of gratitude, but it was more than that—she aroused in him an inner warmth that he had believed he would never feel again.

'Your companion is waiting in the hall downstairs,' Captain Hernshaw said as he met Arabella at the door of the supper room. 'I believe she had been quite unwell and was feeling a little dizzy. I told her to sit and wait while I fetched you to her.'

'Oh, poor Tilda,' Arabella said. 'I should have told her not to eat those dates!'

'Was something wrong with them?' he asked, looking a little puzzled at her tone of voice.

'Yes, I think there may have been,' Arabella said and frowned. 'Excuse me, I may not say more. I must go to Tilda.'

She went quickly downstairs to the entrance hall, discovering her companion sitting near the open door as if in need of fresh air. Tilda looked pale and was clearly unwell, which caused Arabella some disquiet.

'You have been sick I think,' she said. 'I am so sorry, Tilda. Do you have pain in your stomach, my dear?'

'Yes, just a little,' Tilda said. 'I should be pleased if we could go quickly, Arabella. I do not want to be a trouble to you on the way home.'

'You will not be,' Arabella replied. 'You must say if you wish to stop at any time. It must be better for you to bring up anything that is causing you to feel ill.'

'It was probably the dates,' Tilda said. 'I ate several of them before we left and I know they do not particularly suit me, even though I love them—but they were so sweet and delicious.'

'Well, perhaps you should not eat any more of them,' Arabella said. 'I shall arrange to have them thrown away to save you from temptation.'

'Oh, but…' Tilda subsided as a wave of sickness passed over her, making her shudder. 'Yes, perhaps that might be for the best.'

Arabella said no more as she followed her companion into the carriage. She did not know whether it was possible to discover if the dates had been doctored with some foreign substance, but perhaps she ought to find out. Both her aunt and Tilda had eaten only a handful of the sweetmeats and both were ill. What might have happened if Aunt Hester had eaten them all as had been intended?

Arabella herself had never liked the sticky fruit. It was unlikely that she would have tried one even if they had been offered to her. Lady Tate knew that—perhaps Ralph did too?

Her thoughts were whirling with confusion as the carriage clattered through the dark streets. It was a terrible suspicion, but she could not rid herself of the idea that Ralph was planning to dispose of his mother in order to gain control of her estate.

Charles was thoughtful as he made his way home at the end of what had turned out to be rather a pleasant evening. He was a little surprised to discover that he had enjoyed himself far more than he had expected. Now why was that? Could it possibly have anything to do with the fact that Lady Arabella had been present?

No, that was foolish, he decided, dismissing the thought with an impatient shake of his head. She was beautiful, intelligent, generous, brave…but that didn't mean anything. He had met other women with those qualities. Why should this one be any different? And yet she was… Somehow she had managed to get beneath the barrier he had raised against her. He had found himself watching her throughout the evening, listening for her laugh, noticing the way she walked, the unconsciously seductive sway of her hips.

This was leading nowhere! Charles made a conscious effort to put her from his mind. He had no right to think of himself or his own pleasures while Sarah was still lost.

The next morning Lady Tate declared herself much better, but Tilda was still feeling very sorry for herself. She had been sick twice during the night and Arabella insisted that she stay in bed for the rest of the day. She herself took charge of the remainder of the suspect dates, removing them to her room. Her first thought was to destroy them, but she hesitated, wondering if she ought to retain them and see if some kind of test could be made to discover if they had been treated with poison.

It was such a difficult decision. Arabella hated the idea that her cousin could do anything so evil as to make his mother ill. Tilda was the one who had suffered most, but there were only three dates left in the box, which probably meant that she had eaten far more than she had admitted. Could it just be overindulgence? The suspicion that an attempt at murder had been made on her aunt was so awful that she tried to put it from her mind. Surely she was wronging her cousin? He might be selfish and thoughtless—but wicked? No, no, she must be wrong! No gentleman could possibly do such a thing!

Deciding that it would be best to dispose of the dates after all, she gave them to a maid and said that she thought they were not fresh as they had made two of the household ill.

'No one should be tempted to eat them, Maria,' she said.

'They must be thrown away, do you understand? If they are eaten, they may cause sickness and stomach pain.'

'Yes, ma'am, of course. I'll see to it myself.'

'Thank you.' She nodded to the girl. 'I am going out to meet some friends, Maria. If my aunt should ask for me, I shall return before nuncheon—and if Tilda should be worse, please send for the doctor.'

'Yes, ma'am. I'll look in on her again myself.'

Reassured, Arabella put on a green velvet pelisse and tied the strings of a fetching straw bonnet beneath her chin. She had arranged to meet Melinda at a certain milliner's shop that morning. They would spend an hour or so trying on hats and then perhaps visit a little teashop together. She decided to put her uncertainties out of her mind. Her aunt was much recovered and, although Tilda was still feeling a little unwell, neither of them had died. Had Ralph wished to kill his mother, one or both ladies would probably be dead. But of course he hadn't! What a terrible thought to have!

It was just her foolish imagination running away with her.

It was as she was nearing the shop where she had arranged to meet her friend that Arabella came face to face with a gentleman she would have preferred not to meet. She saw him coming and wondered if it might be better to cross the street, but then decided that she would not allow herself to be intimidated. He lifted his hat as they passed, a slightly malicious smile in his eyes.

'Good morning, Lady Arabella. What a delight to see you in town. I trust that you are well?'

'Yes, thank you, Sir Courtney.' She did not return the sentiment for she sensed that it had not been sincere. She walked on quickly, refusing to glance back even though she had a strong feeling that he had turned to watch her. Instead, she moved proudly, head up, refusing to show any sign of apprehension.

She could not like that man! She had never considered his proposal of marriage even for a moment, and perhaps her dislike of him had been a little too evident. She knew that she had made an enemy of him, but apart from feeling a slight discomfort when they met it could make no real difference to her life. She put the small incident from her mind and hastened her step as she saw her friend entering the milliner's just ahead of her.

Melinda inquired after Lady Tate when they met and Arabella was able to assure her that she was recovering. They spent a happy morning together trying on hats and bonnets, both of them buying two additions to their autumn wardrobe before leaving. They parted feeling well satisfied with their outing, and Arabella was smiling as she entered the house just before twelve-thirty. She looked at the calling cards and saw that two had been left for her. It seemed that Captain Hernshaw and Mr Hunter had both called while she was out.

Perhaps it was just as well, she thought. She might have said something foolish concerning those dates had she spoken to Mr Hunter. She had almost made up her mind now that she had been quite mistaken.

Lady Tate came down the stairs even as Arabella was taking off her pelisse and bonnet. She smiled at her, nodding as Arabella handed a bandbox to the maid assisting her.

'Did you buy something nice, my dear?'

'Yes, a rather pretty velvet bonnet for the autumn and a smart hat for riding,' Arabella said. 'Melinda has asked me to visit her in the country next month and I may do so. It is a while since I bought any pretty clothes and I think I must refurbish my winter wardrobe while I am here in town.' She looked at her aunt. 'How are you now, dearest?'

'Oh, quite recovered,' her aunt said robustly. 'It was just overindulgence, Arabella. I should not have eaten three of those dates all at once. I know that they can upset me. I was sorry to learn that Tilda was ill last night.'

'I believe she ate rather more of them than you, aunt.'

'Oh…well, perhaps I ought not to have given them to her. They might not have been quite fresh. I did think that one had an odd bitter taste in the centre, but the next one was very sweet and delicious.'

'It may not have been the dates at all,' Arabella said for she could see her aunt was thoughtful. 'Tilda ate two scones with jam and cream at tea. Perhaps the cream was off.'

'Yes, perhaps,' Lady Tate said and her frown eased. 'I believe I shall come with you this evening, my dear. We are engaged for Vauxhall are we not?'

'Yes, that is so,' Arabella said. 'Sir Harry has taken a booth for the evening and there are to be several of us. It will be a merry party I believe.'

'I am looking forward to it,' Lady Tate said and smiled at her. 'Shall we go and have our nuncheon, my dear?'

'If you will excuse me, I must just wash my hands,' Arabella said. 'I shall not keep you waiting long.'

She ran up the stairs to her own room and tidied herself quickly. As she started back down the stairs she saw that her cousin was being admitted to the house. He glanced up and saw her, frowning as she came down to join him.

'We are about to have nuncheon, cousin,' she said, deliberately keeping her tone flat. 'Would you care to join us?'

Ralph looked at her oddly. 'Mama is with you?'

'Yes, of course.' Arabella's gaze intensified. 'Why should she not be?'

Was it her imagination or did he look uncomfortable? She gave him a direct challenging look and he dropped his gaze. He was discomforted!

'No, of course not. I just wondered.'

'Come into the dining room. I am sure there is plenty of food for you to share, Ralph. Tilda is staying in bed today. She was unwell last evening.' She felt no satisfaction as his head came up, the expression in his eyes similar to that of a rabbit facing a stoat. He was extremely nervous. 'We think she ate something that disagreed with her.'

'Oh…what?' he asked, a belligerent stare on his face now, as if he were daring her to accuse him.

'Who knows?' Arabella said. 'It might have been anything—perhaps the dates you gave Aunt Hester. She had a slight dyspepsia and gave them to Tilda, who ate several.'

'If you are accusing me of something, say it!' He glared at her fiercely.

'Accusing you, cousin?' Arabella smiled coolly. 'Why should I accuse you of anything? You haven't done anything terrible—have you?'

'Certainly not!'

'Then I am certainly not accusing you of anything,' Arabella said. 'Excuse me, I must not keep my aunt waiting.'

She swept past him into the dining room, where Lady Tate was already helping herself from various dishes laid ready on the sideboard. There was a dish of creamed spinach, small new potatoes in melted butter, peas and various meats, besides a baked carp and onions.

'How nice of you to call,' Lady Tate said as she saw her son follow Arabella into the room. 'Please sit down, Ralph. There are plates enough on the sideboard if you care for some nuncheon.'

'No, I shall not stop,' her son replied. 'I came to tell you that I am going down to the country. I have made arrangements to sell the estate and I need to talk to my bailiff.'

'Good, I am glad you have made a decision to do something positive,' his mother said. 'I do not yet have the funds for the necklace I promised you, but I should have it when you return.'

'Thank you,' he said, his eyes holding an expression that might have been sympathy. 'I am sorry if you were unwell last night, Mama.'

'Oh, it was nothing. I am quite recovered now, thank you, Ralph.'

'I am glad to hear it.' He nodded his head at her, turning a thoughtful look on Arabella. 'I may not see you again this visit, cousin. I shall be away for a couple of weeks, I dare say.'

'I wish you a pleasant journey,' Arabella returned. 'But I may still be here when you come back. I think I shall extend my visit for longer than I had anticipated.'

Was it her imagination or did his eyes fire with anger? Arabella could not be certain, but she felt a sense of relief when he left them. Once again her suspicions were raised. Having made one unsuccessful attempt to murder his mother, was he going to wait until Arabella had returned home to try again?

'Is something wrong?' Lady Tate asked as Arabella sat down at the table. 'You look upset, my dear.'

'Oh…no, of course not,' Arabella replied, giving herself a mental shake. She was being ridiculous. She must not dwell on her doubts—she had no true reason to suspect Ralph, though she wished now that she had not instructed that the dates be thrown away.

Arabella went in to Tilda's room before leaving that evening. The companion was feeling better, but sorry for herself because she was obliged to miss the long-awaited treat of going to Vauxhall.

'We shall attend the theatre tomorrow,' Arabella said to cheer her. 'I dare say you will be well enough to accompany us, Tilda. Rest tonight and we shall see how you go on in the morning.'

'It was my own fault for eating so many dates,' Tilda said. 'They were very rich. I shall not do it again.'

Arabella nodded and went out to join her aunt. They were travelling to the pleasure gardens in their own carriage and would meet their friends there. Arabella was wearing a new gown of silver gauze with a deep blue underskirt. She had had her hair dressed high at the back of her head with two shining ringlets allowed to fall on her shoulder, and she carried a fine silk shawl for when the air began to cool. At the moment it was a pleasure to be outdoors in the sultry August night.

The lovely gardens were overflowing with ladies and gentleman strolling here and there, and it was a few minutes before they saw their friends standing by a booth that sold various trinkets. Artists trying to make their way in the world often took a booth there in the hope of attracting a patron, and it was at one of these that they saw Harry and Melinda engaged in buying a picture. Arabella felt an odd fluttering sensation in her stomach as she realised that Charles Hunter was one of the party. She took a deep breath, schooling herself not to show the sudden rush of excitement she had felt on seeing him. It was quite foolish of her, because she knew that he meant to offer her nothing but friendship.

'Lady Arabella, good evening,' he said as she approached. Her heart leapt as he smiled at her. 'You look very well this evening. That gown is most becoming.'

'Thank you, sir. I must admit that it is a new one.'

'Your seamstress is to be congratulated,' he said. 'Melinda has just purchased a picture for her country house. Do you share her interest in art, ma'am?'

'Yes, very much,' Arabella replied. She felt a little breathless, though she was trying to be sensible. Mr Hunter was merely making polite conversation. 'We share many interests. Melinda is one of my closest friends.'

'It was a happy chance that brought you to town at the same time.'

'Yes, indeed.' Harry and Melinda had completed their purchase, and, after greeting the newcomers to their party, had wandered on towards the supper booths. Arabella lingered a few moments longer on the pretence of examining a water-colour. She waited until the others had moved away a little before turning to him. Music was playing at a distance, pleasant but not sufficiently loud to make conversation difficult. 'You offered to help me, sir—may I call on you for advice one day soon?'

'Yes, certainly,' Charles said and offered her his arm. 'Do you wish to discuss the problem now?'

'No, not this evening,' Arabella said with a little frown as Melinda looked back at them, clearly wondering where they were. 'What I have to tell you is of a serious nature or I would not ask for your help—but perhaps you might take me driving one day in the park?'

Charles studied her in silence for a moment, realising that she was truly anxious about something. 'Yes, certainly. I should be delighted. In the morning at about ten?'

'That would be wonderful,' Arabella said, her frown disappearing. She felt so much better now that she had decided to share her anxieties. 'I may be letting my imagination run away with me, but I am worried and there is no one else I may discuss this particular problem with, sir.'

'Then I shall be delighted to help,' Charles said. 'Ah, here comes Hernshaw. He means to ask if you will dance, I imagine—perhaps you will give me the honour a little later?'

'Yes, thank you,' Arabella replied. She smiled as Captain Hernshaw came up to them. Like Charles Hunter, he was very good looking and dressed in the height of fashion. Both men of distinction, they embodied all the qualities of true English gentlemen. 'Good evening, sir. It is very warm, is it not?'

'Very,' he replied. 'Not too warm to dance, I hope? They are about to begin the entertainment.' His eyes dwelled on her face. 'I have been looking forward to securing a dance with you this evening, Lady Arabella.'

'I shall dance with you later, Captain,' Arabella said, 'but for the moment I believe Melinda wants me.'

She left the two gentlemen to exchange a few words of

greeting and went to join her friend, who had lingered outside the booth to wait for her as the others went inside.

'Is everything all right, Belle?' Melinda asked. 'You looked quite serious as you were talking to Mr Hunter just now.'

'Yes, everything is fine,' Arabella said. 'What a pretty gown you are wearing, Melinda. Is it one of your new ones?'

'Yes, it is,' her friend said looking pleased. 'But yours is beautiful. Is it the gown you ordered when we visited the seamstress together?'

'Indeed, it is,' Arabella agreed, linking arms with her as they went into the booth where a cold collation of wafer-thin ham and various accompaniments had been laid for them. 'This looks delicious, Mel. I am so glad that you invited me this evening. I am looking forward to dancing—and to the fireworks later.'

'Captain Hernshaw asked especially if you would be here,' Melinda answered with a sly look. 'He is very taken with you, dearest Arabella. I think you have found yourself an admirer.'

'Captain Hernshaw is a friend,' Arabella said with a little shake of her head. 'You must not think it more—for my part at least.'

'Oh…' Melinda looked disappointed, but then her eyes fell on Mr Hunter and she saw that he was watching Arabella intently. She smiled because, although she favoured her brother-in-law's suit, all she truly wanted was for her dear friend to be happy. And it would distress her to see Arabella live alone for the rest of her life. She was young and beautiful and she ought to be happily married, as Melinda was herself. 'Ah, I see…well, I shall not tease you, Belle, but I do expect you to ask me to be matron of honour at your wedding.'

'No, no, there is nothing of that nature.' Arabella shook her head at her friend, but Melinda's expression was mischievous and there was no time to say more for the gentlemen had joined them.

They seemed to be on excellent terms, talking of a new fencing master that they were patronising, and of their pleasure in becoming skilled in all the finer points. However, when they joined the ladies, the conversation turned, moving to the latest fashions from France and a new production that was now running at Drury Lane Theatre.

'We have made arrangements to see it tomorrow,' Arabella said. 'They say that Mr Edmund Kean has brought a more natural form of acting to the stage. Many people prefer his style to that of Mr Kemble.'

'I think that Mr Kean is at his best when performing Shakespeare,' Captain Hernshaw said. 'His Shylock was a marvellous thing.'

'Then I look forward to tomorrow even more.' Arabella smiled as he offered to refill her champagne glass. 'No, thank you, sir—not if we are to dance.'

'But assuredly we are to dance,' he said and stood up, offering her his hand with gallantry.

Arabella took it and let him lead her out to where other couples had begun to dance under the starlight. As they took up their positions, she glanced back at Charles Hunter. He was watching them, but she was too far away to read the expression in his eyes.

# Chapter Four

Afterwards, Arabella always wondered what had made her wake so suddenly. She had gone to sleep almost as soon as her head touched the pillow that night, drifting off with the sound of music and fireworks in her ears. It had been such a pleasant evening at Vauxhall. She had danced twice with Captain Hernshaw and once with Mr Hunter. She had enjoyed herself with both partners, but only one had caused her heart to behave in the oddest manner. For a moment as she woke it was the memory of that dance that held her, making her sigh—but then she became aware of something. It was an odd sound, a little whimpering cry…like a child or someone hurt.

Jumping out of bed, Arabella lit her candle and then pulled on a dressing robe lying nearby. She went out into the hall, pausing for a moment, waiting, and then the cry came again. It seemed to come from the hall below. Walking to the head of the stairs, she used her candle to light a branch of candles that stood on a side table just there. Holding them aloft, she looked down and saw a huddled figure lying at the bottom of the stairs. She knew at once that it was her aunt.

'Aunt Hester!' Arabella ran down the stairs, standing the branch of candles on a table as she bent over the hunched figure of her aunt. Her heart was beating rapidly, for she sensed that something was very wrong here. 'Are you hurt badly, dearest? What happened?' She knelt down, helping Lady Tate into a sitting position.

'I…I am not sure,' Lady Tate said and gasped as if in pain. 'I must have fallen. My wrist hurts and I have twisted my leg under me. I do not know if I can get up.'

'I shall wake the servants at once.'

'No! Try to help me yourself,' her aunt said. 'Please, my dear. I do not think anything is broken, Arabella. My wrist is painful and I cannot rise without help, but I would rather not wake the servants at this hour.'

Arabella assisted her as she attempted to stand. It was difficult and clearly painful for Lady Tate to put her left foot to the ground. However, after a few minutes she steadied and then begged Arabella to help her return to her room.

'Should I not send for the doctor, Aunt?'

'I would prefer that you didn't, at least until the morning, and then only if I need him. It was just a little fall, my dear. I got up to fetch a book and paused at the head of the stairs. I think I must have turned dizzy or missed my footing in the dark.'

'Did you not bring a candle?' Arabella was puzzled for she had not seen any sign of a chamberstick, which ought to have been lying on the floor nearby if her aunt had dropped it.

'No, I thought I should see well enough without one,' Lady Tate said. 'So foolish of me.'

She leaned on Arabella's arm as they slowly mounted the stairs. Arabella could feel her trembling. The fall had clearly shaken and upset her, and Arabella sensed that her aunt was holding her emotions firmly in check. Once they were inside Lady Tate's room, where several candles had been left burning, she closed the door and looked at her.

'And now, if you please, Aunt, you will tell me the truth.'

'I was afraid someone might hear what we said,' her aunt confessed ruefully—she had known that Arabella would not be fooled. 'I did have a candle, Arabella. I believe someone took it after I fell—and I believe that person pushed me as I hesitated at the head of the stairs.'

'Oh, Aunt Hester, no!' Arabella had feared something of the sort since finding her lying at the foot of the stairs but she had not wanted to admit it, even to herself. She had hoped that she was mistaken, for it was too awful to contemplate. 'Do you have any idea who it might be?'

'I am not sure…' Lady Tate sat down on the edge of her bed. Her hands were shaking as she pressed them to her cheeks in distress. 'I do not want to believe it, Arabella but I think it may have been—' She broke off with a little sob. 'No, no, how could it be? I know he has not been the best of…' Her eyes were wide and frightened as she looked at her niece. It was almost as if she were begging to be reassured that she was mistaken. 'Ralph told us he was going down to the country…'

'Yes, he came purposely to tell us,' Arabella said, hesitating for a moment, then, 'I am sorry to say it, Aunt, but I do not trust him. I do not like to think it, but it could have been my cousin. And it is so odd that it happened tonight after he said he was leaving town, though I suppose he might have sneaked back in while we were out this evening and hidden in the house. If he did, he must have come the back way, through the gardens—and without the servants seeing him. If he went to so much trouble, his purpose cannot have been honourable. Yet how could he have known you would leave your room to go down and fetch a book?'

'I always keep one by the bed in case I wake and cannot sleep,' Lady Tate said carefully, as if considering each word. 'This evening when we came up it had disappeared. I thought it odd, but I did not bother to fetch another for I thought I should sleep. And I did sleep. But then something woke me. I think someone was in my room. I felt something…a breath…a touch of air on my face as if someone bent over me. I was frightened and I cried out. For a moment there was silence—and then a floorboard creaked and the door closed. At first I hardly dared to move, but then I got up, lit my candles and looked about me. I went out into the hall. I could see no one, but I sensed that someone was in the darkness watching. And I felt that Ralph had been in my room, that he was there somewhere. I could faintly smell that distinctive pomander he wears on his hair. I paused at the head of the stairs and called his name…'

'Oh, Aunt, why did you not summon your maid?'

'I did not wish to cause a disturbance. I stood there for a few seconds wondering what to do. I was not sure whether to light all the candles and ring for assistance—and then someone pushed me. I fell and struck my head on something; for a few moments everything went black. When I came to myself the house was in darkness—my candle, which I had placed on the table at the head of the stairs, had gone.' She looked at Arabella in distress. 'I must be going mad, mustn't I? Ralph wouldn't…he couldn't…'

'I do not wish to hurt you, Aunt Hester,' Arabella said, reaching for her hand, 'but I do not think it beyond my cousin to attempt to harm you.' She saw the grief in her aunt's eyes and realised how painful this must be for her to accept. 'Forgive me, dear Hester. Perhaps I am wrong. Yes, I dare say I am mistaken.'

'No, I think you are right,' Lady Tate said and closed her eyes for a moment as if she found the truth too hurtful to contemplate. 'My husband was not a good man, Arabella, and Ralph takes after him. They have both done things of which I cannot approve and I believe I spoiled my son when he was a child. He has violence in him. I have heard stories of his ill treatment of his horses and his servants. These things come back, whether one wants to hear them or not.' She raised fearful eyes to her niece. 'He wants me dead because I will not sell the house and give him the money. What am I to do?'

'It is clear to me that you are not safe here alone.' Arabella hesitated, and then, 'I believe he will have left town by now, having established his intention to go down to the country, to escape any blame for your fall. I dare say he expects me to send word of your accident. I shall not do so. We shall leave him to wonder for the time being.'

'He tried to kill me—my only son…' Lady Tate shook her head sadly. 'Perhaps I should give him the house?'

'You must decide that for yourself,' Arabella told her. She had made her own decision very quickly. 'I think we shall continue as we are for the moment, but when I go home you must come with me. Perhaps we can think of a way to keep you safe.'

'Come with you?'

Arabella nodded. 'You are welcome to make your home with me for as long as you wish, Aunt. I have a large house, which is far too big for one person. You, Tilda and the girl I told you of are the only people I care for and I should be glad to have your company. My house is far too big for one person.'

'I am to allow him to drive me from my own home?' Lady Tate looked more distressed than angry.

'For the moment. Until we can prove his intention and have him restrained.'

Lady Tate gave a moan of despair. 'Have my own son arrested for trying to murder me? No, Arabella, I cannot do it. It would shame me. Whatever he has done he remains my son.'

'You are too upset to think clearly tonight,' Arabella said. 'You must lock your door after I leave, Aunt Hester. I do not think anything more will happen tonight, but you should be careful.'

'Yes, I shall,' Lady Tate said. 'We shall talk again in the morning, my dear. Please say nothing of this to anyone for the moment.'

'No, of course not, though I think we must do something. This may be the second time Ralph has tried to harm you.'

'Those dates…' Lady Tate gave a little shudder. 'Oh, this is terrible…' She put a hand to her chest as if in pain, her face waxen in the candlelight. 'I do not know what to do for the best. Perhaps I am wronging him. I may have turned faint at the head of the stairs. Perhaps no one pushed me.'

Arabella decided to say nothing more. Aunt Hester was making excuses in her own mind, finding it too difficult to admit that her son intended her ill. Indeed, it was such a terrible situation that she wondered if she was in some kind of a bad dream herself. Could Ralph really have been so wicked as to harm his own mother? It did not seem possible and yet she had sensed something when he called on them, and she had always felt that he was not to be trusted.

'Try to sleep,' she said and touched her aunt's hand. 'I shall see you in the morning.'

'Goodnight, Arabella. I am so glad you are here. You are a great comfort to me.'

Arabella went out. She waited outside the door until she heard her aunt turn the key in the lock before returning to her own room, where she also locked herself in. She felt as if a dark shadow hung over her. The suspicion that her cousin had tried to kill his own mother twice was so dreadful that it made her feel sick to her stomach. Surely there must be some other explanation? And yet in her own mind she felt that it was true.

How could Ralph be so callous? It was so awful that she could not bear to think of it, but she must. Aunt Hester was at risk and there was only Arabella to care for her. Her face was set in grim determination as she sat on the edge of her bed. She would not allow Ralph to have his way. Somehow she would protect her aunt from his wickedness.

Arabella went to her aunt's room the next morning before she left for her appointment with Mr Hunter. Lady Tate's personal maid was just leaving and she told Arabella that her mistress was still sleeping.

'She has been overdoing things, ma'am,' Ellen said. 'The doctor warned her last month that she must take things easier now so I didn't wake her.'

'Are you telling me that Lady Tate is ill?' Arabella frowned—this was news to her.

'She isn't exactly ill, ma'am. The doctor left her some powders to take. I think her heart is not as strong as it might be, though I only heard what he said as he left. Her ladyship did not tell me anything herself.'

'I see…' Arabella frowned. If Aunt Hester was unwell, might she indeed have turned faint the previous night? Arabella wondered for a moment if her aunt had imagined that someone was in her room. No, it was unlikely to be that—for where was the missing chamberstick? Whoever had taken it had made a mistake. And she must not forget that Tilda had also been sick after eating those dates, which was too much of a coincidence. 'She did not mention her illness to me.'

'You won't tell her ladyship what I said?' Ellen looked anxious. 'I thought that you would know, ma'am.'

'No, I did not. Thank you for telling me. I shall not betray you.'

Arabella turned away. If Aunt Hester was sleeping, she would not disturb her. She was thoughtful as she went downstairs. The news that her aunt was unwell was worrying. Did Ralph know of his mother's condition? Ellen had told her—had she also told her mistress's son?

The shock of the fall the previous night might have been enough to kill Lady Tate if her heart was truly not strong. Had she lain there all night, unable to get up without help…it could well have meant her death. Was that what Ralph had hoped for—that she would die of natural causes after her fall? Arabella had often thought him a coward, and it might be that he had not been able to bring himself to administer the fatal blow as his mother lay senseless at the bottom of the stairs.

Arabella was still pondering her unpalatable thoughts when a knock at the door heralded the arrival of Mr Hunter. He was admitted by a footman, a smile lighting his eyes as he saw her in the hall.

'Lady Arabella, you are ready. I am not late, I trust?'

'Quite punctual,' she replied with a smile that lit her dark eyes with a silver flame. 'I am glad to see you, sir. There have been some worrying developments during the night.'

'Indeed?' He sensed the burden of doubt and anxiety that hung over her. 'Come, we shall talk as I drive. I can see that you are deeply troubled.'

'I am anxious about my aunt,' Arabella said as they stood for a moment on the pavement outside the house. She glanced meaningfully at his groom. 'What I have to tell you is quite shocking.'

'I understand.' Charles turned to his groom. It would not do for this conversation to be overheard. 'You may go, Brooks. I shall see you later.' He turned to Arabella, taking her gloved hand in his to help her up to the driving box of his curricle so that she could sit beside him. She would feel easier for telling him her troubles in private.

'Thank you,' she said, settling herself as he took the reins. 'I was reluctant to speak in front of your man, for what I have to say must not be repeated. I believe that someone may be trying to kill my aunt.'

'Good grief,' Charles said. 'That is indeed very shocking— but please continue.'

He listened in silence as Arabella told of the dates that had made both her aunt and Tilda feel sick, and then of finding her aunt at the bottom of the stairs the previous night. She explained that her cousin was deeply in debt and that Lady Tate had refused to sell her home for his sake. She also told him that she had learned that morning of her aunt's ill health.

'I think that, if I had not found her, her fall might have led to a severe illness and death.'

'She was lucky that you woke when you did.'

'Yes, indeed. We were fortunate—but it concerns me that it may have been my cousin, sir. I do not like to believe it, but…'

They were driving through busy streets, which were in certain areas clogged by the passage of dray wagons, horses and carriages, and it was not until they entered the park that Charles began to question her. He asked her about her cousin's behaviour in earlier times, frowning and repeating details, as if he wished to build a picture in his mind.

'I believe I may have met your cousin on a few occasions, but he was often in the company of men like Sir Montague Forsythe—and, of late, Sir Courtney Welch.' Charles looked grim. 'I think that his friends may have led him into acts of violence, even depravity—and once a man loses his sense of decency—' He broke off with a shake of his head. It was too dark and painful a story to tell her. She did not need to know of his sister's abduction or the wickedness of men like Forsythe. The loss of her husband and now this fear for her aunt was more than enough to distress her—though she had such spirit that he thought she would defeat her dastardly cousin somehow.

'So you do not think that Aunt Hester has delusions or that I am letting my imagination run away with me?'

'I do not believe you are prone to foolish fancies,' Charles said, glancing at her as he relaxed the reins, allowing his horses to walk at a sedate pace within the park grounds. 'You appear to be a very sensible young woman, if I may say so— and as for Lady Tate, I saw no sign of delusional behaviour last evening. If she said she could smell a certain type of pomade, then she probably did. However, that does not prove that her son was there or that he pushed her.'

'No, it does not,' Arabella agreed. 'Perfume sometimes lingers in the air and others may wear the same preparation. However, her chamberstick had disappeared before I arrived. Someone must have taken it.'

'It could not have rolled away?'

'She said it was on the table at the head of the stairs. I think she must have meant to light the branch that always stands there—as I did. I saw nothing of her own candle.'

'Proof, perhaps, that someone was there.' Charles frowned and looked thoughtful. 'Do not think that I doubt your word, Arabella. I believe your cousin may indeed have attempted to murder his mother. These things have happened in the past, unthinkable as it is! However, I know from personal experience that it can be very difficult to prove someone's guilt— and one must do that for a conviction in law.'

'Aunt Hester does not want that,' Arabella said looking anxious. She sighed and shook her head. 'I was foolish enough to have the dates thrown away. I dare say it might have been possible to have them tested?'

'I believe there are men of science who might have proved the presence of poison in them if it was there,' Charles agreed. 'I know of agents who are skilled in all manner of things concerning detection, though their findings cannot always be used as proof in a court of law—but, had you obtained such proof, would it have helped if your aunt does not wish for the scandal? There would be no escaping it were you to bring this matter to the attention of the law.'

Arabella hesitated, then, 'I might perhaps have been able to threaten him with exposure. To make him promise that he would not attempt anything of that nature again.'

'I think that could prove to be a very dangerous act on your part,' Charles said. 'If he would kill his own mother, I do not imagine he would hesitate to dispose of you.'

A shiver ran down her spine. 'No, I suppose not. I had not considered that I might be in danger.' She was thoughtful for a moment. 'Ralph asked me to marry him. I refused and he was angry, said that I had left him no choice, but he is my only relative other than my aunt. If I died…' Arabella's voice faded away as she realised that it was not only her aunt who might become Ralph's victim. Her eyes opened wide as she looked at Charles. She hesitated a moment, but then realised that she must continue. It was true that she hardly knew him, but somehow a turning point had been found. She was drawn to him in a way she could not explain, and something inside was telling her that this was a man she could trust. And indeed there was no one else to whom she could turn. 'When Ben left me his considerable fortune, I was already wealthy in my own right. As things stand at the moment, Ralph would inherit everything once my aunt was dead.'

'Perhaps you should make a will excluding him—and tell him of it.' Charles suggested. He brought his horses to a halt, turning to look at her, his gaze narrowed and intense. She was a beautiful, intelligent woman and he suddenly wished that he were free to follow his own heart. 'Are you truly all alone? Have you no one to protect you?'

'Only Nana,' Arabella said. 'She was my nurse and has retired to her own cottage. I have my companion Tilda Redmond, and one special friend—and of course a bevy of faithful servants who care for my needs and would protect me to the best of their ability.'

'I meant a male relative or close friend who could protect you,' Charles said and read the answer in her face. Looking into her eyes, he was conscious of an overwhelming desire to hold her close and tell her that he would care for her as long as they both lived. No other woman had ever made him feel quite like this, his stomach clenching with a fierce desire that shocked him by its intensity. And yet it was more than desire, a feeling he had never experienced before that he did not yet understand. He reached out, touching her cheek with one finger. 'Arabella…'

She caught her breath, her lips moist and soft, unconsciously inviting the kiss that seemed to be seconds away. She smiled, his name sweet on her lips.

'Charles!' A voice hailed him from a few feet away and the spell was broken, shattered into tiny fragments that melted like ice in the sun. He withdrew his hand, turning to look at the gentleman who had come up to them, unnoticed until that moment. 'I did not know you were in town.'

'John…' Charles greeted the newcomer with warmth in his voice—they were good friends and John Elworthy had done much to sustain him during the dark months of Sarah's disappearance. 'I am glad to see you. May I introduce Lady Arabella Marshall. She was married to Ben Marshall—you will remember him, of course. Arabella, this is my good friend, John Elworthy.'

'Yes, I do remember Ben,' John said. 'He was a fine officer, Lady Arabella. I am sincerely sorry for your loss, ma'am. We all respected and liked your late husband.'

'Thank you.' Arabella warmed to the newcomer's open, honest manner at once. She sensed that Charles Hunter liked and trusted him. Suddenly, she realised that for the first time she was able to hear someone speak of Ben without feeling an overwhelming sense of loss. 'I am pleased to meet you, sir.'

'And I you,' John replied. 'Shall I see you later at the club, Charles? I've had a letter from Daniel. Something one of his agents discovered about that other business that I think you should hear.'

'At White's at one o'clock,' Charles agreed. 'Excuse me, we must get on. I shall see you later.' He gave the reins a little flick as John tipped his hat to Arabella, and then, after a moment, he turned to look at her again. 'I think that you are probably safe enough for the moment with your cousin out of town. When he returns I shall speak to him, warn him that he must tread carefully.'

'Perhaps…' Arabella hesitated. Her heart had returned to its normal beat, but it had behaved most oddly when his finger touched her cheek. Regrettably, the spell had been broken by Mr Elworthy's arrival. 'But we have no proof.'

'Proof is only necessary if we seek a legal solution,' Charles replied and a little nerve flicked at his temple. He and his good friend the Earl of Cavendish had discovered that to their cost in the effort to bring Sir Montague Forsythe to justice. In the end Forsythe had died in a desperate struggle as he had tried to escape arrest and been killed by his own pistol. 'Sometimes there is a natural justice. Your cousin may be warned in a way that he will not easily forget, Lady Arabella. Please allow me to do at least this for you.'

He had twice called her Arabella; now he was using her formal address once more. He had put a distance between them. Something had made him draw back. She had thought for a moment as he touched her cheek that he felt some-thing—that he was attracted to her in a physical way as she was to him—but now she wondered if she had read too much into that look.

Arabella was thoughtful as she was driven home. She had believed that she would never feel love again, never experi-ence physical attraction to another man after her husband's loss. The lightest touch of Charles Hunter's finger against her skin had made her realise it was possible for her to feel desire. She was not yet certain that she had fallen in love with Charles, but she had wanted him to hold her, to kiss her—to feel the strength of his arms and the hardness of his strong body. In fact, she had discovered a need, a hunger for physical contact in a way that she had not expected to experience again.

Charles spoke only occasionally as he negotiated the traffic, and when he did it was to give her advice about how to handle her cousin. He impressed on her that she must be very careful never to be alone with him and promised that he would do all he could to ensure her safety. He was clearly ge-nuinely concerned for her, which gave Arabella a certain amount of satisfaction. He must like her more than a little to be so anxious for her welfare.

When they arrived back at her aunt's house, he handed her

down from the carriage, holding her gloved hand for a moment or two longer than necessary, his eyes intent on her face.

'Believe that your safety will be one of my chiefest concerns,' he told her. 'Your cousin shall be watched when he returns from the country. And he will know the consequences should anything untoward happen to you, Lady Arabella.'

'Thank you,' she said and her heart missed a beat as their eyes met. He was looking at her earnestly and yet not in the way he had looked at her in the park. For one wonderful moment she had sensed his passion, his need of her, but now his feelings were under an iron control. 'It is good to know that I have a friend, sir.'

'Yes, you have my friendship.' For a brief second a flame leapt in his eyes and she thought he would say more, but then it was gone. 'I know you go to the theatre this evening, but I shall see you tomorrow at Lady Hamilton's card party, I believe. Please give my kind regards to Lady Tate.'

'Of course, sir. Thank you for taking me for a drive. Talking to you so openly has eased my mind and…it was most enjoyable.' For reasons that had nothing to do with her anxiety about her aunt, she acknowledged inwardly.

Leaving him to attend his horses, Arabella went into the house. She saw a man coming down the stairs and recognised him as her aunt's doctor. She started forward at once, feeling alarmed.

'Is Lady Tate unwell?'

'No cause for alarm, ma'am,' Dr Harris said, smiling at her kindly. 'A day or so in bed should put her to rights, Lady Arabella. She tells me she had a little fall last night. Her wrist is hurting her this morning, but it is only a slight sprain.'

'Oh, poor Aunt Hester,' Arabella said, relieved that it was not worse. 'Is there anything we need to do for her, sir?'

'She should rest for a day or so, that is all. I shall call again tomorrow but I am sure she will be feeling better.'

'Is her heart causing her pain, doctor?'

'No, I do not think so,' he said, looking thoughtful. 'I detected a little flutter, a little irregularity, a month or so back, but I think she is in no immediate danger. I believe she worries too much. I have told her she should leave that to others.'

'I am hoping to persuade my aunt to come and stay with me in the country for a while.'

'Yes, the very thing,' he said. 'You can keep an eye on her, Lady Arabella.' He retrieved his hat and gloves from the hall-stand. 'I must be on my way. I shall call again tomorrow.'

Arabella thanked him and ran upstairs, feeling anxious. However, Lady Tate was sitting up against a pile of pillows surrounded by books and her writing materials. She glanced up as her niece entered and smiled a welcome.

'Ah, there you are, my dear. Did you enjoy your drive?'

'Yes, very much. I saw the doctor leaving. Did you feel unwell this morning, Aunt?'

'My wrist hurts a little. I thought it best to be sure nothing was broken,' Lady Tate said. 'It was so foolish of me to fall like that. I must be more careful in future.'

'Yes, but you know it was not just a fall, Aunt.'

Lady Tate glanced down at the bed, her fingers plucking restlessly at the silk covers. 'Oh, I do not want to think about that, Arabella. Perhaps it was my own silly fault. I may have turned faint or missed my step…' She could not meet her niece's eyes as she made excuses.

'Perhaps, but I still think you should come and stay with me for a while, Aunt Hester.'

'Maybe I shall.' Lady Tate patted the bed beside her. 'Sit here for a moment. Tell me, Arabella, do you like Mr Hunter very much? I should so like to see you safely married, dearest.'

'Oh, Aunt…' Arabella shook her head at her '…we are merely friends. You know that, surely?'

'But you might be more one day?'

'I do not think so. I have told you that I do not wish to marry again.' And yet Arabella knew even as she spoke the words that they were no longer true. She had believed that she could never feel passion again, never find another man she could bear to touch her intimately, that no one would ever make her feel as Ben had—but for a moment in the park that morning she had looked into Charles Hunter's eyes and wanted him to kiss her.

'I am sorry if I interrupted something important earlier,' John Elworthy said as they met at White's club that afternoon. Charles dismissed it with a shake of his head. 'I wanted to pass on a message from Daniel from one of his agents.'

'He has heard something important?' Charles was alerted. 'He has news of Sarah?' His own investigations had so far come to nothing. Mrs Lightfoot had heard no mention of a young woman who might be his sister, and so far his agents had little to report.

'Not of Sarah,' John said. 'But the agent has heard of a young woman who might be her. Apparently, she lives near the village of Stapleford Bridge. The cottage is not in the village itself, but just outside—which is why Daniel's agents did not hear of her sooner. It seems that she never goes out alone and, when the report was sent, she had not been seen for a few weeks.'

'Do you have the direction?' Charles stared at him, hardly daring to hope. There had been other sightings of girls who might be Sarah these past months, all of them false trails, ending in disappointment. 'I do not know the village—is it near Forsythe's estate?'

'No, more than thirty miles distant as the crow flies,' John told him. 'Possibly longer, if you follow the roads. It is merely a hamlet, I believe. I had only Daniel's brief note before he and Elizabeth left for France. I was intending to write to you and that was why I was so pleased to see you.' Recalling an odd, intent look on his friend's face when he first saw him in the park, he raised his brows at Charles. 'Have you known Lady Arabella long?'

'No, not really. I attended her wedding to Ben Marshall, but I had not seen her since. We met by chance on the way here. I had had an accident and she found me lying on the road. She took me up in her carriage and she helped to care for me while I lay in a fever.'

'An accident?' John looked at him thoughtfully. 'You are sure it was an accident? Forsythe and Lord Barton are dead and can no longer be a threat to you—but I dare say there may be others who fear exposure, or someone else who holds a grudge against you. Can you think of anyone who might have wanted you dead?'

'I was knocked off my horse by a thief's ruse,' Charles said, dismissing his friend's concern, though he frowned as he recalled a certain game of cards. There was one gentleman who might hate him enough to pay some rogue to murder him, though he still thought it a chance attack for the sake of gain. 'I believe it was for money. I was robbed of my watch and gold, but I don't know if I would have lived to tell the tale had Lady Arabella's carriage not happened along at that moment.'

'You must be careful,' John warned, feeling anxious on his behalf. 'This business with Forsythe has left a nasty taste and I fear it may not yet be ended, even though he is dead. He and Barton had other friends, who may have been involved. Palmer did not name them, but he may have had his reasons. I must tell you that I am at your service, Charles. You may call on me for help at any time until Sarah is found.'

'Pray God that we shall find her safe,' Charles said fervently. 'Thank you, John. I am unable to leave town for a couple of days, because my mother has decided to come up and needs me here. Would it be too much to ask if you would go down to Stapleford Bridge, speak to Daniel's agent and discover if there is any truth in this new rumour? You could make some inquiries of your own, perhaps.'

'I have some business in the morning, but shall go down tomorrow afternoon,' John promised. 'You may rely on me to leave no stone unturned, Charles. If Sarah is found, I shall send word at once.'

'If she is found, I shall come,' Charles said. 'However, I owe Mama a little of my time, John. In my search for Sarah I may have neglected her.'

'I am sure you have not,' John told him, smiling in his own gentle sweet way. 'I know for a fact that you have been a great comfort to her. She told me so when we spoke last. You must stay with her for a day or so, Charles—but if Sarah is found, she will be only too glad to speed you on your way.'

'Yes, though I should not tell her anything very much until I had seen Sarah for myself. Who knows what she may have endured all these months, John? How can we know what might have happened to her? It may have left her badly scarred—both mentally and physically.'

'We must hope that time and the love of her family will cure any ill she has suffered,' John said. 'Tell me, Charles, is there another reason you wish to stay in town?' There was a twinkle in his eyes. 'Lady Arabella is beautiful and surely too young to remain a widow for ever.'

'Yes, she is beautiful—and I like her very well,' Charles said, 'but how can I think of love when Sarah is still lost? And even when we have found her…I must devote myself to making her well again. It may be that I shall take her abroad where no one knows us. If she had been able, she would have come home, John. I can only think that she has been held against her will.' A deep shudder ran through him. 'God knows what she has suffered! I have vowed to care for her and make her safe. I cannot think of myself, John. My wife would have to take second place and that is not right.' How could any woman accept such a situation? It was not to be thought of—even though Arabella had begun to creep too often into his thoughts.

Charles's eyes were dark with grief as he met his friend's gaze. It was true that he felt something more than friendship for the woman who had nursed him when he was ill. He had vowed to help her and he would do all he could to keep her safe—but marriage, children, a happy home were things he dared not hope for. Sarah's abduction had almost destroyed his mother and it had left him bitter and angry, grieving for the sweet sister he had loved so well. He could not offer any woman happiness and it was madness to dwell on something that could never be.

Lady Tate insisted that Arabella and Tilda should go to the theatre that evening without her. Arabella was a little reluctant, but she believed that her cousin must still be in the country awaiting the summons home. The longer he stayed there the better, in her estimation! She was determined that her aunt would accompany her when she returned home at the end of her visit.

The following day, Lady Tate declared herself well enough to get up, though she cried off from their evening engagement once more. Arabella and Tilda attended Lady Hamilton's card party and met up with Melinda, Harry and Captain Hernshaw. Charles Hunter came in just after they had arrived and joined their ranks. However, it was not until suppertime that Arabella had a chance to speak with him privately. It was a warm, still night and they went out into the gardens to take the air.

'How is your aunt, Lady Arabella?'

'Better, I think. She joined us downstairs this afternoon and tomorrow she is expecting a friend to tea.'

'Ah, yes,' Charles said and smiled. 'I believe that may be Mrs Hunter. My mother arrived this afternoon and told me that she would be having tea with her special friend tomorrow— Lady Hester Tate.'

'Oh…' Arabella was surprised. 'I did not realise that, sir. My aunt spoke only of an old friend who was coming up to town after being unwell for some months.'

'Yes…' The shadows were in his eyes. 'My mother has been under a strain for a while.'

'She is not with you this evening?'

'She was a little tired after the journey.'

'Yes, of course.' Arabella nodded her understanding. 'A long journey is often tiring.' She was thoughtful for a moment, breathing in the perfume of a night-flowering shrub. 'I wonder if you could give me the name of an investigative agent I might use, Mr Hunter? It is not for my aunt. She wishes to let the matter drop and I have every hope that a warning will be sufficient in my cousin's case. There is another small matter I wish to have looked into.'

She shook her head as he raised his brows. She had confided in him over her cousin's misbehaviour for she had not known which way to turn, but May's case was different. May was safe enough with Nana for the time being and Mr Hunter could know nothing of her situation. Arabella believed that something bad had happened to her friend to make her lose her memory. She must discover what mystery lay in her past before she revealed her whereabouts to anyone, for she would not risk May being reclaimed by the people who had harmed her.

'This gentleman might help you if it is a confidential matter. He has done good work for me in the past.' Charles took out one of his cards and wrote something on the back of it with a little gold pencil he had in his coat pocket. 'Though if I could be of service I should be only too pleased.'

'No, this is something for which I need an agent,' Arabella said, smiling up at him. 'It was a relief to me to unburden myself in the matter of my cousin, but this is something I can manage myself.' The smile left her face. 'For the moment my aunt is inclined to tell herself that she merely fell, but I do not think she truly believes it.' She shook her head at the thought of her aunt's state of denial.

'You do not believe it?'

'No, I do not, sir. Aunt Hester wants to exonerate her son. I cannot forget that he gave her those dates—and there was a look in his eyes when I told him that they had made two people sick that I found disturbing.'

'You should continue to be careful.' Charles reached out to take her hand in his. The touch of his cool fingers made Arabella tremble inwardly, her heart racing. For one breath-taking instant she thought he might take her in his arms. There was something between them in that moment, a mutual longing and need that made her draw in her breath. But then he gave a slight shake of his head. 'If I were the man I once was…but my heart is dead, Arabella. I could not be the husband you ought to have. You need more than I could give. I am but half a man…' The broken passion in his voice made something deep within her cry out and she wanted to hold him, to love him and take away the pain, but there was a barrier between them.

'Can you tell me what has caused you such sorrow, Mr Hunter? I have sensed it from the first, but I was afraid to ask.'

Charles hesitated. He was on the verge of taking her into his confidence when Melinda came out onto the terrace and called to Arabella.

Arabella turned, sensing the urgency in Melinda's voice. She glanced back, giving Charles an apologetic look and left him to join her friend.

'Is something wrong, Mel? You are not ill?'

'No, I am quite well. A message has come from Lady Tate. She asks that you return to the house immediately.'

'My aunt sent for me?' Arabella's eyes flew to Charles in alarm as he joined her. 'Is Aunt Hester in some trouble?'

'Her note said only that she wished you to return at once.'

'Then I must do so,' Arabella said. 'You will excuse me, Mr Hunter. Perhaps you would call on me soon?' They had unfinished business, but it must wait for another time.

'Yes, of course,' he said. 'Would you like me to escort you to Lady Tate's house?'

'Thank you, no,' Arabella replied. 'You have been kind, sir, but I shall do well enough with Tilda. Goodnight. I shall hope to see you soon.'

She left him to go inside where Tilda was waiting anxiously with her cloak. Glancing back, Arabella saw Charles enter the house a few seconds after her. What had he been about to tell her before they were interrupted? She felt a pang of regret for what might have been. Surely they had been closer than ever before in those few seconds.

Tilda handed Arabella her aunt's note as they went out of the ballroom into the large entrance hall. She paused in the light of some candles to read the brief message. Nothing was said of her aunt being ill or in danger.

'I wonder what can be wrong?' Tilda said, looking at her anxiously. 'Lady Tate seemed quite well when we left.'

'Yes, I thought so,' Arabella replied. 'But we must go at once—she would not have sent for us if it were not urgent.'

'No, indeed. It is very worrying.'

All kinds of thoughts raced through Arabella's head as

their carriage clattered over the cobbles. There were few lights in the deserted streets, for it had turned into a wet cool night that presaged the descent from high summer into autumn. She shivered, feeling apprehensive about what she would find when she returned home. Had her cousin returned unexpectedly and threatened his mother? Or was Aunt Hester ill?

As soon as they arrived and the carriage steps were let down, Arabella got out and hurried into the house. She was met by one of the footmen, who took her cloak.

'Where is my aunt, Jenkins?'

'In her rooms, Lady Arabella.'

She thanked him and flew up the stairs, her heart thumping. She knocked at Lady Tate's door and went in hesitantly, but her aunt was sitting calmly reading a book of poetry. She put it aside as Arabella entered.

'I am sorry to call you back, dearest, but a letter came for you from your home. It was marked urgent so I opened it. Someone called May says that Nana is worse and asking for you. She begs that you return at once—and she is worried about something else, which she will tell you when you get home.'

Arabella took the letter from her aunt, frowning over the beautifully formed script.

'This means that I must cut my visit short, Aunt. I must go if Nana needs me.' She looked at Lady Tate with an anxious frown. 'I do not wish to leave you, but your friend visits tomorrow and you have a dinner arranged for the end of this week.'

'Yes, of course you must go,' her aunt said. 'I shall be perfectly all right. I shall not leave my room at night and if anyone gives me sweetmeats I shall not eat them.'

'Yes, I have to go, but you must come to me next week—

and I shall leave Tilda here with you. I shall tell her a part of what we suspect.'

'No, Arabella,' her aunt begged. 'Leave her with me by all means. I shall feel happier so—and I shall join you next week—but do not tell her what you suspect. Ralph may be innocent. Tilda would never be able to hide her disgust if she guessed that he—' She broke off in distress.

'No, you are right, she could not,' Arabella agreed, knowing her companion's lack of tact. 'Very well, I shall simply tell her that I am anxious about your health. She may drive you mad with her fussing, Aunt, but she will take care of you. If we are fortunate, Ralph will not return until after you leave town.'

'I am sure he will not. He probably means to go to a prize fight or something equally unpleasant, the way that gentlemen do. I dare say he will wait to hear from one of us before he returns.'

'Then I shall go and tell my maid to pack. And I must write two letters. One to Melinda and one to Mr Hunter.'

'Give them to me before you leave. I shall see they are delivered. One of the footmen can go in the morning.'

'Thank you.' Arabella bent to kiss her papery-soft cheek. 'I hate to leave you, but you must keep your promise to come to me next week.'

'I give you my word,' Lady Tate said and looked at her oddly. 'I have decided to sell my house. I shall give half the money to Ralph and half to you, Arabella.' She held up her hand as Arabella protested. 'My mind is made up. I shall have nothing of any real value left. Ralph cannot then see any need to—' She broke off as if it was too difficult to think such a thing, let alone say it. 'You are sure that I shall not be a trouble to you, my dear?'

'Not in the least. My house is so big that we need not meet unless we choose, which we shall, Aunt Hester, every day. I am delighted that you have made your decision—and now I really must go. I shall leave as soon as I am ready.'

'You will travel through the night?'

'Yes, for delay might mean I arrived too late. May is very worried or she would not have sent for me.'

Arabella smiled at her and went out. There was a great deal to do before she could leave and she was anxious to be on her way. Nana had always been special to her. She would feel terrible if the dear old lady died before she could see her again, especially since Nana had asked for her. Besides, May was frightened about something. She had not written down what was troubling her, but Arabella had read between the lines. May would not mention her own distress unless she felt desperate.

Something must have occurred to make her anxious. What could it be? Arabella could only wonder and hope that nothing would happen before she returned home. Perhaps May had begun to recall her past; it would be a good thing and yet it might almost be frightening, for something bad had happened to the girl or she would not have arrived at Nana's door in a state of exhaustion. If someone had discovered her whereabouts… But there was no point in speculating about something she could not know until she had spoken to May.

# Chapter Five

They stopped only to change horses at the various posting houses on their way. Arabella could not think of eating or resting for she was on thorns, anxious to be at home with her loved ones. She prayed that Nana would not die before she could see her again. The old lady had pressed her to keep her promise to her aunt and she could not regret that she had chosen to visit Lady Tate, for something terrible might have happened to her aunt had she not been there. However, Nana had been like a mother to her after Arabella's own mother had died bearing a stillborn child. Arabella had been but five years of age, lonely and frightened until Nana took her to her heart—and it would break Arabella's heart if Nana died feeling that she had been abandoned.

It was dark when they reached the little cottage the following night. Quite isolated, it was situated at the outskirts of Stapleford Bridge, a tiny hamlet that was really a part of Arabella's estate. Some years previously Ben's great-grandfather had built the cottages, which were good red brick and substantial, for house servants who wished to retire from service, and also some of the outside labourers from the estate. Nana had wished for her own home when she retired, though Arabella had wanted her to remain in the big house where she could be looked after. However, the old lady was fiercely proud and had hated the idea of becoming a burden to her young mistress. It had pleased Arabella when Nana had taken May into her home. At first Nana had cared for the girl, who had come to her in the night and collapsed from hunger and weakness, but then, when she was strong again, Arabella had agreed that May should stay to care for Nana as her strength began to fail.

'I would love to have both of you at the house,' she had told May once when they talked about the future. 'But Nana is so independent and I cannot force her to come back to me.'

'She does not want to be a nuisance to you, Belle.'

'She could never be that, for I love her.'

'She has her pride,' May said and looked sad. 'And I owe my life to her—I was starving when she took me in, and ill of a fever. I am happy to stay here and care for her. Besides, it may be best if you do not acknowledge me to your friends, Belle.'

'Do not dare to say that to me,' Arabella said, her eyes flashing with anger. 'I am not ashamed of you, dearest May— and I shall never be, no matter what happens.'

'You and Nana have cared for me and loved me,' May replied, but her eyes held a secret sorrow. 'But how do I know whether or not I deserve your kindness? What kind of a person wanders into someone's house at night wearing only a silken shift? I can never be sure that I am not wicked, Belle, for I may have come from a whorehouse.'

'That is foolish talk,' Belle replied, refusing to listen. 'You are not wicked, May. I know that from my heart, from the way that you have taken on the care of Nana—and whatever you may have been forced to do in the past does not matter to me. I shall still love you, even if you were forced to be the slave of evil men.'

'Oh, Belle,' May replied, tears in her eyes. 'If you and Nana had not cared for me, I might have been forced to become one of those unfortunate women.'

'Well, you were not,' Arabella said. 'And one day we shall discover the truth. We shall discover if you have a family, and who they are.'

'I am not sure that I wish to remember,' May told her and looked pensive. 'Sometimes I seem to recall a house and gardens—a place where I was happy—but it only makes me sad because I can never go back there.'

'If you have a loving family, they will want you back,' Arabella had told her, but May only shook her head. It was perhaps because of her friend's fears that Arabella had waited so long to try to discover the truth. She had intended to ask an agent to start the search for May's past while she was in town, but events had overtaken her. However, she had the card that Charles Hunter had given her and she would write to the agent he had recommended as soon as she had time.

When the carriage at last pulled to a halt, Arabella was feeling very tired. She had slept for a few minutes now and then during the long journey, but her eyes felt gritty and hot as she got down.

'Please go up to the house,' she instructed her servants. 'I shall stay here for a while. You may send someone to me, to await further instructions. In the morning I shall want a hamper of food brought here—and perhaps a change of clothing.'

The cottage door opened as she approached, and May stood in the doorway, looking anxious. 'Thank goodness you came,' she said, and there were tears on her cheeks. 'I do not think she will survive another day. She has been wandering in her mind, Belle—and she asked for you so many times. I hope I was right to send for you?'

'Yes, of course,' Arabella said. 'Darling Nana. I must go to her first, and then we shall talk, May. For I believe something else is bothering you?'

'Yes, that is so,' May said and looked distressed. 'But go to Nana first. She has been waiting for you.'

'Yes, I shall go up to her at once.'

There was a candle burning in the small bedchamber, which enabled Arabella to see the old lady lying back against a pile of pillows with her eyes closed. In the yellow light, she looked waxen pale and very fragile, which made Arabella's heart catch with fright. However, as she approached, Nana opened her eyes and smiled at her.

'My Belle,' Nana said and moved her hand on the covers. Arabella took it, feeling its fragility, hurting because of it as she sat on the edge of the bed to look down at her lovingly. Nana's smile was tender and full of understanding. 'I knew that you would come, my love.'

'Of course I came, dearest,' Arabella said; her throat was tight with emotion and she had to fight her tears. 'You know that I love you, Nana. You cared for me when there was no one else to love me.'

'Your papa loved you, he just wasn't good at showing it

after your dear mama died,' Nana said. 'He never married again—she was the only woman for him. And when he died he was glad to join her in Heaven. But I was not alone in caring for you. You are beloved, Belle.'

'Thank you,' Arabella said and blinked hard. 'Yes, I know that I am fortunate in my friends and those who serve me.'

'One day you will find love again,' Nana said. 'I wanted to tell you not to waste your life, Belle. You were meant to have a husband and children. Ben would not want you to remain his widow for the rest of your life. He was too unselfish and too loving for that—and you owe it to him to be happy.'

'Yes, I know,' Arabella said. She could no longer hold back the tears that trickled down her cheek, but she let them flow unheeded. 'Dearest Nana. You always worry for me. You should be resting. We want you to get better.'

'My time has come,' Nana told her and there was gentle acceptance in the words. 'Do not weep for me, Belle. I am ready to meet my Maker. I want you to promise that you will take May home with you. Look after her, Belle. She has been badly hurt, though she cannot recall what happened to her— but sometimes she weeps and I think she feels so lonely. Take care of her, because she needs you.'

'Yes, I know. It has always been my intention to care for May,' Arabella said. 'I shall try to find her family for her, but if they do not want her—or if she does not want to return to them—she will always have a home with me. I already love her as if she were my own sister.'

'Good. You are a good girl...my little Belle,' Nana said and closed her eyes. 'Always such a good little thing...'

At first Arabella thought that she was sleeping, but then she heard a sigh issue from Nana's lips and the last vestige of colour left her lips so that they were as white as her cheeks.

'Nana…' Arabella gave a little choking cry and bent to kiss her lips. 'Nana, do not leave me….'

'She waited only to see you again,' May said from the doorway. 'She was such a dear woman, Belle. It breaks my heart to lose her and yet I know that she was ready to go. She has been telling me stories of when she was a young girl—and of her sweetheart who went off to be a sailor and drowned at sea.'

Arabella straightened and looked at her. 'She never told me of her sweetheart. Poor Nana…to spend her life in service to others when she might have had a husband and children of her own.'

'I think that is why she was so concerned for you, Belle,' May said. She walked up to the bed, bending down to kiss Nana's forehead. 'She spoke of you so often. I do not think that you need to pity her, for you were her child. She loved you as well as any mother could.'

'Yes, she did,' Arabella said. 'But she loved you too, May. She thought of you at the last. She wanted me to take you back home with me—and that is what I want, too. Please say that you will come and live with me, at least until we find your family.'

'We may never find them. Perhaps I do not have a family— for why would I run away from them if they loved me?'

'Come, let us go downstairs and talk,' Arabella said. 'I shall send to the village so that things can be done for Nana, as they should be. And then we shall talk of the future—of our future, for whatever happens you are my sister, May. We shall never be parted unless you wish it…'

'I have something disturbing to tell you,' May said. 'There

is a stranger staying at the inn and I have seen him outside the cottage.'

'Has he spoken to you? Done anything that frightens you?'

'He asked me for directions once, but he has not harmed me. It is just him—the way he watches me, as if he is weighing me up. Do you think he knows who I am?'

'Perhaps,' Arabella said. 'Or perhaps he is just trying to discover if you are someone he is searching for. You must be careful, dearest. It is just as well that you are coming to stay with me. I should not feel comfortable about you staying here alone now.' She frowned, wishing that she had done something about an agent when she was in town as she had intended. Perhaps he could have discovered who the stranger was. She would certainly write to the address Charles Hunter had given her as soon as she had time, but for the moment there were other more important things that must be taken care of. May would be safe enough living at the manor with her.

Charles finished reading the letter Arabella had sent him. He was relieved to know that nothing untoward had happened to Lady Tate, though obviously the elderly nurse who was dying was very dear to Arabella's heart. She would not otherwise have gone rushing down to the country to see her.

He frowned as he realised that he had been looking forward to seeing her later that week, for he had been invited to accompany his mother to Lady Tate's dinner. In that moment it came to him that his feelings for Arabella were more than the friendship he had claimed. He had tried to deny them as it was an impossible dream, but now that he faced the possibility of never seeing her again, he understood that it would bring him more grief than he had thought possible.

Charles had never taken love seriously. Before Sarah's abduction he had been known in polite circles as a wicked flirt, given to paying extravagant compliments that meant little. He had enjoyed the company of pretty women, and had kept his share of mistresses, though not for many months now. The anxiety over his sister had put all thought of physical gratification from his mind; he had lived only to find his sister, and perhaps now, at last, there might be a chance.

John Elworthy had gone up to Yorkshire—to the hamlet of Stapleford Bridge, which was some fifty-odd miles from the city of York. Charles had at first taken little interest in the exact location for he had expected it to be another wild goose chase, but looking at the directions John had written out for him had caused him to start thinking. If he was not much mistaken, the village could not be that far from what had been Ben Marshall's home…Arabella's home now, for it had come to her through her husband.

If John should send for him, it would be easy enough to make a detour to call on her. She had said that her aunt would be joining her soon. He might even offer to escort her there…

Charles gave an impatient shake of his head. Was he such a fool as to think that she might accept him as he was—a man who must devote his life to searching for his sister? No, she deserved much more of life. It was wrong and stupid even to contemplate such an idea. He must put all thought of her from his mind. John would very likely find that the rumour was a false trail and it would be much better that Charles should stay away from the woman he had fallen in love with against his better judgement.

\* \* \*

Arabella glanced through the letters that had been brought to her that morning. There was one from her aunt to say that she would be joining her in five days, and a few invitations from neighbours asking her to dine with them.

Having read her aunt's letter, she put the others aside for the moment. They were to attend a church service that morning, for it was the day that Nana would be laid to rest. Arabella's first grief had abated a little. Nana had been old and ready to leave this earth, and Arabella had had her blessing. A kind of peace had settled over her after Nana's death, and she knew that May felt much the same. They had both been fortunate to be loved by such a woman and would carry their memories with them for ever.

Dressed in black, Arabella went downstairs. Nana's coffin had been brought to the house the previous night and would be carried by the men of the household, many of whom had known and loved her. The rest of the servants would follow behind May and Arabella as they walked to the church in the village, save a few who had chosen to stay behind and prepare the food that was to be offered to any who came to mourn after the funeral.

May was wearing a black gown that Arabella had given her, which she had altered to fit, being as she was a head shorter than her benefactress. They joined hands as they walked, needing the comfort of physical contact.

It was a pleasant autumnal day. The sun was warm and there was no breeze, which meant that it was not cold in the church for the chief mourners or for the people who stood outside in respectful silence. Arabella was surprised that the whole village had turned out, though perhaps she should not have been—Nana had been kind to everyone she met.

After the service, Arabella and May stood together on the steps outside the church, speaking to friends and neighbours. The sun was even warmer now, as if it smiled on them, and, after a few minutes, the two girls walked towards the carriage, which would take them back to the house.

'Look,' May said suddenly, grabbing Arabella's arm. 'Do you see that man, Belle? The one with the shabby black coat and hat? He is watching us again. What can he want of me?'

Arabella followed the direction of May's gaze and frowned. 'Is he the one you told me of—the one you think has been hanging around the cottage?'

May had said very little in actual fact for they had both been grieving, but Arabella had sensed her fear when she spoke of the man hanging about the cottage.

'Yes, I think so,' May said, her eyes wide and scared. 'He frightens me, Belle. What do you think he wants? He asked me the way to Long Meadows once, but I am sure he did not want to go there. And he asked me my name, but I shook my head and ran away. He did not follow, but he has been watching me, I am sure of it.'

'Well, you are safe enough now that you are living with me,' Arabella said. 'But I shall ask Mr Grant to see what he wants.' Thomas Grant was her bailiff and she relied on him for all kinds of things concerning the estate. She beckoned to him as he stood talking to the Vicar and some of the villagers and he made his excuses, coming to her at once.

'Yes, my lady? How may I help you?'

'That man over there—do you know him?'

Thomas Grant looked at the man standing at the edge of the crowd and then shook his head. 'No, my lady. He is not one of us. A traveller passing through, I dare say.'

'He has been hanging around Nana's cottage and watching May,' Arabella said. 'Please discover what you can of him—and why he has been spying.'

'Yes, my lady. Shall I warn him off for you?'

'If he will give you a reason for his actions, I shall speak to him. Otherwise, please warn him of the consequences if he comes near her again. And tell everyone to be watchful. If he comes on to the estate without an invitation, he is to be asked to leave.'

'Yes, my lady. You leave the rogue to me!'

'Thank you.' Arabella turned to her companion. 'Come along, May. Let us go back to the house. We must entertain our neighbours and those who care to come from the village. The food is to be set out on tables in the garden, and we must try to speak to everyone.'

They climbed into the carriage together. Arabella glanced out as they passed Thomas Grant, who was now speaking to the stranger in an earnest manner. She wondered who the newcomer could be. Was he simply a traveller passing through—or was there a more sinister reason for his being here?

She had little time to ponder the matter that afternoon, for she and May were kept busy talking to their neighbours and the villagers who had come to pay their respects to Nana. As the day wore on great mountains of food and a considerable amount of cider, ale and wine was consumed, and by evening the rather sombre air that had hung over the company had become much lighter. Some of the villagers began to sing old country songs, and a few were a little worse the wear by the time they began to wend their way home again.

'They mean no disrespect,' Arabella told May as they retired to the parlour to drink tea and talk before retiring. 'I shall think of today as a celebration of Nana's life—and I am sure that is what she would have wanted.'

'Yes, I am certain you are right,' May said and smiled. 'I feel much better, Belle. Nana would have enjoyed today, I know she would.'

Arabella looked up as one of the maids entered the room. 'Yes, Maisie—what is it?'

'Mr Grant asks if he may speak to you, ma'am?'

'Yes, of course. Please ask him to come in.' Arabella looked at May as she made to rise. 'No, do not go. I think this must concern you. Stay and hear what Mr Grant has discovered about the stranger.'

'Are you sure?' Arabella nodded and May sat down again, her fingers working nervously at the folds of her silken gown.

'Well, Mr Grant, what have you to tell us?' Arabella said as the bailiff entered the room.

'His name is Brownlow,' Grant said and frowned. 'He apologised if he had distressed the young lady—but he is searching for a girl as went missing about sixteen months ago. A girl of good family she was, ma'am, and the description he gave is very much like yours, miss.' He looked at May thoughtfully. 'I'm not a man to poke my nose in, miss—but you came here at about that time, did you not?'

'Yes…' May's voice was little more than a whisper and her

eyes were open wide. She looked frightened, touching a tiny scar at her left temple with her forefinger. Arabella sensed that she was very nervous. 'But I don't know…' She faltered uncertainly, for she had no idea who she was or where she had come from.

'Did he tell you the name of the girl he was looking for, Mr Grant?' Arabella asked. 'Or give you any indication of her family?'

'He said as her name was Sarah, ma'am. More than that he wouldn't tell me—he said his employer wished him to be discreet.'

'Yes, I see,' Arabella said. 'Do you think he would tell me more if I spoke to him?'

'I don't rightly know, ma'am. Bit of a secretive cove—but then that's the nature of his business. As I understand it, he used to be a Bow Street runner until he retired.'

'Well, I would like to speak to him alone,' Arabella said. 'Please ask him to call on me, if you will.'

'He said as he was off this afternoon, ma'am. Seems he's done his business here and is going to report to his paymaster.'

'That is a pity,' Arabella said. 'For I should have liked to question him as to the nature of his search. Why was he searching for this girl?' She frowned as she pondered the question. Had Sarah's family sent Brownlow in search of her—or was there something deeper, something that might harm the girl? And was May the girl he had been looking for?

'I am glad he has gone,' May said. 'He frightened me—and I do not know my name. I do not know if I am Sarah…' She gave a little sob of fear as she looked at Arabella. 'Do not let them take me away. Please! I beg you as my friend. Whoever comes here seeking that girl, please do not let them take me away.'

'No, my dearest, I shall not,' Arabella said and got up to go to her. She knelt down at May's side, taking her hand in her own and looking at her earnestly. 'I promise you that no one shall take you unless you want to go.'

'You promise?' May looked at her, tears in her eyes. 'But I may be bad, a wicked shameless girl. You do not know what I have done.'

'You have done nothing wicked,' Arabella said and smiled at her. 'But you shall not be taken from me whoever comes—not unless you wish it.'

'Thank you.' May gave a little sob as Arabella drew her into a warm embrace. 'You are so kind to me.'

'You are my sister,' Arabella told her. She looked back at her bailiff, who stood waiting. 'Thank you, Mr Grant. You will please instruct the men that they are to keep an eye out for strangers; if they find anyone hanging round Nana's cottage or sneaking about, they are to surround him and keep him close until you or I have questioned him.'

'Yes, ma'am, we'll do that all right,' Thomas Grant assured her. He looked kindly at May. 'Don't you worry, miss. We look after our own here. None shall harm you while I have breath in my body.'

He nodded to both ladies and took himself off, filled with a new zeal. Life could sometimes be a little dull on an estate that ran itself as well as this one, and it was a while since he'd even had a poacher to deal with. He would enjoy dealing with anyone who came here making trouble!

Charles frowned over the letter he had just received from an agent Daniel had employed. One of many agents they had jointly used, Brownlow seemed to be the first to have found anything significant. He had written that he'd seen the girl he thought might be Sarah on several occasions, but that he had been able to get no more information about her. It seemed that she was a mystery to the villagers themselves.

*Either she does not know her own name or she is frightened. I spoke to her once, but she would not tell me her name. She is called May by the locals and she lived with an old woman at the edge of the village. The woman has recently died and she has now gone to live with the lady of the manor—as a servant or companion, I would imagine, though they seem to get on well. My cover has been exposed and I am leaving at once. I think it best you investigate further yourself. If this girl is not the one you seek, I shall await your further instructions. Yours, H. Brownlow.*

Charles puzzled over the letter. Something about what Brownlow had to say had made him restless. Who did he mean when he spoke of the lady of the manor? Could this mysterious girl actually be Sarah? Was their quest coming to an end at last? His heart leapt with excitement at the thought. He had almost given up hope and yet—

'Charles,' Mrs Hunter said, coming into his study at that moment. 'I have decided that I shall go home tomorrow. I came only to see my dressmaker and to visit Lady Tate. As you know, she is leaving town today. Do you wish to come with me?'

'If you wish it, Mama...' He frowned at his own thoughts. 'There is something I need to do, but I could escort you home first.'

'Does it concern Sarah?' his mother asked, and the shadows were in her eyes. 'Have you heard something new?'

'I am not sure…' Charles hesitated. 'I do not wish to arouse false hopes, Mama. I have heard of a girl, but it might not be her.'

'No, I dare say it is not. I have thought for a long time that she must be dead. It might almost be better if she was. At least we should know…'

Charles heard the grief in her voice and moved towards her, putting his arms about her as she wept into his shoulder. He patted her back, feeling the anger rise inside him. If he ever caught the people who had been holding his sister captive, he would know what to do!

'Do not cry, Mama,' he comforted. 'You must not upset yourself again. You are better now. You do not wish to be ill again.'

'No, I shall not be ill, Charles,' his mother said, withdrawing from his embrace. She was pale, but dignified in her sadness. 'I have faced the possibility of Sarah's death— nothing can be as bad.' She looked at him, calmer now. 'If there is any chance that it is Sarah, you must go. Do not leave it to your agents to discover the truth. Go yourself, Charles. I shall be well enough with the coachman, the grooms, and my maids to escort me.'

'Very well, Mama,' Charles agreed. 'I had hoped that I might hear from John—he went up to Yorkshire a short while back, but he has not sent word. He said he would if he discovered Sarah, but perhaps he has not seen the girl. Brownlow says she no longer lives where she did. Apparently, she has become a servant of some kind.'

'Sarah a servant?' Mrs Hunter shook her head in disbelief. 'You must go at once, Charles. What kind of people would make my Sarah a servant? Oh, it is too awful to contemplate.'

'We do not know what has happened to her in all these months,' Charles said, looking grim. 'I shall bring her home if I find her, no matter what—but you must understand that she may not be your little girl any more, Mama.'

'Whatever she has become, she will always be my little girl,' Mrs Hunter said with dignity. 'All I ask is that you find her—alive or dead.'

'I shall, Mama. If it takes me a lifetime, I give you my word. I shall find Sarah and bring her home to you.'

'They caught him hanging around near the cottage an hour ago, ma'am,' Mr Grant said to Arabella early the next morning. He was slightly uneasy as he looked at her. 'I wasn't with the lads that jumped on him or I might have advised them to use more caution, for I think he may be a gentleman, though I did not discover it until I went to take a look at him. He protested that he knew you, Lady Arabella—but my lads told me he was trying to peer in at the window of that cottage and behaving in a suspicious manner. So we've kept him locked up just to be on the safe side. Gentleman or no, he weren't up to no good in my opinion, and one of my lads says he's been asking about Miss May in the village.'

'Yes that does sound a little sinister,' Arabella said, though she could not help wondering just who they had captured. If the man were indeed a gentleman, he would be well within his rights to complain of his treatment. She had asked her servants to bring him to her, but she hadn't intended them to tie someone up! 'Tell me, where have you kept him prisoner?'

'In one of the barns, ma'am. I set one of the lads to keep guard over him. They told me he was a lively cove and put up a bit of a fight. That's why we left him for an hour or so to calm him down a bit—put the wind up him! He may be more amenable by now. I'll come with you while you question him. You can't be too careful with coves like that, ma'am. And we don't want him getting violent.'

'No, certainly not,' Arabella agreed. 'I shall come at once. I want to get to the bottom of this. May is too frightened to leave the house. I have told her that she will be safe in the gardens but I cannot convince her. I think she has been having nightmares over this business.'

'The poor girl,' Mr Grant said, his brows meeting in a frown of indignant concern. 'I should like to get my hands on whoever hurt her. I'd make them sorry for themselves, ma'am, and no mistake.'

'Yes, I agree with you,' Arabella said, hiding her smile at his fierceness, for he was a gentle, kind man at heart. 'Whoever hurt May deserves a good thrashing, but we must not jump to conclusions, Mr Grant. The man who came looking for a girl called Sarah may have had honourable intentions—and if this man is a gentleman, he may have come here quite innocently.'

'He may,' Mr Grant said darkly. 'But if that were so, why did he not come and ask you about her, ma'am? Everyone knows that you've looked after her. Nana Rose too, by all accounts. You never let them want—no more than any of your dependants. We're all proud to work for a great lady like yourself, ma'am.'

'Thank you.' Arabella blinked back the tears that pricked behind her eyes. She had not realised that she inspired such feeling in her people. 'Shall we go and have a look at your prisoner, Mr Grant?'

'Yes, my lady,' the bailiff said. 'He looks a gentleman by the cut of his jib, but you can't take that on trust. There's many a gentleman with a rogue's heart.'

'Yes, you are very right,' Arabella said with a wry twist of her lips. She went out into the hall and took a paisley silk shawl from the hall cabinet. She was thinking of her cousin Ralph at that moment, and her suspicions that he had tried to harm his mother. Thank goodness her aunt would be with her soon. At least here she could be sure of protecting Aunt Hester, for if she forbade Ralph to enter her house her people would not let him anywhere near. But for the moment she had another problem to attend. Who were these strangers upsetting May?

John Elworthy had at last succeeded in loosening the knots that bound his hands behind him. He was able to slip them free of the ropes that had made an unpleasant red mark about his wrists since his capture. Rubbing them to ease the numbness, he was thinking hard. He had been taken by surprise when the four rogues jumped on him as he was knocking at the door of the cottage, where he understood the mystery girl to be staying. It had looked deserted and empty, and he had been about to open the door and go in when he was pounced on from behind and knocked to the ground. He had struggled valiantly, but was overcome by superior odds.

'Damn them!' John said, rubbing at his wrists again because they were sore from being tied so tightly.

He knew that he was in a barn that was used to store fodder for animals. And that probably meant he was not too far from the cottage where he had been set upon, for he had seen barns and animals in a field close by. He had no idea why he had been captured surely if the rogues were looking for money they would have taken his purse and left him where he lay. He already knew that his watch and his purse were still in his possession—so that must mean that his imprisonment was because of where he had been when attacked.

His mind leapt excitedly from one conclusion to the next. If he had been treading on dangerous ground, it could mean that at last they had found Sarah. But who was trying to prevent him from making that discovery? Was it one of Forsythe's cronies? Sir Montague was dead, killed by Charles Hunter while trying to escape his just arrest for the abduction of Elizabeth and the murder of Lady Roxborough. Forsythe had admitted that it was his bullyboys who had abducted Sarah Hunter, but either he had genuinely not known where Sarah was after she had escaped him or he had concealed the truth.

John was determined to escape from his captors. He must get to Charles and let him know that Sarah was being held by ruthless men who would stop at nothing to prevent her being rescued.

He was alone in the barn, he had known that from the beginning, but he imagined they would have left someone on guard outside the door. He could either try to leave that way and risk being knocked unconscious again—or he could go up into the loft above and escape through the small door that was used for hoisting bales of hay up to the top floor. He climbed the ladder, clambering over the bales of straw and hay that were stored in the loft. It was an easy matter to unbar the small opening. Looking out, he saw that there was a dung heap just to his right, and no sign of anyone. Whoever had been set to guard him must have wandered off, perhaps to have his breakfast, believing that he was safely locked inside.

John took a flying leap into the heap of animal manure and waste, landing in the foul-smelling stuff and sliding down to the bottom. He gagged at the stink, but blessed it for affording him a safe landing. He stood, looking about him for a moment to get his bearings and then, hearing the sound of voices, began to run, away from the farm towards the lane that led to the village and the inn where he was staying.

'You fool!' Thomas Grant looked scathingly at the young lad who had been set to watch over their prisoner. 'You were told to stay here until someone came to relieve you, Jed. Where did you go?'

'Ma called me to have my breakfast,' the youth said, looking shamefaced. 'I told her I wasn't supposed to leave, but she said she would box my ears if I didn't get up to the house. He were locked in, sir. I didn't think he could get out.'

'He must have jumped into the dung heap,' Thomas Grant said, shaking his head. 'We should have tied him tighter.' He looked at Arabella. 'Forgive me for dragging you here on a wild goose chase, ma'am. I never expected this to happen—though I suppose I ought to have thought of it.

'It is not your fault, Mr Grant—or yours, Jed.' Arabella frowned. 'But it does mean that you must keep an extra watch for strangers. If this man came here to try to steal May from us, he might return with others to help him.'

'He'll find a reception committee if he does, ma'am,' Thomas said, his eyes glinting. 'He won't escape twice, I promise you.'

'I must go back to the house and warn May to stay inside today,' Arabella said. 'If she is at risk, we must be very careful until these wicked men are caught and punished.'

Arabella left her bailiff and began to walk back to the house. It was very worrying—surely if the prisoner had been an innocent passer-by, he would have waited to protest his innocence and demand an apology for his treatment. She had not at first believed that someone was out to harm May, but now she was beginning to think it must be so. First the agent snooping about asking questions, and now a man dressed like a gentleman, according to Mr Grant. Just who were these people—and why were they looking for May?

Arabella wished that she had written to the agent that Charles Hunter had told her about, for at least she might then have had someone to help her. It had slipped her mind since her return from London, but she would do it that very day. The card must be somewhere amongst her things, though she had no idea where it might be for she had left town in such a hurry. She would look for it and then she would write her letter—but first of all she must speak to May.

God, this stink was awful! John had stripped off his clothes and was standing naked in the inn bedchamber sluicing himself with cold water, which was left over from the morning. He had ordered more hot water, but could not wait to get rid of the smell of the dung heap that clung to him. When someone knocked at the door, he called out that they might enter, holding a towel to his middle to protect his modesty from the chambermaid. However, it was a man who entered.

'Good grief, John,' Charles said and laughed. 'What on earth are you doing at this hour—and what is that awful smell? Have you been rolling in a pigsty?'

'You may well grin,' John said ruefully. 'I thought you were the chambermaid with some hot water. I have just escaped from the top floor of a barn, in which I had been imprisoned, by jumping into the dung heap.'

Charles whistled, his eyes narrowing as the laughter left his face. 'What happened exactly? Why were you taken prisoner?'

'I was delayed on my journey,' John explained. 'My horse threw a shoe and went lame. I took it to a hostelry and hired another, but it was a sluggard and I did not arrive until late yesterday evening. I asked for Brownlow, but he had gone, so this morning I started to do a little snooping of my own. I asked questions about the girl and directions for the cottage where she had been living. Then I went to take a look, but it appears to be empty. I was about to go in and have a look round when they jumped on me—about four of them, I think. I fought back, but I was overpowered and my hands were tied. They put me in a barn and left me, but I escaped before they returned.'

Charles looked grim. 'Good grief! It is a wonder you lived to tell the tale. Forgive me, John. I never expected this when I asked you to come down here.'

'Nor I,' John said and laughed, shrugging off his imprisonment. 'It has turned out to be more of an adventure than I imagined. Anyhow, I managed to work my hands free and then I climbed up to the loft and jumped out. I heard voices coming towards me so I ran for it, though I have thought since that I should have stayed and demanded an explanation.'

'Did you have a pistol with you?'

'No. I carry one on the road, but left it here at the inn. I did not imagine I should need it—but now I am wondering just what sort of people they are. They must be holding Sarah a prisoner.'

'If it is her, that seems the likely explanation,' Charles said. 'But who are they, John? And where have they taken Sarah?'

'The cottage and the farm buildings belong to Lady Arabella Marshall,' John said with a frown. 'I heard one of the men say she wanted to question me, but when I told them I knew her they seemed not to believe me. While it seems unlikely that she would be involved in such a wicked business, we must remember that Lady Roxborough was once a member of Forsythe's unholy group, even though she turned against him at the last—and she was of good birth too.'

'Explain yourself,' Charles said and stared at him in disbelief. 'Are you saying that you were attacked and imprisoned on Lady Arabella's estate? You must be mistaken! She could never be a party to this, John.'

'It seems a wild idea, I know,' John replied. 'But when we first began the search for Sarah I thought it unlikely that Sir Montague was involved or Lord Barton or Lady Roxborough.'

'But why would she keep my sister a prisoner? And why— if you knew the cottage was on her estate—did you not simply call on her and ask her if she knew of Sarah?

'It was my intention to do so later. Had I not been attacked I should have gone up to the house.' John shook his head. 'It seems unbelievable, I know. I would not have thought it possible either had I not been set upon and tied up that way myself. But I will find out just what is happening here. I meant to call on her—and now we may go together, and we shall both take our pistols.'

'Yes, we must call on her to discover what is going on on her land,' Charles agreed. 'And we shall take our pistols in

case those rogues are still around—but I do not believe that
Arabella could be involved in this affair.'

'I do not know her,' John said. 'I must bow to your
superior knowledge, Charles—but I suspect her of being
more involved than you think. During the struggle, I heard
one of the rogues say that her ladyship wanted to question
me herself—and I think it must be Lady Arabella they were
speaking of—' He broke off as a knock came at the door,
calling out that the maid might enter and retiring behind a
screen as she did so. He came out again as the door closed
behind her. 'If you will be patient for a few minutes,
Charles, I shall finish washing and then we shall pay a
social call…'

'It is only for a day or so,' Arabella told May as they sat in
the back parlour talking. 'Mr Grant had the man tied up, but
somehow he escaped. I do not know who these people are—
or even if you are the girl they seek—but we must be very
careful until we discover their purpose.'

May looked at her, her eyes shadowed by anxiety. 'I
wish I could remember something, Belle. I told you that
sometimes I see a house with lovely gardens, but then it all
goes black and I cannot remember the rest. I know that
something happened in the garden. Before that I was happy,
I am sure of it, but then…' She gave a little shudder. 'I
simply cannot remember.'

'Does the name Sarah mean anything to you? Do you feel
that it might have been your name?'

'I don't know,' May wrinkled her forehead in concentration. 'I have thought and thought but if it was my name I have

forgotten it. Why do you think that is? Surely I ought to remember my own name?'

'Well, do not try too hard, my love,' Arabella said. 'It may come back to you one day, but first we have to make sure that you are safe. My aunt arrives tomorrow, as you know. I shall talk to her, because if someone has discovered your where-abouts it might be best that we go away—perhaps abroad—to escape them. Of course, it might be to your advantage. Perhaps your family is searching for you, May.'

'Would they not have found me before this if they had been looking?' May asked, a hint of tears in her eyes. 'Supposing I have done something dreadful…murdered someone? They might want to arrest me.'

Arabella's laugh was warm and husky. 'Oh, my dearest one,' she said. 'I do not believe that you could kill anyone—unless it was in self-defence, and even that is unlikely.'

'It is one of my fears,' May told her. She hesitated, then, 'I have nightmares sometimes, Belle… I see these strange crea-tures in the firelight and it frightens me. I scream out and then I am running…running into the darkness. Then I wake up and I cannot remember anything more—except the darkness.'

'What a horrid dream,' Arabella said, looking thoughtful. 'What kind of creatures, May?'

'I do not know. I think one had a mask and horns on his head, but the other…had the body of a man, and he was naked…' She blushed a bright pink. 'How could I dream such a thing unless I had seen it?'

'I do not know,' Arabella said. She had turned cold of a sudden, and she shivered as she heard shouting from outside the house. Something was happening! 'Go up to your room quickly, May. I think my men may have caught someone snooping. Stay inside and do not unlock the door until I come to tell you it is safe.'

May gave a little squeak of fright, her face turning pale. She did not need to be told a second time and ran out of the room and up the stairs. She could hear shouting outside the front door, and it hastened her steps. She did not pause to hear the outcome of what was obviously a struggle, hurrying into her own room to lock the door.

Arabella rose to her feet. The shouting and argument was growing louder, and then, all at once, the door of her sitting room was thrown open and a group of men came in. Four of her servants were surrounding the two visitors, who carried pistols in their hands. They were all watching each other warily. It might even have been comical if it had not been so startling.

'They threatened us, ma'am,' Thomas Grant said. He and two of the other men were carrying pitchforks and it seemed to be a stand-off between the opposing factions, though, had they cared to use them, the gentlemen with pistols would have won the tussle. She could only be glad that no blood had been shed. 'Said as they'd come to call, Lady Arabella—but that one is the cove we caught sniffing around the cottage, and he'd been asking for Miss May.'

'Charles! Mr Elworthy…' Arabella stared at her visitors in dismay. 'What is going on here? Why have you threatened to shoot my servants?'

'Why did you surround us with pitchforks?' Charles asked, clearly angry. 'And what have you done with my sister? Have you been keeping her here against her will?'

'Your sister?' Arabella was stunned. 'Are you saying that

May is your sister?' She recalled hearing her aunt say something about Mrs Hunter's daughter who had gone to stay with friends in Scotland. 'The girl you seek is Sarah Hunter…'

'Yes, Sarah is my sister,' Charles said and his eyes glinted with anger. 'We have been searching for her for nearly seventeen months since she was abducted—and, from information received, I believe that she may have been here on your estate for much of that time.'

'Yes, perhaps,' Arabella said. 'Put your pistols away, gentlemen—and you may go, Mr Grant. I do not think these gentlemen mean to harm me.' She looked at John Elworthy. 'I think I owe you an apology, sir. My men had instructions to bring anyone acting suspiciously on the estate to me—and you were at the cottage doing just that—but that does not excuse the way you have been treated. Please forgive us. We had a particular reason for doing what we did, but I am sorry that you were tied up.' She turned to her bailiff. 'Please tell Mr Elworthy that you are sorry your men were a little too hasty, Mr Grant.'

'Ah, well, that's as may be,' Thomas said, reluctant to let his prisoners go. 'He were where he shouldn't ought to have been, ma'am, and that's a fact. I'll stay close by if you need me. Just you call and I'll deal with them right enough.'

'I hardly think that necessary,' Arabella said as the pistols were slipped into coat pockets. 'Please sit down, gentlemen. I think we should attempt to discuss this in a civilised manner, don't you? Perhaps you would care for some refreshment?'

'No, I damned well should not,' Charles said and glared at her. 'I want to see my sister at once, ma'am—and I demand an explanation.'

'Do you, indeed?' Arabella drew herself up, her manner

cold and haughty, as he had only once seen her before. Her eyes gleamed with a silver light and she gave him a look that would have slain most men. 'I think that if anyone is owed an explanation it is I. It is true that I have a young woman living with me who may or may not be your sister. She came to us in great distress…to Nana, actually. She was dressed only in a white silk shift, which was torn and filthy, and she was near starving. Her feet were bare, covered in cuts and dried blood for she had walked a long way. She was very ill and Nana nursed her back to health. Later she repaid that favour by caring for Nana until she died. I do not know where she came from, for she cannot tell us—but it was quite a distance by the state of her feet.'

'Nearly thirty miles as the crow flies,' John remarked. He looked at Charles who was tense and tight, veins standing out at his temples. 'Sit down, Charles. We may as well hear what Lady Arabella has to say. I am prepared to forget what happened in the circumstances, for I should perhaps have come to her instead of trespassing on her land. I think perhaps we have taken the wrong end of the straw. If I am not mistaken, those men we thought rogues have been protecting Sarah.'

'Yes, of course.' Arabella's eyes snapped with temper. 'Did you imagine that I had held her here against her will for some nefarious reason? It has always been my intention to search for May's family when she was ready, but until now she has been too distressed—and now she is terrified. I sent her upstairs to lock herself into her room until I called her, because I thought someone was trying to take her from us, for what purpose I knew not. She has been badly hurt, that much I do know, and I am not prepared to let it happen again.'

'Yes, she has been hurt,' Charles said and flung himself down into one of the elegant elbow chairs. 'But not by her family. She was abducted by evil men who sought to use her for their foul purposes. We were told that she had run away from them by one of the rogues, who confessed his shame in the affair—but all our efforts to find her have come to nothing. Unless she is the girl you call May.' His eyes narrowed. 'It was at the beginning of that month last year that she was taken.'

'And at the end of it when she came to us. She was begging for food, but she fainted and was very ill,' Arabella said. 'She lay in a fever for a long time and we feared that she would die. Nana cared for her and she sent for me. I visited them every day until I came up to London. It was my intention to set an agent to search for her…'

'Why did you wait so long?' Charles demanded, still angry. 'My mother was ill for months. She despaired of seeing her daughter again. You have neglected your duty, ma'am. Did you not think that her family would be in agony all this time?'

'I did not know what to think,' Arabella replied in a gentler tone. Her anger had passed and now she understood that bleak expression she had seen in his eyes. 'May could recall nothing but a beautiful garden. Of late she has begun to have nightmares concerning some kind of ritual, I think…' Charles started up from his chair and she knew that she had touched a nerve. 'Forgive me. She only spoke of it today.'

'I must see her! I must know if she is Sarah.'

Arabella hesitated and then got to her feet. 'Wait here, if you please. I shall go upstairs and see if she will come down. You must accept that she may have changed, Mr Hunter. And she may be afraid of you. The man you sent to search for her frightened her—and then, when we knew someone else had come to look for her, it made her nervous.'

'I shall go out into the garden,' John said as Arabella left the room. 'If it is Sarah, she will not want me here, for I know her only slightly as your sister. I shall wait for you, Charles.'

He rose and went out through the French windows, walking towards a little summerhouse at the far end of the garden. Charles got to his feet and went over to the window, watching his friend walk away. For a moment he was tempted to follow. What would Sarah look like? Would it be her? He was not sure that he could bear the disappointment if it was yet another false trail. Hearing footsteps outside the parlour, he tensed, his shoulders squared. Whatever happened, he would stand by Sarah, care for and love her for the rest of her life. He turned slowly as he smelled a certain intoxicating perfume and knew that Arabella was once more in the room.

At first glance he thought that the girl with her could not be Sarah. Sarah had long golden hair and she was a child… this girl's hair had been cut short and now brushed the back of her neck, just above the lace collar of her black gown, and it had streaks of white in the front where it was caught back from her face. She looked much older, older than her years, but as he stared at her his heart missed a beat and he knew that she was indeed his sister.

'Sarah, my dearest,' he said and started towards her. She gave a little cry of fear and clutched at Arabella's arm for protection. 'No, do not be afraid. I shall not hurt you. I am Charles—your brother. Do you not know me?'

May shook her head. 'I do not know you,' she whispered. 'How can you be my brother? I do not know you…' Her voice caught on a sob and tears trickled down her cheeks. 'I have never seen you before. Who are you? Why have you come here?'

His face contracted with grief at her rejection. 'I am Charles Hunter and you are Sarah Hunter, my only sister. I love you, Sarah. I have been searching for you since you were abducted. I have come to take you home to your mama, who has been breaking her heart for you all these months.'

'No!' May shrunk against Arabella, trembling. She turned frightened eyes on her. 'Please do not let him take me, Belle. I do not know him. How do I know that he is my brother? I do not want to go with him.'

'You must come home,' Charles said, his frustration getting the better of him. Why was she behaving this way? Surely she must know him? 'I have been searching for you for so long. I shall take care of you, Sarah. We shall go home and then perhaps we shall go abroad and you will learn to know us again.'

'No!' May moved behind Arabella. 'I shall not come with you. Do not let him take me, Belle.'

'I shall not let anyone take you unless you want to go,' Arabella promised, turning to take her in her arms and comfort her. 'You must not be frightened. I do not believe Mr Hunter means you any harm—but he shall not take you. Your home is with me for as long as you please.'

'You cannot keep her here,' Charles said. 'I do not know what you have done to her—what you have told her to poison her mind against her family—but she belongs with us.'

Arabella's manner became cold and haughty once more. 'I have done nothing that would turn May against you, sir. You harm your own cause by this display of temper. If you will listen for a moment, I may have a solution to your problem.'

'And what is that, pray?' Charles glared at her, blaming her unfairly for a situation that he found unbearable. To have found Sarah at last, only to be told that she would not allow him to take her home!

'May will remain with me and you will fetch your mama to her,' Arabella said. 'She is welcome to stay with us until they become accustomed to each other.' She smiled at May, drawing her forward. 'You would like to see your mama, I think?'

'Yes…' May lifted her head, pride conquering her fear now that she knew herself safe. 'If you are my brother, I am sorry for the trouble I have caused you. I wish I knew you, sir, but I do not. Please bring my mother to me—and perhaps then I shall remember. Surely I must remember my own mother?' She looked at Arabella, trembling on the brink of despair.

'I shall ask John to bring her here,' Charles said and looked grim. 'I shall stay at the inn. I do not intend that Sarah should disappear again. I shall call every day to see her—and hope that time will ease her fear of me.' He inclined his head to Arabella. 'If I have offended you, ma'am, I apologise. I may have been too hasty—but I believe you ought to have sought Sarah's family before this. Excuse me. I shall send for your mother at once, Sarah.'

May nodded, her face pale as she watched him leave via the French windows. She saw another gentleman come to join him and a little shiver went through her as she turned to Arabella.

'Do you believe that I am Sarah Hunter?'

'Yes, I think it is likely to be true,' Arabella said. 'You must not be frightened of Charles. He is very angry, but I think he must care for you a great deal. We shall wait until your mama comes, and then I think we shall know for certain who you are.'

'Why can I not remember?' May asked, her eyes wide and dark with distress. 'Why can I not remember my own brother—if he is indeed my brother?'

'I do not know, except that you were very ill when you came to us,' Arabella said. 'But whatever happens, I shall always care for you, May—and no one shall take you from me until you are ready to go.' She smiled at her. 'I believe that it is perfectly safe for you to walk in the garden when you choose and even as far as the village—for I believe neither Mr Elworthy nor Mr Hunter is a threat to you.'

'No, perhaps not,' May admitted. 'But he was very angry. The way he looked at you…'

'Yes, I know,' Arabella agreed. 'But he is angry with me, not you. He thinks I should have done something to find your family a long time ago—and perhaps he was right.'

'But I did not want you to…'

'Which is why I made no enquiries. Yet Mr Hunter does have some right on his side. But do not be anxious. As I told you, I am sure you stand in no danger from him or Mr Elworthy.'

Arabella thought that if anyone was in danger from Mr Hunter it was she herself. The look he had given her before he left was angry and bitter, as if he blamed her for keeping his sister from her family. In London she had hoped that perhaps he was coming to care for her, but now she thought that it was a forlorn hope. Charles Hunter did not like her at all!

## Chapter Six

Fortunately, Arabella did not have long to dwell on her unhappy thoughts for even as she finished speaking to May there was the sound of wheels at the front of the house.

'That will be Aunt Hester,' she said and looked out to see the carriage in the drive. 'I must go and greet her at once. I shall bring her to meet you in a few minutes.'

'But how shall you introduce me?' May asked. 'Am I May—the girl you befriended—or Sarah Hunter?'

'I think that perhaps you are both for the moment. You must make up your own mind, love.'

Arabella left her to ponder the problem and went out into the hall to greet her aunt. Lady Tate was accompanied by two maids, from whom she had told Arabella she could not bear to be parted; she was at that moment being greeted by Arabella's housekeeper, who knew her well from previous visits, and was helping her off with her bonnet and pelisse.

'How was your journey, Aunt? I am so very glad to see you here. I suppose you have not heard from Ralph?'

'Not a word,' Lady Tate said, 'But I did not expect it. He quite often does not visit me for ages. Indeed, the only time—' She shook her head, conscious that they were not alone. 'The journey was very tolerable, my dear, but I am glad to be here.'

'Your rooms are ready for you,' Arabella told her. 'The pink suite is where my husband's parents lived for some years. I had it refurbished only last year, for I thought I might move there myself. The bedchamber looks out towards the south and has a pleasant view of the lake. I believe you will be comfortable there, Aunt, and you may be private when you wish.' She extended her hand in invitation. 'Will you come and meet someone? She was staying with Nana until recently, but now she has come to live with us—at least for the time being.' She glanced behind Lady Tate at Tilda, who had been organising the disposal of a mountain of luggage that was to be taken up the back stairs. 'Welcome back, Tilda. I trust your journey was comfortable?'

'You know I am an indifferent traveller, Arabella. I am glad to be home again. I have several boxes and parcels for you. They were delivered to Lady Tate's house only yesterday. Was that not fortunate? We have brought them with us. So many that I thought we should not have room for everything.'

'Some of them must be clothes and trifles I ordered for May,' Arabella said. 'Would you continue to oversee everything for us, Tilda? I shall ring for tea in ten minutes, if you would care to join us then.'

'Oh, but…yes, of course.' Tilda looked a little put out. She had a great deal to tell Arabella, things which she considered of some importance, but she knew better than to argue when her employer made such a request. She could not help but feel a little jealous. She could hardly justify her own presence in the house now that Arabella had her aunt to live with her on a permanent basis and she was secretly dreading the day when she would be asked to leave.

Arabella was aware that Tilda's nose was a little out of joint over the new arrangements and regretted it. She would talk to her later, explain that she was still needed, and hope that would settle her feathers. However, she wanted to explain about May to her aunt and did not wish Tilda to hear what was actually May's secret.

'You recall that I told you someone was looking after Nana until she died?' she said as they moved towards the parlour at the back of the house.

'Yes, my dear—so sad, but of course she was almost eighty, was she not? A good age, Arabella. Didn't she take in a young girl or something of the sort?'

'That is what I wanted to tell you, Aunt. We called her May, but now it appears that her name might be Sarah. She has no memory of what happened to her or who she is, but her family have been searching for her and now they have come here.'

'Goodness gracious, how very odd,' Lady Tate said. 'You are sure that they are her family and not impostors? One hears such terrible things at times.'

'We cannot be sure, but I do not think that Mr Hunter would lie about such a thing—do you?'

Lady Tate gasped and stared at her in dismay. 'You do not mean to say that little Sarah is here? Her mama told me that she had been abducted some months ago, though it is being kept as quiet as possible. Well, I never! It makes me feel quite upset…poor dear Sarah!'

Arabella stared at her aunt. 'Do you know Sarah?'

'Yes, naturally, though it must be all of two years since I last saw her—but I am sure that I should know her again.'

'Then come and meet her and tell us what you think.'

Lady Tate placed a hand to her chest. 'It makes me feel quite breathless to think of it. Selina has been in such distress, for no one knew what had happened to Sarah. They thought her dead or…' Lady Tate shook her head as if she could not bear her own thoughts. 'It is quite shocking, Arabella.'

'Yes, I know. It must have been terrible for them. Mr Hunter was very angry with me for not contacting her family long before this, and practically accused me of keeping her a prisoner, but of course I did nothing of the kind. Besides, May was too distressed to talk about the past until recently. I did ask her a few questions now and then, but it upset her for she could remember nothing.' Arabella paused outside the sitting room door. 'Do not forget that she has been ill. She may be changed a great deal.'

She opened the door and went in, her aunt following. May was standing by the window looking out at the garden, but she turned as they entered, smiling a little uncertainly. She dipped a graceful curtsy at the older woman.

'This is the young lady I told you of, Aunt Hester. Dearest, come and say hello to Lady Tate.'

Lady Tate stood for a moment, staring at the girl. She looked older than her years, partly because of the white streaks in her golden hair, where it winged back at her temples, and partly because of the shadows in her eyes. It was evident that she had suffered. However, there was no doubt in the older woman's mind as she went forward to greet her.

'Sarah, my dear,' she said warmly and held out her hands. 'How glad I am to see you safe with Arabella. Your mama will be so happy that you have been found.' Tears stood in her eyes. 'Come, embrace me, my love. We have always been fond of one another and I was greatly shocked when your dear mama told me the truth just a few days ago.'

'Lady Tate…' Sarah said hesitantly. She felt no fear of the kind woman, though even now she had no memory of ever having known her. 'Then I am truly Sarah Hunter? Charles Hunter is my brother?' She took a few uncertain steps towards Lady Tate and was gathered into a motherly embrace.

'I have always been Aunt Hester to you, Sarah,' Lady Tate said. 'It was a joy to me to come here today, but finding you makes it all the sweeter.'

Tears trickled down Sarah's face as she let herself be embraced and kissed. She could not fear Arabella's aunt, and she knew now that she was truly Sarah Hunter. She still had no memory of her abduction or of anything until she woke up in Nana's bed, but she knew instinctively that Lady Tate was telling her the truth.

'You must let Mrs Hunter know that Sarah is here, Arabella.'

'Mr Elworthy has gone to bring her here,' Arabella said. 'She must stay with us for the time being…just until she and Sarah get to know one another and Sarah feels ready to go home. She did not wish Charles to take her home and he has agreed to the arrangement.' Reluctantly, but with the knowledge that he had no choice unless he wished to drag Sarah screaming and kicking from the company of her friends.

'Well, that is very proper of you, Arabella. Just exactly what I would have expected, my dear.' Lady Tate beamed at her. 'Now, I should like to go up to my room, if you don't mind, my dears. I need to make myself comfortable before we all have tea together.' She patted Sarah's face. 'Isn't this nice? Your dear mama is my greatest friend. I was sorry to part with her when she returned home, and now we shall all be together again.'

Tilda entered as Lady Tate was about to leave. She hesitated on the threshold, as if unsure of her welcome, which made Arabella frown.

'My aunt is going upstairs for a few minutes so I shall not ring for tea just yet, Tilda. Please come in and talk to Sarah while I take Aunt Hester up to her rooms. I shall come down shortly and we will all have tea together in half an hour.'

'Oh, but I wanted to—' Tilda shook her head as Arabella and Lady Tate went out together. She glanced sullenly at Sarah. 'So you have remembered your name, then—or did you know it all along? Have you been pretending all this time in order to take advantage?'

'No, of course not,' Sarah said. 'Why should I?' She blushed as she saw the jealous look in the companion's eyes. They had met previously, but hardly knew each other. Sarah had not expected to see that look of dislike in Tilda's eyes. 'You think I have been playing on Belle's sympathy. Well, it is not true. She has been kind to me—but she is kind to everyone.' She blinked hard—it had been a difficult morning and she was feeling emotional. 'Excuse me, I must go to my room.'

Tilda ignored her. She walked over to the French windows and looked out, her shoulders shaking with the tears she held inside. Arabella found her fussy and irritating. She knew that she had long outstayed her welcome at Long Meadows, but she had nowhere else to go. Now that Arabella had her aunt staying and so many new friends she would not need Tilda any more. Blinking back her foolish tears, she went out into the garden. Perhaps she would pick a few flowers to arrange in Arabella's sitting room. Her only hope was to make herself so useful that Arabella could not do without her.

Somehow Arabella did not manage to have a private talk with Tilda that evening. It was impossible, for Lady Tate was full of gossip about the friends she had left in town, and her friendship with Selina Hunter. She talked endlessly about when they were young, and told stories of Sarah and her mother, which kept both Arabella and Sarah hanging on her every word.

Tilda complained of a headache when dinner was over, asking if Arabella would mind if she went to bed early.

'No, of course not. I know you do not travel well,' Arabella said kindly. 'Please go on up, Tilda. I wanted to talk to you alone, but it will keep for tomorrow.'

'I can stay if you need me for anything,' Tilda said, her face paler than usual. 'But you have Lady Tate to keep you company.' Her manner was one of righteous hurt, as if she had been slighted but was determined to rise above it.

Arabella ignored her sulky look. 'You must get some sleep. You will feel better in the morning. Ask Mrs Bristol to make you one of her tisanes, Tilda dear.'

'Thank you, Arabella. You are always so thoughtful, but *I* do not like to take advantage of your good nature.'

Arabella frowned, but did not answer her. She knew what was upsetting her companion, and she would try to set Tilda's mind at rest as soon as she could, but she did find her constant need of reassurance a little irritating.

'No one here takes advantage of me, Tilda,' she said, a sharper note than usual in her voice. 'Sarah and my aunt give me pleasure with their company. Go up now. I shall speak to you tomorrow.'

Tilda turned away quickly, going out without another word. Arabella considered going after her, but surely it wasn't necessary. Tilda was just being very silly and a little jealous when there was really no need at all. She turned as her aunt began another anecdote about when Sarah was learning to ride her pony. It was wonderful to watch the girl's face, to see the confidence beginning to return with the knowledge that she had a loving family. It was so fortunate that Aunt Hester had arrived at an opportune moment—it would help Sarah to face her mother's imminent arrival more easily.

Later that evening, Arabella accompanied her aunt to her bedchamber, seeing her settled comfortably before retiring herself.

'Thank you for being so kind to Sarah,' she said. 'She needs all the love and kindness she can get until she begins to trust in herself. I hope that her memory will return when her mama comes, but we cannot be sure that it will.'

'She may never remember what happened to her,' Lady Tate said. 'And perhaps that may be for the best, Arabella. We do not know what ordeal she may have suffered before she knocked on Nana's door. It may be that she is deliberately blocking it from her mind.'

'I think sometimes she has flashes of memory,' Arabella said. 'But now we must talk of you, Aunt Hester. Is everything to your liking? Can you be comfortable here?'

'Yes, perfectly,' her aunt said. 'You have provided all I could wish for, my dear, and once all my own things are unpacked I shall be quite at home.'

'Good, I am so pleased, dear Aunt. I was anxious for you while you remained in town, but now that you are here I can be sure that you are safe.'

'Oh, please do not let us talk of that,' Lady Tate said with a little sigh. 'I cannot bring myself to believe that Ralph… though I know what happened. I am not so entirely foolish as he believes, but I must excuse him if I can. Do you understand, love?' She gave Arabella a look of appeal.

'Yes, of course. We shall not talk of it—but if he comes to visit I shall stay with you. If I should be out, you must make sure that Tilda or Mrs Bristol is nearby.' Her housekeeper was a sturdy woman and would stand no nonsense!

'Yes, I suppose so,' Lady Tate said. 'But surely when I tell him that I have decided to sell the house…' She shook her head, refusing to think of something that made her so unhappy. 'It was so good of you to ask Mrs Hunter to stay, Arabella. You are always so generous.' She dabbed her eyes with her lace handkerchief.

'It was the best arrangement for us all,' Arabella replied. 'Had I not done so, I think Charles might have snatched her from us there and then, even though the very idea distressed Sarah. I suppose I must call her Sarah now, though it still seems strange—she has always been May to me.'

'Did Charles really think to snatch her away?' Lady Tate frowned. 'Surely he could not be so foolish? Anyone must see that it would be the worst thing he could do. It would seem to Sarah that she was being abducted all over again.

Besides, he cannot possibly blame you after all you have done for her?'

'I assure you he does,' Arabella said. 'I fear that he actually dislikes me, Aunt, but perhaps he will forgive me in time.' She forced herself to smile, though she did not feel inclined to do so. 'You must be tired. I shall leave you to sleep.'

Arabella kissed her aunt's cheek and walked along the landing to her own suite of rooms, which were up a small staircase and looked out over the wild garden—her favourite place, especially in summer when the dog roses were in bloom. Beyond the garden was a small wood and then the high wall that guarded her estate from intruders. She opened the door to her bedchamber and went in, dismissing her maid before sitting down at her elegant satinwood dressing table. She looked at her reflection in the little shield-shaped mirror that stood on top, taking the pins from her hair to let it cascade down her back. It was thick, shining like a curtain of black silk in the candlelight.

She had kept the thought of Charles's anger at bay all day, but now it returned to haunt her, making her heart ache. Could he truly believe that she had detained Sarah here against her will? If he could think so ill of her, he could not like her at all. He must think that she was unkind and careless, which was quite unfair.

It was such a painful thought that Arabella felt the sting of tears. She held them in check as she climbed into bed, putting out her candle with a long-handled silver snuffer. Closing her eyes, she snuggled into the feather mattress and tried to forget the ache in her heart. Life was so complicated. She had grieved for Ben so long and now, when she had begun to feel a little better, it seemed that the man she had allowed herself to care for did not return her feelings.

Standing in the gardens below her room, Charles watched the light go out as Arabella snuffed her candle. He did not know what had brought him here to the house, for he understood that he must take things slowly with Sarah. She had been frightened of him! His own sweet sister, whom he had loved and spoiled all her life, had been afraid of him. To see the look of fear on her face had caused him such pain that he had struck out without thinking, blaming the woman who had saved her from more suffering.

Now, alone with his bitter thoughts, he admitted that if it had not been for the kindly old woman that had taken her in Sarah might truly have died. That woman had been Arabella's nurse and Mr Grant had told him that it was Arabella who had supplied them with everything they needed, food, warmth and clothing—and now that Nana was dead, she had taken Sarah to live with her. Instead of lashing out in a temper, he should have been thanking her for all that she had done.

If Sarah could recall nothing of what had happened until she was nursed back to health by Nana and Arabella, then no one could tell him what had happened to her after she was abducted. Only Sarah could reveal that, if and when she regained her memory.

He wondered if she were pretending not to remember. Might it be that she was ashamed of what had happened to her? Clearly she was frightened of men, which made him fear the worst. It might be that his sweet sister would never remember what had happened to her during that time, never lose her fear of men—because she had been too badly scarred.

Charles uttered a muffled curse. He had imagined that when Sarah was found he would be at peace, but now he knew that his agony of mind would go on. Just what had those devils done to her? He turned, striding through the shrubbery towards the wooded area that led to the lane and eventually to Nana's cottage, now empty and forlorn. There was actually a wall that kept the estate private, but the gate had been unlocked. Charles had had no difficulty in gaining entrance, which he had thought a little strange, although perhaps Arabella's people were no longer on the alert for intruders?

Lost in thought, he walked past the cottage without glancing at it, and it was thus that he did not see the thin stream of smoke issuing from its chimney. The cottage was no longer empty.

'I am going for a ride,' Arabella announced at breakfast the next morning. 'I did not ride in London and I have not done so since my return. My poor mare will believe she has been deserted, though I know my grooms have seen to it that she is exercised.' She smiled at Sarah and Tilda, who had both come down to take breakfast in the small parlour used for that purpose because it had the benefit of the morning sun. 'Aunt Hester will not come down much before nuncheon, but if she should ask for me, please tell her that I shall not be more than an hour. I think I shall ride down to the village.'

'I should like to arrange the flowers for you,' Sarah said. 'Where may I cut flowers? I do not wish to upset your gardeners.'

'I always do the flowers for Arabella,' Tilda said, giving her a look that was not far short of hatred. 'I know what to do, for I have lived here for some years and I understand these things.'

'Then you may take Sarah with you and show her,' Arabella said, ignoring the sullen flash in her companion's eyes. 'Sarah is to live with us for the time being, Tilda. She will not want to be idle and I am sure you have plenty of other things to occupy you.'

'Yes, I suppose I have,' Tilda said. 'I was going to start an inventory of the linen this morning, but I dare say I can show Sarah where to cut the flowers first.'

'Thank you,' Arabella said. 'I shall see you both later.'

She left the house and headed towards the stables, which were in a courtyard at the far end of the outbuildings that made up the kitchen area. It was an ideal arrangement, for the stables kept the vegetable garden in good heart but were far enough away from the house not to be unpleasant in summer.

Arabella had sent word that she intended to ride and her mare had been saddled ready for her. One of the grooms had brought out his own horse in order to accompany her, but she dismissed him with a smile.

'I shall not need you this morning, Robert. I am only going as far as the village, thank you.'

'As you wish, ma'am,' the groom said, smiling in return. She was a popular mistress, for, though she owned a large estate, she was never unfair and always had a pleasant word for her people. 'With your permission though, my lady, I have an errand for Master Coachman in the village—he needs something from the blacksmith. Would you mind if I rode a little distance behind you?'

'No, of course not,' she said and laughed as she tipped her

head to one side. 'I am not sure if poor Blackie can keep up with Windflower—but you are welcome to try. I have a mind to give her a good gallop. You would like that, wouldn't you, my pet?'

She patted the mare's head and gave her the treat she carried in her pocket, enjoying the feel of the horse's soft nose against her hand before she pulled on her riding gloves and allowed the groom to help her up. They trotted out of the yard together, but Arabella had meant what she said; as soon as they reached open ground, she gave the mare her head and was soon racing far ahead of her groom.

Arabella did not notice the odd flash of light that glinted in the autumn sunshine as she passed a small copse to her right, for she was enjoying her ride too much. She had not felt this free in an age and it was good to have the wind in her face. However, it did not go unnoticed by her groom, who was not attempting to do more than keep his mistress in sight. Mr Grant had told them all that they must keep a sharp eye. He was not yet convinced that the two gentlemen callers were to be trusted and it was best to be careful. And so Robert saw the man in the trees. He had been using a spyglass and his purpose was to watch her ladyship. Robert would have something to tell the bailiff when he returned to the estate, and he would make sure that his errand for the coachman lasted just long enough for him to be able to follow Lady Arabella home again.

Arabella was completely unaware that she was being watched over by her faithful servants. She had decided to ride into the village to speak to Charles Hunter. She would tell him that her aunt had recognised Sarah and that she now accepted she was his sister. She also intended to ask him to take nuncheon with them, and to consider himself free to visit as often as he liked.

* * *

The inn was quite large and, though ancient, was reputed to be comfortable. It was used as a staging post for Scotland and also for London because it stood a short distance from the crossroads. The yard was a hive of activity; a coach had recently arrived and the passengers were disembarking to partake of refreshments before going on—in this case to Scotland. Arabella avoided the horses and grooms milling in the yard, an obliging potboy sweeping a path over the cobbles for her to reach the inn, and taking her horse by its reins.

'I shall not be long,' she said, giving him a shilling. 'Let my mare drink at the trough if she wishes, for I have pushed her hard this morning.'

'Right you are, my lady.' The urchin touched his forelock—he knew Lady Arabella well and had received many a silver coin in his palm. His father worked on the estate as a gardener and he hoped to follow when he was older.

Arabella nodded at him and went into the inn. The host was busy seeing to his customers and she was standing in the hallway waiting to be noticed when a gentleman came down the stairs. She went forward to greet him, for it was Charles Hunter, dressed as if for a morning call, in pale buff riding breeches and a blue coat that fitted his broad shoulders like a second skin. His long boots had a gloss that would not disgrace him in the eyes of the *ton* and she sensed that he had taken care with his dress that morning.

'Sir,' she said in a tone of studied politeness, 'I have some news that will please you. Lady Tate arrived yesterday afternoon, and she knew Sarah despite the changes that you too must have noticed. She is very fond of your sister and assured

Sarah that you were indeed her brother. Sarah now accepts the truth—and I am sure she will be pleased to see you should you care to join us for nuncheon today.'

'I had intended to pay a social call this morning,' Charles said a slight frown creasing his forehead. 'However, it would be pleasant to stay a little longer at your house—if you are sure I shall not be inconveniencing you, ma'am?'

'No, of course you will not be in the way. I rode here this morning for that purpose—to tell you that you will be welcome to call as often as you please while Sarah is living with me. Your mama should be with us in a day or so and you must feel free to spend time with her and your sister.'

'Thank you.' Charles inclined his head a little stiffly. 'I have ordered my horse brought round, Lady Arabella. Shall we ride back together—or have you other commitments?'

'None at all,' she replied. 'I have given my mare the exercise she sorely needed. If you do not mind, we shall go back past Nana's cottage. I want to see that it is securely locked—it is my intention to offer it to one of my people. I believe one of the grooms is hoping to marry as soon as he can find a home for himself and his wife. We abandoned the cottage when Nana was brought to the house, and I do not think anyone has been back since. I told Sarah that she could send one of the servants for anything she needed—and then I shall offer it to Henry.'

They walked outside to where Arabella's mare was being jealously guarded from the other grooms by her dedicated urchin. Seeing Charles, one of the senior grooms led out his horse and stood waiting while he assisted Arabella to mount. The touch of Charles's hand made her tremble inwardly, but she gave no sign that she was affected, bestowing a cool nod on him. She had offered him the hospitality of her home, but she was not about to lay her soul bare to him.

Once Charles was mounted on a magnificent black stallion that Arabella felt was more than capable of keeping up with her mare, they trotted out of the inn yard together. Arabella had ridden off her frustrations and she was content to canter sedately as they left the village, this time taking a narrow wooded lane rather than the open moor. Neither of them spoke, though each was aware of the horsemanship of the other, silently approving. It was only when they reached Nana's cottage that Arabella gave a muffled cry.

'The door is open,' she said and dismounted without help, walking swiftly inside the cottage. The remains of a fire smouldered in the grate and she saw an empty wine bottle and the crumbs of a loaf on the kitchen table. 'Someone has been here!'

'I saw nothing as I passed last evening,' Charles said and faltered as Arabella shot a suspicious look at him. 'I came up to the house. I was restless and walked through your woods. The gate leading into your estate was not locked. I intended to tell you that this morning. It might be as well to instruct your bailiff that it should be locked at all times.'

Arabella stared at him. 'Are you thinking of Sarah's safety—or my aunt's?'

'Actually, I was thinking of you,' Charles said, looking serious. 'It might be best if I told you what I know of Sarah's abduction…' He paused, eyebrows raised and Arabella nodded, sitting down on a chair at the kitchen table. 'We know that a man called Sir Montague Forsythe and his bullyboys took her. He and some others were members of a satanic cult and they performed strange ceremonies in the woods of his estate, of which the main purpose was to sacrifice virgins to their deity. I do not mean that they were to be killed, but rather to be used in ghoulish rites that included the rape of innocent girls—girls who afterwards disappeared into a whorehouse. Forsythe owned several of these houses, which have, since his death, been closed. Some of the girls were glad to be rescued and sent home to their families, though some had nowhere to go. Daniel—the Earl of Cavendish—has helped as many as he could. Most of the girls were maidservants, though I believe there were one or two girls of good family who had fallen on hard times…'

'Wicked!' Arabella cried, a feeling of disgust curling through her. 'It is difficult to believe that a gentleman could do such things, though I knew that these places existed—but to keep girls there against their will is evil! Unbelievable!'

'Is it?' Charles looked at her, his eyes dark with cynicism. 'I know more of the world than you, Arabella. I find it easy enough to believe that certain types of men will do these things. However, the two most influential members of the cult are dead—one by Forsythe's hand, and he by mine.' He saw her flinch. 'It was as we struggled for possession of his pistol. We were trying to arrest him for murder and the ab-duction of another lady, and it went off by accident. However, if I am honest, I had vowed to see him dead. Daniel insisted that he must be tried and condemned by law, and I sought only to prevent his escape—but in other circumstances I might have killed him.'

'I see. Thank you for telling me, sir.' His expression was so grim at that moment that an icy shiver ran down her spine.

She understood that in his anger and bitterness he might have killed in cold blood…but he had not. 'I am glad that this evil man is no longer able to harm Sarah or any other girl.'

'His death was a blessing, except that he might have given us more information about Sarah…' Charles frowned. 'I believe I must offer you an apology. I still think you ought to have tried to discover Sarah's family before this—but I know that she owes her life to you and your kind nurse.'

Arabella's expression did not change. 'Sarah owes her life to Nana, who took her in and cared for her. I helped her to recover as she regained her strength and we became friends— but it was Nana who saved her life. That is why she wished to care for Nana when she became ill some weeks ago. I wanted them both to come up to the house, but Nana did not want to be a trouble to me, which she could never have been. I could not force Sarah and she did not want to know who she was at that time. She was reluctant to come to the house, because she was afraid that she had done something evil…that she might have killed someone…or that someone wished her harm. She felt safe in Nana's cottage and hardly ever went out. It was my intention to discover what I could by engaging an agent to search for clues, but, as you know, I was forced to leave town in a hurry.'

'Yes, I see,' Charles said. 'Well, it is in the past now.'

'Yes, it is in the past.' Arabella stood up. She was tight with nerves, for his expression made her heart race. Was he still angry with her? She could not tell—but he was angry about something. 'I think we should leave now. I shall tell Henry to come and secure the cottage. He may wish to make changes here before he brings his sweetheart to see it—though it was made comfortable for Nana when she retired.'

'I dare say he will think himself fortunate to have the offer of such a good house,' Charles said as he followed her outside. 'It is odd that someone should have been here. Do you often have vagrants on your land?'

'No, not that I know of. Occasionally, a tinker family will pass through looking for work, but the magistrates maintain a poorhouse at Marsden, a village some ten miles south of here, and any homeless folk found in the parish are sent there.' She wrinkled her brow. 'Your agent stayed at the inn, I know. It is rather puzzling.'

'Have you heard from your cousin since he left town?'

Arabella stared at him. 'My cousin? I cannot see Ralph spending even one night here. He is too fond of his own comfort.'

'Always providing that he is in funds.'

'You mean…' She felt cold all over. 'But why would he stay here? He could have come up to the house.'

'Would you have welcomed him with open arms?'

'No, I suppose not,' Arabella said. 'He knows that I suspect him of giving my aunt sweetmeats that made both her and Tilda ill. And there was that fall, which might have killed her had I not found her in time…but I could not refuse him if he came to visit Aunt Hester. He is her son, after all.'

'Then I think you should be careful,' Charles said and gave her his hand to help her into the saddle. 'If it was your cousin, he came here for a purpose—and, as I believe we discussed once before, he is the main beneficiary from your will, Arabella. If you left everything to your aunt, it would eventually come to him.'

'Yes, I know. I have been thinking about that,' Arabella said. 'I believe I must go into York and speak to my lawyer soon. Tilda is a distant cousin of my mother's and I would wish her to have something, but I am not sure what to do for the best otherwise.'

'You need someone to look after your affairs,' Charles said. 'Is there no one at all who could be trusted?'

'I have many friends and my people are very loyal,' Arabella said, lifting her head proudly. She refused to feel sorry for herself—or to accept his pity. In London she had thought he truly cared, but now she knew that he had merely been showing concern as a gentleman for a lady living without the protection of a male relative. Something he might as well show for Tilda or her aunt. 'Thank you, but I shall speak to my lawyer on the matter. I dare say he will advise me—and now we should return to the house.'

'Yes, of course,' Charles said and mounted his own horse. 'I am eager to see my sister now that she accepts I am her brother.'

Arabella nodded, but said nothing. She had issued the invitation to make free of her home because it was the proper thing to do in the circumstances, but she must keep her distance—she did not want to betray herself. She was glad that they had discussed Sarah's abduction, for it had helped her to understand what must have happened—and it explained Sarah's nightmares. She could not know what had happened prior to Sarah's escape from the wicked men who had captured her, and she would not press the girl for answers. It would not make the slightest difference to her genuine affection for Sarah even if she had suffered a dreadful fate. Indeed, the possibility that she had been abused only made Arabella more desirous of protecting her.

She thought that perhaps she might make Sarah one of her

beneficiaries. It was true that she had a family to care for her, but it might be that she did not wish to return to them. If her memory returned and she could not face living in the bosom of her family, a small independence would make it possible for her to live as she chose.

She flicked her reins and set off a little ahead of Charles. He was deep in thought—he sensed that she was keeping her distance from him, despite her invitation to make free of her home. Had he hurt her pride by holding her to blame for the months of agony his mother had endured, to say nothing of his own distress? He blamed himself for this rift between them, but he had apologised and only time would tell whether they could ever be true friends again.

Neither of them noticed the man creeping out from behind the cottage as they rode away. Nor could they have known that through an open window at the back of the cottage, he had heard everything they said as they talked. Ralph stood staring after them as they disappeared round a bend in the lane, a look of fury in his dark eyes. Damn the fellow for his interference! What right had Hunter to advise Arabella to make a will excluding him from what he believed was his by right of kinship?

His mother had little left to leave him but the house and he knew that its sale would hardly touch the mountain of debt he had built up these past months. He had lost much of his fortune to Forsythe and others of the same ilk—damn them! He had been promised a chance to redeem his debt to Forsythe by some favour, but with Forsythe dead he had no chance of getting a penny of what was owed. And there was the other debt, which far outweighed it. He had no chance whatsoever of paying that whatever he did.

In his anger he blamed the couple who had just ridden away. It was all the fault of Charles Hunter and Arabella! If she had not interfered, everything would have gone according to his plan. Ralph had hoped that his mother would die after her fall and that her estate would see him through until he could recover. It was not possible to go on losing at the gaming tables for ever—his luck was sure to turn eventually. His plan had not worked and now his mother was living with Arabella. It would be too dangerous to try to arrange another accident for her, because the suspicion would be bound to fall on him.

Damn them all to hell! Ralph ground his teeth in frustration. In truth, his mother's death would profit him little—it was Arabella who was rolling in it. She had been blessed with far more money than she needed! She could have offered to help him out with his problems, but she was a selfish bitch. If she had the least consideration, she would fall off that wretched horse and break her neck. He had watched her riding hell for leather earlier that morning, and hoped that she might have an accident, but no such luck.

Supposing he were to arrange an accident for her? The thought popped into Ralph's head out of the blue. He must get some funds soon, for his creditors were pressing for their money. He cared little for the tailors and other tradesmen to whom he owed huge sums; they could whistle for their dues and he would not give a damn—but it was the other one.

Sir Courtney Welch was a devil. He had been one of Forsythe's cronies and it was to him that Ralph owed the most—twenty thousand guineas, thrown away at the card tables in a drunken fit. Sir Courtney had given him one month to come up with the dubs, but he could not find the half of it.

'Fail and you will regret it,' Sir Courtney had told him, a gleam of menace in his eyes. 'I take payment one way or the other, Tate—let me down and you are a dead man.'

Ralph hadn't been scared of Forsythe. He'd known about his little secret, though he had never been present at the meetings in the wood. He was not interested in that kind of affair. In fact, he wasn't really interested in much other than gambling, drinking and the horses, and his besetting sin was laziness. He was actually a bit of a coward, which was why he hadn't dared to put a significant amount of poison in those dates—just enough to make his mother ill. Damn it! He hadn't known she would give them to the stupid companion. He had wanted to cause his mother some stress in the hope that she might die of natural causes. Her heart was supposed to be weak, wasn't it? At least that was what that stupid maid had told him. Why couldn't she just pop off and let him have what was his? He had pushed her down the stairs, but then, when she lay whimpering for help, he hadn't dared to finish her off. He had simply taken her candle and made a dash for it down the back stairs. As a young man always in trouble with his bad-tempered father, he had learned how to enter the house without being discovered, and it had stood him in good stead that night. He had hoped his mother would lie on the floor all night and take a turn for the worse from it.

And of course Arabella had found her and now she was living up at that huge house with no money worries, and he had nothing. His own fortune had been insignificant, compared with all that Arabella had inherited, and soon spent. His cousin had so much money! If she were not so damned selfish, she might have made a part of it over to him. And yet if he could get his hands on the whole… Ralph's eyes gleamed with greed. Why not? She hadn't made a will yet, which meant that everything would go to his mother—and she would be easy to persuade once Arabella was gone.

The thing was—how could he get rid of her? She was an excellent horsewoman. He had watched her through his spyglass that morning, and he knew that she was in good health, confident and assured in all she did. If he wanted her dead, he would have to kill her. The idea made him shiver all over. He had thought of his attempts to kill his mother as just a little help in the right direction—after all, she couldn't have much longer, could she? But his cousin was another matter.

Ralph knew that he hadn't the guts to do it himself. He would have to pay someone to do the thing for him—but where would he find someone willing to murder for money? He had some guineas in his pocket and a few items of value that were still left to him. He needed to find a cut-throat who would do it for a handful of gold—but where?

A little smile touched his mouth as he realised there was only one person he could turn to for help. Sir Courtney wanted his money—well, he would tell him of his plans and ask him to point him in the right direction. Yes, yes, it was a good plan, he thought, eyes lighting with excitement. Sir Courtney would know that he was trying to get the money and he would be willing to wait a little longer if he believed that Ralph was going to inherit what must amount to almost three hundred thousand pounds—maybe more, for all he knew. It was a huge fortune and wasted on his cousin, who spent her time rescuing people in distress and repairing cottages on her estate for the benefit of her labourers. Ralph could find a better use for a fortune like that!

He would go back to London at once and seek out the man who could help him get his hands on what was, after all, his by rights.

# *Chapter Seven*

Arabella stood looking out of the back parlour window. Her aunt and Tilda had settled with some needlework and were chatting contentedly about something they had done together in London. Arabella wasn't listening. In the garden Charles and Sarah were walking together. Sarah had consented to her brother's request to be private with him for a while, though she was keeping a little distance between them and she had gone no further than the oak tree, which could be seen from the house. Clearly she was not yet ready to trust him completely.

'Shall I ring for tea?' Lady Tate asked as the clock chimed half past the hour of three. 'Do you suppose Mr Hunter intends to stay?'

'Please do ring,' Arabella said. 'I shall go out and ask.'

She opened the French window and walked down the steps of the terrace. A few sweet-scented roses still scrambled over the old stone balustrade, spreading their perfume on the air.

Sarah turned to look at Arabella as she approached, a slightly hesitant expression in her eyes.

'Charles was saying that I should go into York with you and order some new gowns. I told him that you had bought me several while you were in London. He says that you must give him the account, Belle.'

'I shall do no such thing.' Arabella's eyes sparked with pride. 'They were my gift to you, Sarah. If your brother wishes to buy more for you, that is his own affair. However, I shall accept nothing, either for your clothes or board. You are my guest for as long as you wish to stay.'

Charles gave her a frowning look. 'Sarah is my responsibility. I have been telling her that she may have or do whatever she wishes. I am at her disposal.'

'You have been most considerate,' Sarah said, looking at Charles. She was still uncertain, a little anxious, as if she did not quite feel comfortable with her brother's protestations of undying devotion. 'Perhaps if Belle will allow me I shall go to York with her to buy some things—but my mother will be here by then, I imagine.'

'I shall put off my visit for a few days and then we may all go together,' Arabella said. 'But your mama will want to rest after her journey, Sarah. She will be overcome when she sees you. You must get to know one another in private for a while.'

'Yes, of course. I would not want to distress her. I fear I must have caused everyone so much trouble and grief.' Sarah's eyes misted with tears. 'Excuse me, I think I shall go up to my room for a little. Please do not wait tea for me, Belle.'

'I shall come again tomorrow,' Charles said as she walked quickly away. He looked ruefully at Arabella. 'Is it my fault? I did not intend to upset her. I wanted her to know that her family still loves her—and that we shall do whatever she asks of us. I would die rather than cause her one moment's distress, believe me.'

'I think she is overcome with it all,' Arabella said. 'For months she has suffered from the loss of her memory. Neither of us can properly understand how bewildering that must be. She did not know whether she had a family or not. To suddenly discover that she has caused so much grief to you and her mother must distress her. She is not sure how to behave towards you, sir.'

'I do understand her reticence towards myself,' Charles said and frowned. 'I must seem impatient to you, Arabella. I want so much for Sarah to be as she was, to be happy again!'

'You must not expect it, sir. At least, not for some time yet. Now that she knows she was abducted, she will wonder what happened to her before she escaped from her captors. She may fear that she is ruined—that you will censure her for it.'

'Never! Even if she—' He broke off, his face working as he struggled to control his emotions. 'Sarah is my sister. I love her and I shall never blame her, whatever the truth. That is what I was trying to tell her. She is not to be hidden away in shame. She will be a part of our family as always, loved and spoiled, but if she does not wish to meet people she once knew, we shall take her away—perhaps abroad. I am sure that in time she will learn to trust us and be happy again.'

'Yes, in time,' Arabella agreed. 'But you must be patient. She is not yet ready to leave us. She feels safe here with me, Charles. You must not force her to do things she finds too difficult. Perhaps she would rather live quietly than be forced to live as you suggest?'

'You think that I would force her?' His eyes met hers in a challenge. 'Do you really believe I am so cruel?'

'Not intentionally cruel,' Arabella replied, a half-smile on her lips. 'I think you are not naturally a patient man, Mr Hunter. I think you have a quick temper and sometimes you are harsh when you do not mean to be. I think that some people might find your manner intimidating.'

For a moment his expression vacillated between indignation and disbelief, and then he laughed. 'I dare say I deserved that,' he said and now his eyes were warm with amusement. 'I have not been at my best of late. I assure you that I used not to be this way. I was perhaps too easy going…too careless…' Something flickered in his eyes that made her wonder. 'My fear and grief at knowing my sister lost have taken a bitter toll on me.'

'But she is restored to you,' Arabella reminded him. 'She is well and I believe she will come to trust and love you again.'

'Do you? I fear that I have lost her for ever.'

Arabella hesitated and then reached out to touch his cheek, her eyes warm with sympathy. 'You must not chastise yourself like this, Charles. You were not to blame for Sarah's abduction, and you have done all you could to find her.'

'It was not enough! She would have died if it were not for Nana. She has told me of Nana's kindness—and of yours. I cannot thank Nana, but…' He suddenly seized her hand in a fit of passion, turning it to his lips to kiss the palm. 'I can never thank you sufficiently, never tell you what it means to me.'

Arabella trembled inwardly. The touch of his lips against her skin was enough to make her knees feel as if they would give way, and her heart was racing. 'I only did what anyone would do for a young girl in distress.'

'No, that is not so,' Charles said, a fervent light in his eyes.

'You are a great lady, Arabella. Everyone speaks of you with respect and I…' He let go of her hand, staring at her strangely. 'No, I have no right, forgive me. Excuse me, please. I shall call to see Sarah tomorrow.'

'Charles…' Arabella was not sure if she spoke his name aloud. It was a sigh on her breath, a hopeless cry. He was a man tormented by his grief and he had thoughts for only one person. He could not give his heart because it had been broken.

Arabella spent a restless night, finding it difficult to sleep. She could no longer hide her love for Charles Hunter from herself. She suspected that he was attracted to her, that he felt something—but not enough. He was determined to spend his life caring for his sister, and his guilt over her disappearance was so strong that he would not allow himself to think of his own happiness.

Would he never turn to her? Perhaps if he could let go of his guilt they might be happy together. Sarah was dear to them both. There was no real need for Charles to sacrifice himself as he seemed determined to do. If they were married, they could care for Sarah between them, but he had not considered such an outcome—perhaps because he did not want Arabella as his wife. He might feel something for her, but it might not be the kind of love she felt for him. Or maybe it was simply that he was overcome with grief and self-blame.

Why? Why was he so tormented? Sarah was safe now. Had he done something that he believed made him responsible for her suffering? Grief and anger against those who had taken her were understandable, but why guilt?

Arabella got up and went to gaze out of her window at the

moon, which was casting its silvery glow over trees and bushes alike, giving the garden a mysterious, magical atmosphere. Why was Charles willing to cut himself off from personal happiness because of what had happened to Sarah? Had he done something for which he could not forgive himself?

Charles stared out of the inn window. It was impossible to sleep when his body was tight with tension and his mind seethed with too many doubts and regrets. He knew that the feeling he had for Arabella was not just mindless lust, even though he had wanted her so badly as they stood together in the garden. He had found it difficult to keep from catching her in his arms and kissing her until they both succumbed to the desire that swirled between them. When she had touched his cheek it was as if a fire had been lit inside him. He had wanted to hold her, to tell her that he loved her, to know her intimately—but he had no right.

He owed Sarah a lifetime of care and devotion, because it was his fault that she had been abducted. At last, after all these months, Charles faced the monster that had lurked in his subconscious mind. It was because he had thrashed Sir Montague Forsythe at the card table that Sarah had been snatched from her family. He had seen anger in the rogue's face that night, anger and a thirst for revenge, and it had amused him. He had smiled as he took the gold he had won and stuffed it into his pockets, careless of any danger to himself—but he had not understood that something much worse than his own death could happen.

He had not wanted to play cards that night, drawn into the game by Barton and Sir Courtney Welch, who had insisted that he join them. Charles had been a little drunk. He was at that time often a little drunk by that hour of the evening, and against his better judgement he had taken up the invitation.

However, he was perhaps not as foxed as they had thought, for he had won. Not at first, for they had been cheating him, but he had understood what they were doing after going down badly on the second hand. He had waited his chance, losing small amounts to them until the last game—and then he had started to bet large sums, which they had had to match to keep with him. First Sir Courtney had dropped out and then Barton. Forsythe held on to the bitter end—losing two thousand guineas to Charles when he finally laid his winning hand.

The disappointment and anger, the realisation that he had played them at their own game, had made Forsythe furiously angry. He had said little, but he did not need to—it was in his eyes. Charles had laughed, thinking that it would teach them a lesson, leaving the table to join some of his friends to tell them of his conquest. He had done to Forsythe and his friends what they so often did to others, but without cheating as they did. It was just three days later that Sarah had been abducted from the gardens of her home.

Charles had not imagined that Forsythe and his cronies could have done it. He had confidently awaited the ransom note that would restore her to her family unharmed, but as the days and then weeks passed without word hope began to fade. Yet it was not until Elworthy's young sister-in-law had fought off a similar attack that it began to dawn on them that the culprits might be Forsythe and his cronies. Daniel had seen it first and he had forced Forsythe to a desperate act, which had resulted in his death. In his anger, Charles had thought only of finding his sister and destroying his enemies. It was only now that he understood what had driven him so desperately.

If he had not deliberately set out to antagonise Forsythe that night, Sarah might never have been taken. She might never have suffered all these months. How could he ever make up to her for what he had done? There was only one way and that was to dedicate this life to making sure that she was safe and happy.

'Tilda, I want a word with you,' Arabella said as she came downstairs the next morning. 'I am sorry that I have not managed it before this, but there has been so much to do with one thing and another.'

'Oh…' Tilda looked like a startled rabbit caught by a stoat. 'I was just going to see Cook about the menus for the week. I know you said that you would do it, Arabella, but you are always so busy.'

'I can find time for that,' Arabella said. 'Come into my private sitting room, Tilda. I do not want to be overheard.'

Tilda hesitated, but did as she was asked, standing defensively just inside the door as Arabella went over to her desk. She watched as Arabella began to write something, her heart thumping.

'Are you angry with me?' she asked at last. What was Arabella writing—was it her dismissal? She did not want to leave, for it would mean that she must seek a post elsewhere, and no one would be as kind to her as Arabella. 'I know that I irritate you sometimes, but I do try to please you, Arabella.'

'It might be better if you did not try to please me so much,' Arabella said and frowned as she finished what she was doing and sanded her letter. 'In particular, I would prefer it if you let Sarah do a few small tasks. She is new to the house and you could help her rather than hinder her, Tilda.'

'I thought that you would take her side.' The companion looked sulky. 'I can do things so much faster because I know how you like them.'

'But Sarah wants to help, and actually you do not always know how I like things, Tilda. I do not tell you, but I prefer to speak to Cook myself—and sometimes I should like to pick my own flowers.'

'Oh, but…' Tilda blinked as tears pricked her eyes. Defiantly, she tried to face it out with pride. 'Perhaps you would like me to leave?'

'I have not said so,' Arabella replied. 'I have been grateful for your company often enough, Tilda—but my aunt lives with us now and for the moment Sarah is my guest. I will not have you say spiteful things to her. She has not complained, but I have heard and seen you.'

'If you were in my position, you might feel uneasy too,' Tilda said with a little burst of spirit. 'I know that you prefer her company to mine—and you like to be private with Lady Tate.'

'Yes, I do sometimes,' Arabella admitted. 'But you are welcome to join us most of the time. If you let yourself be one of us, it would be better, Tilda. You are not an outsider, but you do not have to prove to Sarah that she is—she knows it only too well. If I make more fuss of her, it is because she needs it. After what she has been through, we should all be kind to her.'

'I did not mean to offend you.' Tilda looked upset. 'When do you wish me to go?'

'There is no need for you to leave, unless you are unhappy here?' She looked at Tilda inquiringly, her brows raised. Tilda flushed and shook her head. 'My house is big enough for all of us and there are still enough rooms to spare for guests. However, I do understand your position better than you may think, Tilda. What I have written here is a draft on my bank for ten thousand pounds. It is for you, to give you your independence. I had considered leaving it to you in my will, which I shall make when I go into York—but I thought you should have it now. It does not mean I wish you to leave, but if you feel out of place here it will help you to make a life of your own.' She stood up and held out the piece of paper to Tilda. 'Come, take it, my dear, and let us have no more of this sulking.'

Tilda stared at her, eyes filling with tears that began to trickle down her cheeks. She took the bank draft, staring at it in disbelief—she had never owned more than fifty guineas in her life, though she had received many generous gifts from Arabella previously, but nothing like this. Invested wisely, she could quite easily live on the income from this money, if she chose not to work.

'Why have you given me this?' she asked on a sobbing breath. 'I do not deserve it. I have been spiteful to Sarah, and—' She shook her head, suddenly turning and running from the room.

Arabella frowned as she stared after her. It would have been easy to send Tilda away, for now that she had independent means she could quite well live alone. She had not had the heart to do it, and only hoped that Tilda would feel easier in her mind for this little talk.

Hearing voices in the hall, she went out to discover that her aunt and Sarah had met there and were discussing whether or not it was warm enough to walk in the gardens.

'I think I should prefer to sit in the parlour by the fire,' Lady

Tate said, smiling at them. 'Arabella will walk with you, Sarah. I shall rest until it is time for nuncheon. I have a few letters to write and I need some ink. Unaccountably, I have none in my rooms, Arabella, though I thought I had brought my own from London. May I borrow yours, my love?'

'Yes, of course, Aunt,' Arabella said. 'Please use my desk. I shall find a shawl and walk with Sarah in the garden, for it is quite pleasant out and we do not know how long the fine weather will last.'

She collected a wrap from the hall cabinet where several bonnets, shawls and walking sticks were kept, sometimes used by her, but not exclusively. It was so easy to take a shawl from the shelves of the cabinet, rather than running upstairs to fetch one, that they had made it a habit to leave one or two there. Arabella wrapped a plaid shawl about her shoulders, and Sarah took a plain red silk one.

They set out to walk through the gardens at the front of the house, venturing as far as the park, which stretched for some distance to the main highway. It was after they had been walking for some twenty minutes that they saw the carriage bowling through the park towards them. Sarah caught Arabella's arm, looking apprehensive.

'Do you think that is Mama?'

'Yes, I think it very probably is,' Arabella said smiling at her as it went straight past them. 'Do not be frightened, my love. Mrs Hunter will be so pleased to see you.'

'Supposing she is angry with me for causing her such distress?'

'Why should she be angry with you? It was not your fault that you were abducted—how could it be?'

'Perhaps I did something to make those men choose me,' Sarah said, her eyes dark with anxiety. 'Do you think I said or did something wrong?'

'Whatever makes you ask that? I am sure that you did not, Sarah.'

'Then why did they take me? Why me and not some other girl? I have been wondering about it, Belle. Am I wicked? Is there something about me that made men like that want me?'

'You could never be wicked,' Arabella assured her, squeezing her arm. 'I think it may have been because you were so pretty, dearest.'

'There are lots of pretty girls,' Sarah said. 'I cannot think why it should have been me—unless I did something wrong.'

'You are not to blame yourself,' Arabella said with a frown. 'Put all such thoughts from your head, Sarah. And now we must go back to the house. Your mama will be waiting.'

'Yes, of course.' Sarah clung to her friend's arm. She was very nervous about the coming meeting, though she also longed for it. She had not known her brother—but surely she must know her mother when she saw her? 'We must not keep her waiting long.'

'We shall be there by the time my housekeeper has taken her pelisse and bonnet from her,' Arabella said. 'And I know that she will be so happy to see you. Come, let us walk a little faster, for she will be wondering where you are.'

The carriage had gone round to the back of the house to unload Mrs Hunter's baggage by the time they arrived at the front door, which stood open, but she herself was still lingering in the hallway, being greeted by the housekeeper and Lady Tate. The two ladies were embracing each other and exchanging greetings. As the girls walked in through the open door, they were in time to hear Mrs Hunter's question.

'Where is she, Hester? Is she all right? Has she changed terribly? Oh, my darling little girl…' Something made her turn at that moment and she gave a little shriek as she saw Sarah, rushing towards her to gather her into a tight embrace and sobbing audibly. 'My poor, sweet Sarah. What has happened to you, my love? Oh, it does not matter. I am here now. I shall never let you out of my sight again…'

'Mama?' Sarah gently eased herself from Mrs Hunter's embrace. 'I am sorry…' Her eyes filled with tears of disappointment. 'I do not know you…'

'You do not know me?' Mrs Hunter was thunderstruck. 'I know Mr Elworthy said something of the sort, but you must remember me? I am your mama.' She looked at Lady Tate in bewildered appeal as Sarah shook her head. 'But she must know who I am…'

'Please come into the sitting room and sit down,' Arabella said. 'We are serving a cold luncheon today, for we were not sure when you would arrive—but that may wait. I suggest that we sit down and talk for a while.' She glanced at her housekeeper. 'I think we need some tea, Mrs Bristol—and perhaps a cordial or a little brandy.'

Arabella led the way into the sitting room, smiling at Mrs Hunter as she sat down uncertainly. 'Mr Elworthy told you that you are to be my guest until Sarah comes to know you better?'

'Yes, but I did not realise that she would not know who I was.'

'It was a shock for Charles too,' Arabella said. 'I believe he will be calling later today. You will see him then and perhaps it is best if he explains everything, Mrs Hunter. I can tell you that Sarah was ill when she came to us. My nurse looked after her and she lived with her until a couple of weeks ago when Nana died. Sarah came to me then and she is welcome to make her home here if she chooses.'

'Her home is with me. I am her mother.'

'Yes, of course—but Sarah must make up her own mind,' Arabella said. She looked up with relief as the housekeeper brought in a large butler's tray, which she set down on a stand next to Arabella's chair. 'Thank you, Mrs Bristol. Yes, I shall pour myself. You may go.'

'Sarah…' Mrs Hunter looked at her daughter who had chosen a chair opposite her mother. 'Surely you wish to be with your family?'

'Arabella has been kind to me,' Sarah told her. 'I should like to come home one day, but I am not ready yet…Mama. I must feel comfortable with you and my brother.'

'Feel comfortable… Yes, milk and one sugar, please," she said in answer to Arabella's question. Mrs Hunter looked bewildered as she was handed a delicate porcelain cup filled with tea. 'I do not understand any of this. Hester, pray tell me—what has been going on here? Did you know that Sarah was staying here with Lady Arabella?'

'No, Selina. We none of us knew. Arabella had mentioned something about a young girl living with Nana, but she did not go into details—and in any case I had no idea that Sarah was missing. I thought she was staying with friends in Scotland.'

'That was what we told people,' Mrs Hunter said with a little frown. 'We did not wish it known that Sarah had disappeared.'

Sarah blushed and looked down at her hands. 'I have

caused so much trouble for you—all of you. I have brought shame on your name. You must be angry with me.'

'Indeed we are not…' Her mother looked flustered. Clearly she did not know how to handle this girl who was her daughter and yet not the Sarah she knew. Fortunately, there was an interruption at that moment as the door opened and Charles walked in. Mrs Hunter was on her feet at once. 'Charles! Thank goodness you are come. Tell Sarah that I am her mama. She does not know me.'

'She does not know me either, Mama,' Charles said and walked to his mother, stooping to kiss her cheek as she sat down again. His eyes met Arabella's across the room apologetically. 'Forgive me. I assume you are about to have nuncheon. John came to see me in the village. He escorted Mama that far and then decided to find me. We have been talking and the time went on. I do not wish to impose on you, but I wished to see how Mama was doing…'

'You are very welcome to stay. A cold collation has been laid in the dining room because we did not know when Mrs Hunter would arrive,' Arabella said. 'I suggest that you take Mrs Hunter upstairs, Aunt Hester. She will want some time to herself before we eat. Sarah, perhaps you would like to walk in the garden for a moment with Charles? I shall speak to Cook and tell her that we shall be two extra for dinner this evening— if you would care to stay, Mr Hunter?'

'Yes, thank you,' he said. 'Could I impose on you to make it three? I believe John might wish to dine with us this evening. He said that he might call later and he has been of great help to me in this affair.'

'Yes, certainly,' Arabella agreed. 'It will be pleasant to

have guests in the house. I have not given a dinner party for some time and I must do so while you are here, Mrs Hunter.' She stood up, leaving to make the arrangements with her staff. It was several minutes before she returned.

Arabella was grateful to her aunt for whatever had been said while they were upstairs together. Mrs Hunter seemed to be much calmer when she came down. Although she could not take her eyes off Sarah, she did not complain of the situation. Indeed, she spoke little until after they had eaten.

'I have several gifts for you in my trunks, Sarah,' she said, smiling at her tenderly. 'They were purchased for last Christmas and for your birthday. You were eighteen last month, my love.'

'Eighteen? I had thought I must be older.' Sarah touched the little wing of white hair at her right temple. 'I believe my hair was much longer before I was ill? Nana cut it because the doctor said it was taking my strength. Was it very long?'

'Yes, it was, Sarah. It reached to the small of your back. You used to say it was too long when I brushed it, for it often tangled, but I begged you not to have it cut.' Mrs Hunter blinked hard to keep away the foolish tears. She must not distress Sarah, for it was clear that she was already nervous. 'I think it suits you very well as it is, my love. You are even lovelier than before.'

'Sarah is beautiful,' Arabella said as she led the way into the larger sitting room at the front of the house. 'She deserves a lot of pretty new clothes. We are thinking of going into York in a few days. Shall you come with us, Mrs Hunter? Or would you prefer to keep my aunt company here until we return? We shall not stay more than two days at most, for my local seamstress may come to us to finish the gowns.'

'I am not a good traveller,' Mrs Hunter said. 'Perhaps I shall stay here with Hester—but Charles must go with you as your escort for protection.' She looked so anxious that her son hurried to reassure her.

'I shall be happy to do so, Mama,' he said. 'I have already told Sarah that I am at her service whenever she wishes.'

'Oh, you must not,' Sarah protested, looking uncomfortable. 'I do not wish to give anyone any trouble. I have caused enough grief already.'

'Do not be foolish, my love,' Mrs Hunter said, clearly upset. 'You were not to blame for any of this unfortunate business—was she, Charles?'

'No, Mama, certainly not.' He turned his intent gaze on his sister. 'No blame attaches to you, Sarah. It is my fault. I should have protected you better.'

'What could you have done? If I was taken from the garden of my own home—how could anyone have expected it?'

Charles did not reply. He walked over to the window, looking out into the courtyard just as a curricle came bowling smartly up to the front entrance.

'I believe you have another visitor.' His gaze narrowed as he watched the driver of the curricle throw the reins to his groom and get down. 'I think it is your cousin, Lady Arabella.'

'Ralph? Good grief!' Arabella went to join him at the window as the visitor mounted the steps at the imposing front door and wielded the knocker vigorously. She turned to her aunt to confirm it. 'Ralph has come to visit you, Aunt Hester. I shall go down and greet him, tell him that we have guests staying.'

She left the room and went down the main stairway as Ralph was being admitted. She had reached the bottom of the stairs when Charles came to the top and stood looking down. He watched as a footman helped Ralph off with his driving cape, gloves and hat, alert and ready should he be needed.

'Good afternoon, cousin,' Arabella said in a pleasant tone. 'This is a surprise. You did not let us know of your intention to visit. I am afraid that we have several guests. I am not sure that I can offer you a bed for the night.' It was a lie—there were rooms to spare, but she would not have felt comfortable with him staying in the house.

'Oh, you need not bother,' Ralph said airily, though his eyes glinted with suppressed anger as he looked at her. She was beautiful, wealthy and proud—but she would be humbled soon enough. He had Sir Courtney's word on that. Remembering their conversation, he smiled suddenly. 'I have just come from London. I had heard that Mama was staying here and I wanted to see how she was now. I remember that she had been a little off colour before I left town.'

'Yes. Something she ate, we think,' Arabella reminded him. She did not like the way he was smiling—as if he were gloating over something. She had no intention of mentioning his mother's fall. Let him stew over it a little longer!

'Well, she should be more careful,' Ralph said arrogantly. Had his cousin wished to accuse him of harming his mother, she would have done it by now. He was in the clear as far as that other business was concerned and he had regained his courage. 'I trust she is better now? I had thought she might let me know—or that you would, Arabella.'

'I should have let you know if there was cause for concern.'

'Perhaps.' Ralph looked uncertain again. Arabella appreciated his difficulty: he could hardly ask if his mother had recovered from a fall that no one had told him of. 'I suppose I may see her?'

Arabella resisted the temptation to tell him that he was not welcome in her house. Until she had proof of his intentions, she could hardly prevent him from seeing his mother, though she would not encourage his visits.

'Yes, of course. Please come up. As I told you, we have several guests, but you are welcome to join us. We shall have tea in a little while.'

'I would prefer to speak to Mama alone.'

'You are at liberty to ask her, cousin.'

Arabella turned and walked upstairs, her bearing almost regal. Charles had remained at the top, watching, ready to spring to her defence if necessary. Their eyes met, but neither spoke until Ralph was with them.

'I believe you know Mr Hunter, Ralph?'

'We have met.' Ralph stared at him coldly. 'Didn't expect to see you here, Hunter.'

'You must know that Lady Tate and Mrs Hunter are great friends, Sir Ralph.' Charles addressed him formally, meeting his challenge with one of his own. 'And of course Lady Arabella and I are becoming good friends.'

Something in his eyes dared Ralph to deny it. He did not, merely inclining his head. He had taken a bold step in coming here like this, but Sir Courtney had demanded it and he dared do no other than fall in line with his plans. He had been promised that his debt would be at an end and he would receive a substantial gift if things went as Sir Courtney intended.

'Indeed? That is new, Arabella. Thinking of making a match of it, are you?' They would have to work fast if she were to be married! It would be too late if she made a will in Hunter's favour.

'I think you presume too far, cousin,' Arabella said, her face impassive, giving nothing away. 'If I were contemplating marriage, I should not feel the need to inform you.'

'Head of the family,' Ralph muttered. 'Not that you've ever shown me the slightest respect. You always go your own way, Arabella.'

'Yes, I have and shall continue to do so.'

They had reached the drawing room. It was on the first floor and, being large, used only when there were several guests. Arabella went in first. Charles stood back and allowed Ralph to precede him, the cold glint in his eyes making Arabella's cousin uncomfortable. Lady Tate looked at Arabella, frowning slightly as she saw her son following behind.

'Good afternoon, Ralph. It was good of you to call.'

'I shall not stay long,' he replied in a perfunctory manner that bordered on rudeness. 'I must be back in London tomorrow. I hoped I might speak with you alone, Mama.'

Lady Tate hesitated. She did not particularly wish to be private with him, though she knew that she was safe enough. Ralph would do nothing to harm her when there were so many other people in the house.

'Very well, Ralph. We shall go downstairs to the back parlour.' She glanced at Arabella. 'I shall only be a matter of minutes, my dear. Selina has promised to play a hand of whist with me. Ralph, walk in front of me if you please. I recently had a fall and I watch my step more carefully now. You will walk more quickly.

Ralph shot a look at her and then at Arabella, but neither of them displayed any emotion. It was as he had thought—he could not be blamed in connection with his mother's fall; there was no proof, no matter what his nosy cousin might think.

Arabella watched as her aunt went out. She moved to the far end of the room, appearing to study a collection of Chinese porcelain in the mahogany display cabinet. Charles came to stand beside her.

'She is safe enough,' he said in a low voice. 'He would not dare to harm her with so many of us present to testify against him.'

'I have warned my housekeeper to stay close whenever he visits,' Arabella said. 'She will be within call should my aunt cry out—but I believe you are right. I do not know why he has called, but he will not dare to attempt anything at this time. I dare say he has come to ask for money again.'

'Yes, that is probable,' Charles agreed, his expression serious as he looked at her. 'You have a great deal to worry you, Arabella. My offer holds good. Shall I go after him and warn him off? It may be done discreetly.'

'Would you? Just a hint might be a good thing.' Her lovely face was clouded by doubt. 'I am sure that he did push Aunt Hester down the stairs—though he did not dare to mention it.'

'At least he will not be staying here tonight.'

'No…' Arabella turned to look him in the face. 'Would you and Mr Elworthy accept my hospitality for a few days—just until we go to York? I should feel much safer. If Ralph thought that you and Mr Elworthy were our guests, he would hesitate to try anything underhand. I know my cousin. He is a coward at heart.'

'Would you truly allow both John and I to stay here?' Charles gazed down at her, his eyes burning with a hot light.

He knew that he was a fool to accept, because it meant that he would be close to temptation, but she had asked and he could not refuse. 'I should be delighted and I am sure that John would also. He talked of going back to town, but I know that he would prefer to be of use to Sarah. He was always quite fond of her, you see. There was a time when I hoped…but that time has gone.'

'Please go back to the inn and bring him here,' Arabella said. 'You may leave at the same time as Ralph. If you were to hint that we were closer than friends, he might realise that I am no longer unprotected and take himself off—perhaps abroad where he might live more easily on what money he will have once my aunt has sold her house.' She blushed slightly. 'It is a great deal to ask, but no one else will hear of it.'

Charles shook his head, not daring to reply on that subject. 'Lady Tate is to sell her house for his sake?'

'She thinks it best,' Arabella said. She glanced over her shoulder and saw that the others were looking through the fashion journals she subscribed to, which had been delivered via the receiving station only that morning. 'I do not wish my aunt to know this, but I intend to ask my lawyer to buy the house. When Ralph has been persuaded to leave us alone, I shall tell her that she is still at liberty to use it when she wishes. Indeed, we shall all use it when we go up to town. I do not have a town house and I think it is the ideal solution for us all.'

'You mean that you wish to preserve it for Lady Tate.' Charles looked at her with warm approval. 'You are as generous as you are lovely.'

'It is nothing…' Arabella moved towards the window and

glanced out. 'I think Ralph is about to leave. His groom is preparing the curricle.'

'Then I shall take my leave,' Charles said. 'John and I will return very shortly.' He nodded to his mama and Sarah. 'I shall see you both later. Lady Arabella has been kind enough to ask John and I to stay so that we can all be together.'

Arabella went to join Sarah as he went out. She had been showing Tilda a fetching ensemble that she liked in the monthly journal, and Arabella was pleased to see that Tilda had responded in a friendly manner. She smiled at her and sat down, taking the journal to look at the fashion plate that had captured Sarah's interest. It was a pretty spotted muslin with short puffed sleeves and a high waist.

'Yes, that is charming,' she agreed. 'I think it would suit you very well, Sarah, my dear.' She looked at Tilda. 'Mrs Hunter is to stay here with Aunt Hester. There will be room in the carriage for you, Tilda, should you wish to come with us to York.'

'Oh…thank you, Arabella. Yes, I should like that.' She flushed and glanced away as Lady Tate entered the room. 'Would you like me to ring for tea? I could go down and save Mrs Bristol the trip, if you wish it, Arabella.'

'Yes, if you would,' Arabella said, looking at her aunt's face. Lady Tate looked a little pale, but she was otherwise composed. 'Ralph has gone, Aunt?'

'Yes. He did not wish to stay as he is returning to town at once—at least that is what he says…'

'I am sure he will, Aunt. I should tell you that I have invited Mr Hunter and Mr Elworthy to join us here. They will stay for a few days—until we leave for York.'

'Ah, that was a sensible idea,' Lady Tate said and looked relieved. 'How nice that will be for everyone.'

'You are so kind,' Mrs Hunter said. 'I think we shall be for ever in your debt, Lady Arabella.'

'Not at all,' Arabella replied. 'It is a pleasure to me to have your company.'

She walked back to the window, glancing down at the courtyard. Both Charles Hunter and her cousin were standing there; to a casual onlooker it might seem that they were merely passing the time of day, but Arabella saw that her cousin's manner was defensive and angry. Obviously Charles had kept his promise to issue a warning, though whether it was discreet or not, she could not know.

Ralph climbed into his curricle, taking the reins from his groom. He whipped his horses and went off at a furious pace. He was very angry. She watched until Charles had mounted his horse, setting out at a much more leisurely pace. A little smile touched her mouth. Charles had accepted her invitation to stay. She would see him every day, a mixed pleasure when she was torn between loving him and keeping her distance for fear that he would guess that her feelings were stronger than they ought to be. And yet, if Charles would only allow himself to love her, she thought that they might find happiness together.

Perhaps when he saw her every day he would realise how much he was throwing away.

'Ah, tea is here,' Lady Tate announced, breaking her train of thought. 'Would you like me to pour, Arabella dear?'

'Yes, please, Aunt,' Arabella said and turned to face her with a smile that hid her inner turmoil. 'That would be very nice…'

# Chapter Eight

John Elworthy had been taking a walk in the woods that bordered the Long Meadow estate to while away the time. He knew he ought to think of returning to London. He had nothing to do here now, for Sarah was returned to her family and all danger was surely at an end and yet he had lingered. He was not sure of his reasons, for he was hardly needed at this time. It was as he turned to retrace his footsteps to the inn, where he intended to pay his shot and leave a note for Charles, that he heard voices and something made him pause. Surely he knew that laugh? It had a high-pitched titter to it and was most unpleasant. John frowned. What on earth was a dandy like Sir Courtney Welch doing so far from London?

John felt a sliver of ice at the nape of his neck. Sir Courtney was a devil! He had killed two men in duels for slight offences, and there were rumours that he had killed others in a more sinister way. He had sometimes been seen in the gaming hells with Forsythe and Lord Barton, but John did not believe that Sir Courtney had been a member of their cult. He would scorn such rituals, dismissing them as nonsense. He was, in John's opinion, a far more dangerous man than Forsythe. No, he would not have taken part in rituals, but would have used Forsythe when he needed him, as he used others. John knew perhaps more of him than most might, for a friend of his had disappeared after an argument with Sir Courtney. His body had been found in a ditch on a lonely country road some months later. The general verdict had been robbery, but since his friend had been identified by a gold ring on his finger, John had always wondered if the motive had truly been murder.

Something made him decide to get closer to see what he could hear of this conversation. He caught sight of four men; two of them appeared to be ruffians, but the other two were gentlemen—Sir Courtney and Lady Arabella's cousin, Sir Ralph Tate. He knew them both by sight, though he avoided their company whenever possible.

John shrank back behind the trunk of an ancient oak tree as Sir Courtney glanced his way, as if sensing something. Yet he could not have seen anything, for he continued to berate his companion in a loud voice.

'You are a fool, Tate. If you had not bungled your own business, you might have been a guest in that house and the thing would have been easier. We could have taken her while the house slept and none the wiser. As it is, we must take her from the garden in broad daylight.'

'I still think it would be easier to lay a trap for her when she goes riding. Charles Hunter is made free of the house, damn him! He was acting as if he owned the place. I dare say he has his eye on her fortune, if the truth be known. We must wait until he is out of the way.'

'And what do we do in the meantime? Sit around and twiddle our thumbs?' Sir Courtney's tone was scathing. 'I shall deal with Hunter if necessary. I have a little score to settle with that gentleman. It would please me if he did interfere. He would not live to tell the tale. You said yourself that she plans to make her will shortly. We must act soon. I want her and the money.'

'She's my cousin,' Ralph complained in a sulky voice. 'Why should you have it all? It was my idea to kill her, before she has time to make her will. Mama will inherit then and I can twist her round my finger.'

'But you came to me for help and you will do as you are told,' Sir Courtney replied. 'That proud bitch made me angry once and I have pondered on my revenge. When you came to me I saw that I could have everything. Once she has been in my bed she will beg me to wed her—and then, once my ring is on her finger, she will not survive long.' He threw a gloating look at the other man. 'When the money is mine, I may toss you a few crumbs now and then if you please me.'

'You are a devil, Welch,' Ralph said bitterly. 'I wish that I had never told you my idea.'

'Your idea would have landed you at the end of a hangman's noose,' Sir Courtney sneered. 'Mine is foolproof, for she would never admit what had been done to humble her. She will learn to obey my every whim until I decide I have had enough of her, and that may not be for a while. I like a woman with spirit, the taming is so much sweeter. But please yourself—you either help me and the debt is ended or you write your own death warrant. The choice is yours.'

'Damn it! I don't have a choice…'

John had heard enough. He moved away, silently, careful not to make a sound. He would take a different route back to the inn. There was no thought of leaving for London now. He must tell Charles what he had overheard, and they must send immediately for Tobbold. His men had guarded Elizabeth and Lady Cavendish for Daniel, and they would be needed here if Sir Courtney and Tate were to be stopped from carrying out their evil plan.

Quickening his stride, John's mind was working hard as he thought about what was happening. At least this time, they knew that a kidnap was planned, and they must make sure that the culprits were caught before they could do any harm. A grim smile touched his mouth as he went into the inn and saw Charles inquiring for him of the innkeeper's wife.

'Well met, Charles,' he said. 'I have something to tell you—something I think you will find disturbing.'

'We have been invited to stay up at the Manor,' Charles said. 'Let us go up and pack our things at once. You may tell me your news and I shall tell you mine.'

Everyone had gone up to get ready for the evening. Tilda had not spent long changing her gown, for she was desperate to find something that she might do to please Arabella. She had hit upon the idea of bringing her some wild roses. She knew that they were Arabella's favourite flowers, but those in the garden had finished flowering. She had noticed that there were still a few in the wood at the far end of the garden and it would be worth the walk to pick a small posy and place it by Arabella's plate at dinner that evening. Perhaps she would understand then how very grateful Tilda was for her kindness.

It was only when she got downstairs that Tilda realised she would need a shawl. She seldom borrowed one from the hall cabinet, for they were Arabella's and she did not like to use them without permission, as they were heavy silk and good quality. However, it would waste time to go back for her own shawl and she was sure no one would notice. She would be back at the house before anyone else had come down for dinner.

Selecting a heavy red silk, Tilda slipped it around her shoulders and went out quickly. She would need to walk quite fast or she would keep everyone waiting for their meal and that would never do. Arabella would be cross then, and she did so want to please her. She was smiling to herself as she walked through the shrubbery towards the wood. Ten thousand pounds was such a lot of money. She could have her own cottage if she chose…or she might even travel. She had heard that it was very cheap to live in countries like Spain and Italy, and she had always wanted to see some of those exotic places she had only read of in books.

Walking with her head down, thinking only of Arabella's pleasure when she saw her flowers, Tilda was quite unaware that anyone was lurking behind her; when a heavy blanket was suddenly thrown over her head from the rear, she gave a little shriek of fear.

'Be quiet, girl,' a man's gruff voice spoke close to her head, making her moan in terror. 'Give me any trouble and you'll be crows' meat by mornin'—but if you behave yourself nothing will happen to you. It ain't you we want, but I was told to bring whichever one of you came out. I dare say as you'll come in mighty handy for fetchin' her out where we want her.' A coarse laugh sent Tilda into a spasm of fright and she began to struggle helplessly as she was picked up and tossed over her captor's shoulder. As he walked carelessly through the wood towards the gate through which he had come, Tilda's head was banged against the heavy branch of a spreading oak and the blow rendered her unconscious.

'Isn't it nice to have gentlemen staying in the house?' Lady Tate said as they gathered for a glass of sherry before dinner. 'I am so glad you could come, Mr Elworthy. One gentleman would hardly be enough with all these ladies.' She glanced around the room. They were all gathered except for Tilda, which was a nuisance because Mrs Bristol had just come to announce dinner. 'Where is Tilda, Arabella? It isn't like her to be late for meals.'

'No, she is usually down before the rest of us,' Arabella said and looked at her housekeeper. 'Have you seen Tilda this evening?'

'I believe she went out for a walk earlier,' Mrs Bristol said. 'She was wearing your red silk shawl, ma'am, and she set off through the wild garden—heading for the woods. At least I think it was her, though at first I thought it might be Miss Hunter, but then she came downstairs with you.'

'What on earth is Tilda doing going for a walk at this hour?' Arabella said. She felt a flicker of irritation. She had believed that Tilda had accepted the situation and was settled in her own mind, but this was outside of enough. If she was trying to upset Arabella's plans for the evening, she would be disappointed. 'We shall not wait for her, Mrs Bristol. She may join us when she comes back.' She stood up, smiling at her guests. 'I think we should go in, everyone. Cook will not be pleased if we keep her waiting.'

'Good cooks are so hard to come by,' John Elworthy said. 'Lady Cavendish—the dowager, you know—lives in terror of losing hers.'

'Oh, I understand how she feels,' Lady Tate agreed, taking his arm. 'I have suffered badly in the past, but Arabella has an excellent cook here.'

Charles had offered his arm to his mother, Sarah and Arabella walked in behind the others, talking of Lord Byron's work. Sarah had been reading a copy of *Childe Harold's Pilgrimage* that she had discovered in Arabella's library.

'Oh, I do love poetry,' Sarah said, smiling at her friend. 'But I think that Colonel Lovelace wrote some of the most romantic poetry to his lady during the Civil War, don't you?'

Arabella looked at her oddly. 'And where did you read Lovelace, Sarah? I do not believe that I have more than one copy and that is always beside my bed.'

'I read his poems long ago, at home. Mama is very fond of him too.' Sarah stared at her, her eyes opening wide with surprise. 'How did I know that, Arabella? I am sure she has not mentioned anything of that nature to me since she has been here.' She was a little startled at herself for having come out with such a statement—it was the first time she had ever referred to anything from the past as if it were natural to her.

Arabella gave her arm a little squeeze. 'I think it is as I hoped, my love. Now that your mama and brother are with you, you may begin to remember things. Not everything at once, and perhaps not the things you would most wish to remember—but silly little things like poetry.'

Sarah nodded, her expression serious. 'Do not tell anyone yet, Arabella. If Mama knows that I have begun to remember she will expect me to know her, and I do not. I feel that I like her very much, and I am not afraid of either Charles or Mr Elworthy now. Indeed, I feel happy that they are here—but I do not remember anything, other than that I liked Colonel Lovelace's poems.'

'I shall say nothing, Sarah. When you are ready, you will wish to tell your mama what you remember. However, if she keeps telling you things about your home and the way you were, it is bound to help you feel comfortable—even if you cannot truly remember.'

'Yes, I am already feeling better since she came,' Sarah said. 'But I also feel guilty because I have caused her and my brother so much suffering.'

'You must not,' Arabella told her. 'It truly was not your fault.'

'I keep thinking that I must have done something. I must have made someone angry. Why else would they take me? It could have been anyone—so why me?'

'I do not know,' Arabella said. 'Does it really matter, dearest? You are safe now and I do not imagine that anything like that will ever happen again. We are well protected here— I am sure that my people would notice anything untoward as soon as it happened.'

'I wonder why Tilda went out,' Sarah said. 'She told me earlier that she was feeling hungry. It seems odd that she should not be here for dinner, doesn't it?'

'Yes…' Arabella frowned. 'I dare say she will come rushing in soon full of apologies, but if she does not come in to dinner I shall go up and speak to her when we retire to the drawing room. It really is most inconsiderate of her to disappear like this!'

\* \* \*

Arabella did not begin to worry until after they had finished dinner and she led the ladies to the drawing room, leaving the gentlemen to their port. She suspected that they would not be long in following. She left her aunt to oversee the ordering of the tea tray and went upstairs.

She paused outside Tilda's door and then knocked. 'Are you there, Tilda? We are about to have some tea in the drawing room. Will you not come down and join us?'

Arabella frowned when she did not receive an answer. It was not like Tilda to behave like this. She could be a little sulky, but for her to miss dinner altogether was strange. She tried the door handle and when it turned easily went inside. Tilda's room was immaculate as always. She was meticulous about keeping it tidy herself, everything in its place—but she was not there, her bed untouched.

Surely she could not still be out walking? It was not yet quite dark but why would Tilda stay out so late? Arabella felt coldness at the back of her neck. Tilda had been wearing her red shawl—and the last person to borrow that had been Sarah. Had someone abducted Tilda, thinking that she was Sarah?

She had a sick feeling in her stomach as she turned to return to the drawing room to join the others. Mrs Bristol was coming from the dining room carrying a tray of used dishes. Arabella stopped her.

'I suppose you have not seen Tilda?'

'Not since she went out earlier. It is a little odd, isn't it, ma'am? She never misses her dinner—unless she is feeling unwell.'

'She isn't in her room,' Arabella said. 'Thank you, Mrs Bristol. You will let me know at once if you should see her come in?'

'Yes, of course, my lady.' Mrs Bristol hesitated, then, 'I have noticed that a valuable box is missing from the cabinet in the downstairs drawing room, ma'am. I believe it was a musical one with a singing bird?'

'The box that Ben gave me as a wedding present?' Arabella frowned—that particular box had more sentimental value for her than anything else. 'Are you sure it is missing, Mrs Bristol?'

'I sent one of the girls to clean the silver in that cabinet, ma'am. Afterwards, I checked to make sure that she had done her work properly—and I saw that it was missing. Annie believes it was there when she cleaned the silver early this morning.'

'I see.' Arabella frowned. 'Perhaps I moved it. I shall look and see if it is in another cabinet. We shall not say anything about this for the moment, Mrs Bristol.'

'As you wish, my lady.'

Arabella was frowning as she went into the drawing room. It was odd that the box had gone missing, for she did not recall having moved it. However, she wished to be sure that it had gone before jumping to conclusions. Besides, she had more important things on her mind just now. She was not surprised to see that the gentlemen had not lingered over their port and were sitting with the ladies.

'Tilda isn't in her room,' she announced. 'She hasn't returned from her walk. I am afraid something may have happened to her.' She saw Charles shoot a look at John.

'What? Is there something I should know? Please, you must tell me. I am worried about Tilda.'

'In private,' Charles said. 'John, stay with Mama and Sarah, if you please.'

'My sitting room,' Arabella said, leading the way along the hall to her private apartments. She turned to him as he closed the door behind them. 'Something is wrong, isn't it? I should have guessed when she did not come in to dinner. I thought she was sulking. She is a little jealous of my aunt and Sarah, though she has no need to be.'

Charles looked grim. 'John overheard something in the woods earlier today. Your cousin was with three men, two of whom were clearly ruffians—but the third was a gentleman, though he disgraces the term. It seems that there may be a plot to kidnap you and force you into marriage for the sake of your fortune.'

'I would never marry Ralph, no matter what he did. He must know that,' Arabella said. 'How can he be so foolish?'

'It was not his idea. He meant to arrange an accident for you when you were out riding, hoping to inherit through his mother. Apparently, someone else has other ideas.'

'This other gentleman?' Arabella looked at him in bewilderment. 'I do not understand.'

'Do you know Sir Courtney Welch?'

'Sir Courtney…' Arabella was shocked. She put a hand out, clutching the back of a chair to steady herself. 'That man! I refused his offer of marriage last summer. I believe he was offended and is now my enemy.'

'He hates you,' Charles said, looking grim. 'He plans to marry you and then arrange your death when he is ready, but

that is not the worst of his intentions towards you, Arabella—
though I am sure that, like your cousin, he has plans for your
fortune that do not include your happiness.'

Arabella closed her eyes for a moment. She shook her
head as if she could not believe this was happening, then she
opened them and looked straight at Charles. 'Have they taken
Tilda? They might have thought that she was me because she
was wearing my shawl.'

'I doubt she was mistaken for you,' Charles said. 'I think
they may hope to get to you through her. They will have a ruse
of some kind. I think we may expect a letter in her hand, asking
you to meet her somewhere—or something of that order.'

'And then they will grab me as well,' Arabella said. 'What
am I to do, sir? If a letter comes, I cannot simply ignore it.
Otherwise, they might harm her. Tilda has been a good friend
to me. She does not deserve this…'

'No, indeed she does not,' Charles agreed. 'No woman
should be treated so disgracefully. That is why I would gladly
have killed the men who snatched Sarah from her family. We
blamed Forsythe for that and he was certainly the one who had
her abducted for his own foul purpose—but I wonder now if
Sir Courtney had a hand in it.' He hesitated, then, 'You see, I
think they took Sarah to punish me. I had played cards with
Forsythe and Sir Courtney some days earlier. They thought I
was drunk and planned to fleece me as they have others before
me, but I was not as intoxicated as they imagined and I beat
them at their own game. Forsythe was furious. I knew I had
made an enemy of him, but I thought Welch had accepted it,
with a bad grace perhaps, but shrugging it off, as one does
when gambling.'

'Is that why…?' Arabella nodded to herself, for she understood now why he felt so guilty regarding Sarah's abduction. 'Thank you for telling me. I understand why Sir Courtney wishes to punish me—but they should have taken me, not Tilda.' She frowned. 'I had wondered if they meant to snatch Sarah, because she was the last one to wear that red shawl before Tilda—but I see now that they did not care who they took. It would have had the same effect, for I should have been even more distressed had it been Sarah, because she has already suffered too much.'

'We meant to warn you this evening,' Charles said. 'But we expected them to make their move against you. It did not occur to me to wonder what had happened to your companion. You did not seem concerned at the time and I assumed she had simply decided not to come down for reasons of her own. I am sorry that I did not think of it sooner.'

'It was not your fault. I should have started a search as soon as she failed to join us, but I imagined that she might be sulking again, though I thought I had cured that…' Arabella gave a little sob of distress. 'Poor Tilda! I feel so guilty.'

'You are not to blame for what that evil man has done,' Charles said and reached out to touch her hand. He caught it, holding it in his own. 'Please do not think along those lines, Arabella. I know how painful it can be. We shall find her and bring her back. I promise you.'

'But how can you?' Arabella asked. 'We do not know where they have taken her. They may even have—' She shook her head. 'No, I must not let my imagination take over or I shall not be able to think clearly. You are right in your assumption. It is me they want, not Tilda, therefore they will send a letter to lure me into their trap.' She turned and began to pace about the familiar room, hardly noticing the comfortable arrangement of her personal things, her books and the collection of delicate Chinese porcelain, which usually gave her so much pleasure. She felt that by snatching Tilda these rogues had invaded the sanctity of her home, destroying her peace. Her brow was furrowed in thought, her mind working furiously. She paced for some minutes and then came back to where he stood, meeting his gaze steadily. 'If they send a letter, I must do whatever they say.'

'No, you shall not!' Charles cried in outrage. 'To sacrifice yourself for her is beyond the call of right or reason, Arabella.'

She raised her head, her face proud, eyes sparking with a silver flame. 'I have no intention of sacrificing myself. I shall carry my pistol with me, sir. I know how to use it—and I shall arrange for my men to be somewhere close by. If I cry out, they will come to my aid.'

'You would dare to do that?' Charles stared at her, a gleam of appreciation in his eyes. 'Then, if you are willing, I think that we may be able to trap them, Arabella. Your own men from the estate may play a part, but I have sent for others—men who know how to track their quarry silently; men who understand violence and have no fear of a fight. We shall set a trap for Sir Courtney and your cousin. And this time they will both pay for their evil deeds.'

'Yes, they must, of course,' Arabella said. 'I would rather my aunt did not know that her son is involved in this just yet, sir. It would distress her and I do not wish to cause her more pain.'

'That is why I asked to speak to you in private,' Charles said. 'We shall tell the others that we have discovered a plot to kidnap you for a ransom, but nothing else. Let the others think that Tilda was taken by mistake. They must understand that much, for no lady in this house must go walking alone until this business is finished. But it is best not to disclose the whole—it would distress my mother and your aunt too much.'

'That is understood,' Arabella said. 'You cannot watch all of us. It means that we must put off our visit to York for a while, because that would be too dangerous. On the open road we should be more vulnerable. Besides, I could not enjoy myself while Tilda is their captive.' She frowned. 'None of this could have happened if I had attended to my lawyers. They wanted to tie up the bulk of my money in trust for any children I might have in future, but I refused. I thought I should not marry—' She broke off because she could not look at him for fear of betraying herself. 'I am perhaps too wealthy for my own good, sir.'

'Yes, it seems so. Were you married, all this could have been avoided,' he said. 'I understand that your grief turned you against marriage, Arabella—but you might be safer.'

'Maybe.' She turned away from him. The only man she could bear to marry was Charles, but she was too proud to let him see it. 'I could put the money into some kind of trust… I must speak to my lawyers soon.'

'Could you not ask them to call on you?' Charles suggested.

'Mr Holden is always busy and quite elderly,' Arabella said. She turned to face him again, her emotions under control now. 'However, he could send his clerk to take my instructions. Mr Jones is a pleasant young man and would not mind the journey.'

'I suggest that you send for him,' Charles said. 'The sooner it is done the better for your own sake. In the meantime, I think there is little we can do except wait for their next move. Tobbold's men should be here by the morning. He may be able to find where they are holding your companion—but in any case I shall feel more satisfied once they are here. John and I will take it in turns to sit up this evening, Arabella. It is fortunate that we are staying here.'

'Yes, very,' she agreed. 'I thank you for your help, sir.'

'Will you not call me Charles? You have done so once or twice, Arabella.'

'Of course, if you wish it.' She smiled at him. 'I think we should return to the others. They will be anxious to know what is going on.'

'John has told them what we have agreed,' Charles said. He hesitated, seeming as if he wished to say more, but gave a slight shake of the head. 'I shall tell him privately that you are willing to be the bait for our trap—much as I dislike the idea, Arabella. It means you will be in danger, but I think it may serve. At least we know what is planned.'

'Yes, that was a stroke of good luck,' Arabella said and then gave a little sob of distress. 'Poor Tilda. How frightened she must be…'

'They should never have brought her here.' Ralph's voice had a sulky whine to it. 'I don't see how you can trade her for my cousin. She would tell everyone what we had done and then my neck would be in the noose. Those idiots should have blindfolded her if they were going to take that damned blanket from her head. It was me she saw when they removed it and started screeching. I've never heard such a row in my life. God save me from complaining women!'

'Who said we were going to let her go anywhere?' Sir Courtney drawled, giving a high-pitched titter. 'Once she has lured our proud lady into our trap, it hardly matters what happens to her.'

'You're going to kill her too?' Ralph's face turned a yellowish white. He felt sick as he saw the expression in the other man's eyes. He was a devil and mad at that! He wished fervently that he had never played cards with either him or Forsythe, and even more that he had kept his idea about getting Arabella's fortune to himself. He was unlikely to see a penny of it once Welch had his ring on her finger. Indeed, he might think himself lucky if he came out of this business alive. 'But that is a hanging matter…' He swallowed uncomfortably, already feeling the rope around his neck.

'Did you think this business was without risk?' Sir Courtney asked, scorn in his eyes and on his tongue. 'You lily-livered coward! You'll not run out on me now or I'll slit your throat. We are in this together. If I hang, then I'll see you go with me.'

Ralph turned even paler. He didn't want any more to do with this mad scheme and at the first opportunity he would run. Damn Arabella's money! All he wanted was to disappear somewhere, perhaps abroad, and forget this whole thing, but for the moment he was too afraid.

'Supposing she refuses to write the letter?' he said. 'Supposing Arabella ignores it?'

'She will write what I tell her,' Sir Courtney said, and Ralph's forehead broke out in beads of sweat as he felt the menace of those words. 'She is too damned ugly to have any appeal for the rogues I hired, but they know how to inflict pain. I doubt if she will hold out for long.' He smiled nastily.

'Wishing you hadn't started it now, aren't you? Well, it is too late, far too late to draw back. By tomorrow night I intend to have that hellcat in my coach and be on my way to Scotland. I'll soon teach her to know her master!'

'Is it my fault that they are planning to kidnap you?' Sarah asked later that night. Lady Tate and Mrs Hunter had retired to their rooms, and the gentlemen were busy somewhere preparing the house against any attempt at a break-in during the dark hours. 'Is it because you have looked after me? Have I brought danger to this house?'

'I am afraid it is simply because I have too much money and no husband,' Arabella told her. 'I refused a certain gentleman's offer of marriage last summer, and this is his revenge. He thinks that he can force me into paying a large sum of money as a ransom. It has nothing whatsoever to do with you, my dear. It would have happened even if you had never come into my life. I am fortunate that you did, for Charles and Mr Elworthy are here to help me.' Arabella stuck very much to the story she had agreed to with Sarah's brother, for she did not wish to cause her friends more distress than they already felt. Had it only been a matter of money, she would have felt very much easier in her mind.

'Mr Elworthy is so kind, isn't he?' Sarah said and gave a little sigh. 'He says that we were good friends, but I cannot remember. I wish that I could.' She frowned and gave a little shake of her head. 'That does not matter. Poor Tilda! She must be so frightened. Those wicked men—what do you think they will do to her?'

'I am hoping they will ransom her to me,' Arabella said,

bending the truth a little. 'We expect to receive a note from them at any time.'

'Will you pay it?' Sarah looked at her anxiously.

'Perhaps. Yes, if it will serve,' Arabella said, crossing her fingers behind her back. 'But we shall see what the note says. Your brother and Mr Elworthy are making arrangements to protect us all. You must not be frightened, Sarah. You are safe enough as long as you do not leave the house alone.'

'Yes, Charles told me,' Sarah said, but her eyes were anxious. 'I do not want anything to happen to you, Arabella— or Tilda. I know that it is very frightening to be taken against your will.'

'Has this brought it back to you?' Arabella looked at her in concern.

'I am not sure,' Sarah said. 'I keep shivering and I see flashes of something…firelight and a man's face.' She wrinkled her smooth brow. 'It is only the old nightmare. I still cannot remember what happened that day…except…' She looked thoughtfully at Arabella. 'I think I may have been going to feed the swans on the lake that morning. It was a lovely day and the sun was shining and then…' She sighed and shook her head. 'Am I remembering what actually happened—or just what Mama told me? I cannot be sure.'

'Do not worry about it,' Arabella said. 'It will come back when you are ready. Just be careful not to leave your window open tonight, and do not go out alone until this is all over. I am sure it will only be a few days.'

Arabella said goodnight to the younger girl and went to her room. As she approached her apartments, she saw that Charles was just coming from them. She knew that he had conducted a search to make sure that no one was hiding inside the house, and he and John Elworthy were to take turns in sitting outside her door throughout the night.

'No one is hiding under the bed,' Charles said, a grim smile on his mouth. 'I shall be here should you need me, Arabella— and some of your men are patrolling the grounds.'

'Thank you. I shall sleep easier for knowing that you are here,' she said. 'Sarah is a little disturbed by all this and…I am not certain, but she may be beginning to remember what happened to her the day she was taken.'

'I am not sure whether that is a good thing or not,' Charles said with a frown. 'It is a pity that this had to happen, but it cannot be helped. All we can do now is wait until that ransom note comes.'

'Yes, if it does,' Arabella said. 'I think that Tilda is possibly too old to be of any use as a whore, and she is not pretty, so we can be sure that she will not suffer that fate—but they may kill her. I know that she seems to be a fussy old maid, but she has more wit than they may imagine. If they realise that she would know and repeat things about them…' She shook her head. 'I must not speculate or I shall lie awake all night. Goodnight, Charles. Thank you for all you are doing.'

He smiled and shook his head. 'I can never repay you for what you did for us,' he said. He hesitated, and then touched her cheek with his fingertips. 'My sister would have died if it were not for Nana and you. I would give all I have to help you, Arabella. My life if need be.'

'Thank you, but I should never ask so much of you,' she said in a voice husky with tears. Something in his manner was making her long to be in his arms, to weep on his shoulder, but she knew that she must not give way to her feelings. 'I prefer that you should live and be my…friend.' For a moment their eyes met and something passed between them. She thought that he would cross the barrier he had erected between them and take her in his arms, and she longed for him to do so—but he did not. She turned away before she could betray herself. 'Goodnight…'

Inside her own room, Arabella felt the sting of tears, tasting the salt on her lips as they trickled down her cheeks. Would it always be like this between them? She was almost certain that Charles felt something for her. Was it merely physical desire? Even that would be acceptable to her—she would welcome the chance to lie in his arms if only for one night of passion. And yet she wanted his love to be a lasting thing. Every fibre of her body ached for him as she thought of him sitting outside her room, guarding her. She was tempted to open her door, to invite him in—into her bed—and yet pride would not let her.

She would not beg him to love her. Charles had chosen his own path of denial and he must take the first steps towards the chance of happiness that might be waiting for them both.

It was nearly time for luncheon the next morning when Mrs Bristol came into the parlour where the ladies were sitting, pretending to be busy with their needlework, but in truth on thorns for anything that might be happening outside the house. They had seen men patrolling the grounds and knew that the men Charles had sent for had arrived and were helping to protect them.

'A young lad says he has a letter for you, ma'am,' the

housekeeper announced. 'He comes from the village and says that he was told to give it to you and no one else.'

'Thank you—you may bring him in,' Arabella said. She stood up, her nerves jumping as she wondered if this was what they had been waiting for. As the housekeeper reappeared with a young lad, she gave a little start of surprise, for it was the lad who had so often held her horse for her. 'Sam—do you have something for me?'

'Yes, milady,' the urchin said, taking off his greasy cap and extracting the note from inside. 'There's a gent staying at the inn. He gave me a florin and said as I was to bring this here and see as you had it—no one but you, ma'am.'

'Thank you.' Arabella took it from him. 'Did this gentleman say anything else?'

'He said I was to wait and see if there was an answer, milady.'

'Very well.' Arabella smiled at him, and then looked at her housekeeper. 'Please take Sam to the kitchen and give him something to eat—and a florin, if you please. I shall read this letter and if I wish to reply I shall send for you, Sam.'

'Yes, milady.' The urchin looked at her. 'Did I do right to bring it, milady? Only I don't much like the look of the gent what give it to me.'

'You did very right,' Arabella said. 'Go with Mrs Bristol now, if you please—and should the gentleman ask, tell him that I was alone when you gave me the note, will you?'

'Yeah.' The urchin grinned at her. 'Do anything fer you, milady.'

'Thank you. Go with Mrs Bristol now.'

She sat down on a chair by the window to read her note. Tilda had certainly written it for she recognised the way she had of curving her capital letters with some style, but there was something odd about it, which was hardly surprising since it must have been written under duress.

*Forgive me. I am in some trouble and I need Your help. Please come to the summerhouse by the lake this evening at nine. I hope that I May rely on your help, Arabella. I would not ask if it were not desperate. Your loving friend, Tilda Redmond.*

Arabella was still puzzling over the letter when Charles came in. He crossed to her immediately.

'You have received a note? What does it say?'

'It is from Tilda. I recognise her hand—but it is not a ransom note and there is something odd about it.' She handed it to Charles who read it and frowned. 'Do you see that she has formed a capital M in the middle of a sentence? Now why would she do that? Tilda is meticulous in all things. She would never make a mistake like that…'

'Yes, I see…' he agreed. 'Do you imagine that it is some kind of clue?'

'Perhaps, yes, it may be. As I told you, we called Sarah "May" when she came to us,' Arabella said. 'I think Tilda is trying to tell us something, Charles. I believe that she could be being held at Nana's cottage. Sarah lived there for some months when we knew her as May—but these rogues might not know that. We discovered that someone had been using the cottage, did we not? And they could hardly hold Tilda a prisoner at the inn…' She frowned. 'I had intended to give the cottage to the groom I told you of, but in all the excitement it slipped my mind.'

'Nor would certain gentlemen wish to have the trouble of looking after her,' Charles said. 'They would leave her to their bullyboys. If by chance she should be discovered before their plan could be put in place, they would not then be connected with her abduction or anything else.'

'Yes, I think that is what she was telling us,' Arabella agreed. 'And there is something else. She has used capital letters in the wrong place twice and she has also used the same phrase twice. Do you think that…?'

'Two men are guarding her?' Charles was struck by her logic. 'You have broken the code, Arabella. How clever of Tilda to have thought of it. Most people would not have noticed anything amiss.'

'I should not if she were not always so meticulous about everything,' Arabella said. 'This gives us some advantage, does it not?'

'Yes, indeed,' Charles agreed. 'We have enough men to guard the house and to attack the cottage, Arabella. I shall show Tobbold this and leave the rescue of Tilda to him, for he is more adept at such things than your own men.'

'You do not think that they will kill her rather than let her go if they are attacked?'

'Do not concern yourself,' Charles told her. 'Tobbold has more sense than to go storming in there. He will know how to do the thing. We shall wait until this evening—perhaps half an hour before they expect you to meet her in the summer-house when it is getting dusk…'

'Must we wait so long?' Arabella asked. 'Oh, I know I should not be impatient, but I cannot help feeling uneasy about poor Tilda.'

'If she had the presence of mind to send you this message, I think she is managing quite well,' Charles said and smiled.

'I take my hat off to Miss Redmond, Arabella. She is not as foolish as some might think her.'

'No, indeed she is not,' Arabella said. 'Well, if we must wait I suppose there is nothing more we can do for the moment.' She raised her brows at him. 'Do you still intend that I should keep this appointment this evening?'

'I think you should send a reply promising to meet Tilda. However, I do not believe it will be necessary if Tilda is where we think.' Charles smiled grimly. 'I have quite another plan in mind, which I shall tell you, though I must ask you not to disclose it to anyone else…'

Tilda had been working at loosening her bonds for hours. It was not easy and her wrists were quite sore, for those ruffians had bound her tightly. However, the knots were beginning to give way and she thought that she might be able to free herself soon. She could hear the men talking in the room downstairs and she wondered if she dared try to escape once she was free. It was ages since she had woken up with a headache from the bang she had received on the back of her skull, and as yet she had been given nothing to eat.

They had freed her hands to make her write that letter to Arabella. At first she had tried to resist, but when they had told her that she would be killed if she did not she had given in. She was glad of that, for they had neglected to tie her as tightly the next time, and at last the knots were beginning to give way. Soon she would manage to get free and then one way or another she must escape. She did hope that Arabella would guess what she was trying to say and would not be foolish enough to go to the summerhouse alone. Somehow she did not believe that Mr Hunter would allow it, because she had observed that he was more interested in Arabella than he permitted to show.

She tugged frantically at the ropes that bound her, wanting to be free. She thought it must be past eight in the evening and she was very hungry. Her stomach was rumbling and she did not think that she could bear it much longer. Once her hands were free, and that could not be many minutes now, she would make her bid for freedom. She thought that she would rather die trying to escape than lie here and starve to death, for she believed that they intended to leave her here when they went to the summerhouse. Either someone would return to kill her or she would be left to starve. Unless Arabella had deciphered her message…

'I do not think I want to be there when you grab Arabella,' Ralph said as they were preparing to leave the inn that evening. 'You said that you would return my notes if I helped you, Welch. I have done what you asked. Surely you do not need me for this part of the business?'

'You are a coward and a fool,' Sir Courtney said and his thick lips curved in a sneer of derision. 'You want to run away, don't you?'

'I shall not be of much help to you in this,' Ralph said. 'Perhaps I should go to the cottage and deal with the other one?'

'Please yourself,' Sir Courtney said. 'It is true that you will not be of much help to me. I dare say you have served your purpose. Ride with me until the parting of the ways, and then you may go to the cottage. Brice and Jackson will have left there by now and be on their way to the summerhouse. My groom will have the carriage in place and I shall be waiting to carry off my blushing bride. I shall not need you again— but don't come crawling to me next time you want something.'

'No, I shan't,' Ralph said, relief spreading through him. He had discovered that he had no stomach for this sort of thing and he was glad that Welch had agreed that he should be left out of it. He would go to the cottage, but he would not kill the companion. It had occurred to him that he could act the hero's part and let her go free. No one could prove that he had ever been involved in this affair. Arabella was sure to be grateful and she would probably offer to pay some of his debts—if Sir Courtney failed in his kidnap attempt. The more Ralph thought about it, the more certain he became that Arabella would not simply walk into their trap. His cousin was too clever to be so easily taken in. He was well out of the business. 'Yes, I'll ride with you, Welch—and I'll deal with the companion for you. You get on with your own affair. I'll not interfere.'

Their horses trotted out of the inn yard. For a few minutes they rode in silence until they came to the crossroads. Ralph reined in and turned to look at the other man.

'I'll leave you here, then,' he said. 'Don't worry, I'll keep silent, Welch. No one shall hear of this from me.'

'You are damned right they won't,' Sir Courtney said and drew his pistol. He aimed it directly at Ralph's chest and fired, grinning as he saw the surprise in the other's eyes. Ralph's body jerked as the ball struck, and then, as his horse reared in fright, he was thrown from the back of the terrified beast, which went racing off, its reins hanging loosely. 'Fool! Did you think I would trust you? Dead men don't talk—that is a certainty.'

Sir Courtney scarcely wasted a glance at Ralph as he lay still where he had fallen. Digging his heels into his horse's flanks, he set off at a furious pace. His men would be in place by now. They would not need his help to capture one female. He would watch from a safe distance. No one could know that he had masterminded the whole affair—the companion had seen only Tate's face and he was dead. If the thing should go wrong, he would have plenty of time to escape and no one could prove that he had ever been involved.

'You must stay here,' Charles told Arabella. They were alone in her sitting room because he had again asked to speak to her in private. 'Whatever you hear, do not leave the house this evening. We have set up a trap for them, but you must not become involved.'

'But if I do not go, they may kill Tilda…'

'Someone will take your place,' Charles told her. He drew her to the window, standing behind the curtain so that they could see, but not be seen. 'Look out, Arabella, and tell me what you see.'

At first Arabella could see nothing, for the darkness was falling fast, but then, caught in a sudden burst of moonlight as the clouds parted, she saw a woman crossing the lawns. A woman wearing a red dress and a paisley shawl over her head…and yet something puzzled her. She had never seen a woman walk quite that way before.

'Who is it?'

'John,' Charles said and chuckled. 'He makes an attractive lady, does he not? We drew straws for who should go and who should stay to guard you, and he won, Arabella. He said that

I must take care of Sarah and you, and that it were best he be the one to take your place. However, our men are crawling all over the estate, and all of them armed. They have instructions to stay hidden until those rogues try to capture John. We need to catch them in the act, but I doubt that he will be in much danger.'

'Charles!' Arabella looked at him in astonishment. 'Surely they will know he isn't me?'

'It is dark out there and will be more so by the time he reaches the summerhouse,' Charles said. 'With his head and face covered by the shawl, they are unlikely to realise until it is too late. He has his pistols and so have Tobbold's men. And more of my men are at the cottage, intent on rescuing Tilda even as we speak. I do not think you need to fear for her.'

'I pray that you are right,' Arabella said, understanding his plans, which were clever and seemed to cover all eventualities. 'Oh, this is terrible. I do not like to think that John is risking his life for me.'

'It isn't just for you,' Charles said. 'Haven't you realised that he cares for Sarah deeply? He needs to do this because he can do nothing to help her.'

'Yes, I see,' Arabella said. 'But I hope that he will not be killed. I should feel that it ought to have been me—and I think Sarah is beginning to like him very well.'

'John will survive, I promise you,' Charles said with an odd smile. 'I wanted to go, but he would not have it. And perhaps it is harder to be the one that waits. I should have liked to be there. Sir Courtney would have rued the day he hatched this little plot with your cousin.'

'What of Ralph?' Arabella asked. 'I know that he is as

much to blame as Sir Courtney, but my aunt would be so distressed if she knew.'

'We shall keep him out of it if we can,' Charles said. 'Tobbold knows of ways to dispose of tiresome rogues without putting a pistol to their head—and it may be best if Ralph were to just quietly disappear. A sea trip to the West Indies, perhaps?'

'Oh, yes, that would be an excellent way to solve the problem,' Arabella said. 'Yes, that could not upset my aunt. If I told her that Ralph had decided to begin a new life in Jamaica, I think she would be quite pleased for him.'

'Then we shall see what happens this evening,' Charles said. 'Now, go and join the others and play cards. Try to act as if nothing unusual was happening. We do not want to distress your aunt or my mama, do we?'

'It is Sarah I am most concerned for,' Arabella told him. 'She has been very quiet all day. I have asked her if something is wrong, but she just shakes her head and says that she is well enough.'

'I dare say she is upset by all this,' Charles agreed. 'But she will be better again once Tilda is back and the rogues who planned this wretched affair have been dealt with as they deserve.'

'Ralph is to be sent to the West Indies,' Arabella said. 'But what of Sir Courtney?'

'That depends on whether or not we take him alive.' Charles looked angry. 'He deserves to hang, but I do not know whether it may be done. After all, we only have John's word for what was said in the wood—and I know well enough that that is not sufficient to have him arrested.'

'Then what…?' She became aware of his grim determination. 'Charles, you cannot! Please, you must not take the law into your own hands.'

'We shall do what must be done,' Charles said. 'Until that man is either in prison or dead, you can never be safe again…' He gave her a straight look. 'Join your aunt and the others, Arabella. You may safely leave this to John and I…'

# *Chapter Nine*

'Is something happening?' Lady Tate asked as Arabella joined them in the drawing room after leaving Charles. 'Mrs Bristol told us that Mr Elworthy has gone out. She seemed amused about something, though she would not tell me why. And where is Charles this evening?'

'I have just been talking to him,' Arabella said. 'There is nothing to worry about. Charles is just making sure everything is all right, and I dare say John will be back soon.' She smiled reassuringly, though she sensed that neither her aunt nor Mrs Hunter accepted her words at face value. Everyone was a little uneasy. She could only pray that nothing terrible would happen to cause further distress. 'Now, shall we play a hand of whist?'

'Yes, why not?' Mrs Hunter said. 'It is very upsetting that poor Tilda has been taken hostage like this, but I am sure that they will find her soon.'

'Mama, how could you?' Sarah said. She jumped to her feet and went over to the window to look out. It was clear that she was restless and on edge. 'It took months to find me. Just think of how Tilda must feel. She will be so frightened. She cannot know what they mean to do with her…' Sarah broke off as she saw something moving outside. 'Someone is there…in the shrubbery. I think… yes, I am sure it is a woman. Arabella, come and look! I believe it is Tilda.'

Arabella hurried to the window. She was in time to see a woman running towards the house. 'Yes, I believe you are right, Sarah. It does look like her! Excuse me, I must go down…' She turned and rushed from the room, moving swiftly along the hall towards the top of the main staircase just as a wild hammering started at the door. A footman looked up at Arabella. He was plainly hesitating, for he had been instructed not to open it without orders.

'Open it, Thomas,' Arabella said. 'It is Miss Redmond.'

He did as she asked, and Tilda almost fell into his arms. 'Arabella,' she cried. 'Tell her she must not go…'

Arabella ran down the stairs. 'I am here, dearest,' she said. 'We understood your message, telling us that you were being held at Nana's. Do not worry for my sake, Tilda. Mr Elworthy and Mr Hunter have everything under control. I am just so glad that you are safe. We have all been very worried about you. Are you all right? They did not harm you too much?'

'I am a little bruised, no more. I ran all the way to warn you,' Tilda said, gasping for breath as she flung herself into Arabella's arms. 'They tied my wrists again after they made me write that wicked letter, but I managed to get free at last. I could not escape immediately, for they had pistols and I dare not go downstairs until I heard them leaving. As soon as I knew they were going, I went down and climbed out of a back window at the cottage. And then I ran all the way here. I heard some shouting after I escaped. Something was happening at the cottage, but I did not stop to find out what.'

'You were so brave,' Arabella said and embraced her warmly. 'Charles planned to rescue you, but they had to wait until those rogues left, because we needed to catch them in the act of attempting to kidnap me. He was certain that they would keep you alive until after they had me, just in case they still needed you. He had instructed his men to watch the cottage; however, it seems that you managed to escape yourself, love—and I am very glad of it.'

'I had to do something. I had no idea what was happening and I could not bear to think of what they might do to you. I heard one of them say that you would be crows' bait before long, and that made me angry. I wasn't frightened of them then, Arabella. I simply wanted to get free so that I could warn you. At first I thought that I would rather die than write that letter, but then I realised that I could give you a message and warn you. You did understand, didn't you?' Tilda's manner was so fierce that Arabella was tempted to laugh. What had happened to her timid companion?

'Tilda!' Arabella exclaimed, her eyes moist with tears. 'You were so courageous and so clever. You told us exactly where you were and that helped us to plan what we should do. Some of our men have been close by the cottage preparing to rescue you as soon as your guards left it, while others waited near the summerhouse to catch them when they try to capture me. Only it will not be me.'

Tilda clutched at her. 'I was so afraid that you would go there yourself, though I suspected that Mr Hunter would not let you.'

'I believe I should had it been necessary to find you, but

as we knew where you were being kept, Mr Elworthy has gone in my place. He is wearing one of Mrs Bristol's gowns and has my paisley shawl over his head.'

'Oh…' Tilda's mouth opened in surprise and then she laughed. 'Oh, how splendid of him! I should so like to see him dressed as a woman, Arabella. It will just serve those awful men right. I do hope he makes them very sorry for what they planned to do to you. It will be a shock for them when he turns up in your place.' Her laughter died suddenly. 'Oh, dear, I have just realised that I have lost your shawl—and it was a silk one. Very expensive, I dare say.'

She looked so distressed that Arabella laughed and embraced her. 'Do not be so foolish, my very dear Tilda. Do you imagine that I care for a shawl? I am just so happy to know that you are safe.'

'Arabella…' Tilda's eyes brimmed with tears '…I have been so silly, haven't I? I was jealous and unkind to Sarah because I thought that you would not need me now that you have others to keep you company. And then you gave me that money…so very generous. I wanted to pick you some wild roses to show how grateful I was, and instead I caused you all this worry.'

'But you made up for it by sending that message,' Arabella assured her. 'If it had not been you they captured, Tilda, it might have been Sarah or me.'

'Then I am very glad it was me,' Tilda said stoutly. The look of determination was back in her eyes. 'Sarah has suffered enough and I should not want you to be harmed, Arabella.' She hesitated uncertainly. 'I know your cousin was one of the men who planned this wickedness, for I saw his face when they took the blanket from my head—but there was another gentleman. I did not see him, but I heard his voice.'

'Yes, I know. Sir Courtney Welch. He intended to force me to marry him for the sake of my fortune,' Arabella said. 'I refused his offer of marriage last year and this is his revenge.'

'The wicked man!' Tilda cried indignantly. 'How dare he do such a thing—and why was your cousin mixed up with him?'

'I would appreciate it if you did not mention that part of it to anyone else,' Arabella told her. 'It must be between the gentlemen and us, dearest. I do not wish to cause my aunt more pain. Now, I think you must be in need of a change of clothes and some rest, Tilda. Go up to your room and make yourself comfortable again.'

'I am very hungry,' Tilda said. 'I suppose it is too late for dinner?'

Arabella smiled her relief. Tilda was a little battered and bruised by her experience, but she did not seem too affected by it.

'I shall speak to Mrs Bristol,' Arabella said. 'I am sure that she will find something delicious for your supper, dearest— and I shall come in to see you before I go to bed.'

'Thank you,' Tilda said and smiled at her. 'You are always so kind to me, Arabella.'

'That is because I am fond of you,' Arabella said and kissed her cheek.

She saw Tilda on her way upstairs and then went in search of her housekeeper. Mrs Bristol promised a supper fit for a king, praising Tilda for her courage and cool head.

'I declare I never thought she had it in her, my lady.'

'No, I did not think it either,' Arabella said. 'I am very

proud of her, Mrs Bristol—and grateful that she has been spared to us. I should never have forgiven myself if she had been seriously harmed.'

She left her housekeeper and was about to mount the stairs once more when she heard two shots. She thought that they must have come from the direction of the summerhouse and her pulses raced. What was happening? She silently prayed that Mr Elworthy was not killed or injured. Sarah had come to the head of the stairs as Arabella walked up them.

She looked anxiously at her. 'Did you hear the shots?'

'Yes, but we must not go outside, Sarah, even though we might wish to discover what is happening. Someone will come and tell us soon enough.'

They went back to the drawing room together. The two older ladies were looking anxious, meeting Arabella with a barrage of questions.

'Tilda is a little bruised and tired,' Arabella said, 'as we might expect—but otherwise seems in good spirits. She was held prisoner at Nana's cottage, but managed to work her hands free and escaped. She ran all the way here to warn me that I must not keep the tryst with her at the summerhouse, which of course I have not. Charles and Mr Elworthy set a trap for the kidnappers. Mr Elworthy went in my stead. He was wearing one of Mrs Bristol's gowns—that's no doubt what she found amusing, Aunt. I expect the shots came from the summerhouse. For the moment I can tell you no more.'

They were not to be so easily satisfied and Arabella was obliged to tell them the whole, leaving out only her cousin's part in the sordid affair. She had come to the end of her tale when Charles entered the room, looking pleased.

'Have you news?' Arabella asked.

'We have two of them,' he said. 'One has been wounded in the leg; the other surrendered as soon as he realised that there were too many of us. I am afraid that Sir Courtney has escaped. I expected that he would take no part in the abduction itself, and I sent three men to look for him at the edge of the woods. A carriage was seen waiting in a secluded spot and a man on horseback. He made off as soon as he saw our men coming. The carriage went in another direction. I believe two of my men are pursuing him; the other came back to report to me.'

'Then that means he is at liberty to try again,' Lady Tate said, looking alarmed. 'Arabella will never be safe while he is free.'

'He is certainly a danger to her,' Charles said, his expression grim. 'However, we shall not relax our vigil—and perhaps he may be brought to justice.' He glanced at Arabella and then back at her aunt, seeming to hesitate before continuing, 'I must tell you that your son was shot this evening, Lady Tate. He survived by sheer chance, for he carried a silver card case in his breast pocket and the ball struck that instead of penetrating his flesh. He was, however, thrown from his horse and he struck his head as he fell.'

'Ralph was shot?' Lady Tate was startled. Her face went very pale. 'But what was he doing here?'

'Perhaps on his way to visit you,' Charles said, giving Arabella a warning glance. 'However, I must tell you that Mr Henderson of Marsden witnessed the attempted murder as he approached the crossroads from another direction, and he stopped to investigate. Ralph was found to be alive, apparently unhurt apart from the blow to his head, and he has been taken to the inn. He was not conscious, but the doctor has been summoned to tend him.'

'Mr Henderson is a Justice of the Peace,' Arabella said and looked thoughtful. 'You said that he witnessed the attempt—did he actually see the person who shot Ralph?'

'Yes, he saw the incident quite clearly. Some of my men were nearby and they saw another man riding away—a man they were able to identify as Sir Courtney Welch. It would appear that he tried to kill Ralph.'

'But why? I do not understand,' Lady Tate said, shaking her head. 'That wicked man was here to—' She broke off, shock and distress in her eyes. 'No! Please tell me that Ralph was not involved in that dreadful affair!'

'I dare say it was just chance,' Arabella said. 'Perhaps my cousin had some private quarrel with him, Aunt. Pray do not distress yourself.' Her gaze turned in Charles's direction. 'Do you know how my cousin is? Will he recover?'

'I cannot tell you that at the moment,' Charles said. 'One of my men brought the news, but the doctor had not visited when he left the inn. The rest of them followed my instructions, which were to go on to the cottage and help to rescue Tilda.'

'Then it was possibly the delay that made them a little late,' Arabella said with a wry smile. 'The kidnappers threw a blanket over Tilda when they took her, and she received a blow to the head, which made her lose consciousness for a while. It must have been afterwards that they tied her hands. Tilda made her own escape by freeing her hands from the ropes. She then ran all the way here to tell me I must not go to the summerhouse. She too was a little late, but I have not told her so—it was a brave effort and I am proud of her. And I am very grateful to you for all you have done, Charles.'

He shrugged as if it were of no consequence. 'I had hoped

that we might take all of them,' he said. 'Sir Courtney has escaped, but Mr Henderson is a witness to the attempted murder of Sir Ralph. My men saw Sir Courtney riding away hell for leather—between them they might be able to see him hanged. Until he is caught, we must keep our vigil, but I do not think he will attempt anything more just yet. He will need to lie low and lick his wounds—and to think about what to do next.'

'Would that he had been wounded!' Mrs Hunter said, giving way to anger. 'What a wicked man he must be—' She broke off as she saw Sarah's face. 'What is it, my love? Something has distressed you…'

'Everything is suddenly so clear to me. I remember that I was going to visit the swans that morning,' Sarah said, her face ashen. 'I saw a man at the far side of the lake and I hesitated, and then someone threw a blanket over my head from behind. It was very thick and it smelled of horses. At first I couldn't breathe, but then I kicked and struggled. I heard someone laugh. He said something like… "I told you it would be easy, Forsythe. When you have finished with her, let me have the whore. It will give me great pleasure to get even with Hunter." And then he laughed again. He had such a horrid laugh…a high-pitched titter…' Sarah stared at her brother. 'I do not know who he was, but I remember what he said.'

'Sir Courtney,' Arabella and Charles spoke together. 'He has a distinctive laugh.'

'I think the man named Forsythe called him Walsh or something similar…' Sarah added, her brow wrinkled in a frown of concentration.

'Welch,' Charles said, and his mouth thinned. 'Of late I have suspected that he might have had a hand in it—both of them had cause to feel anger against me, for I had beaten them at the card table.'

'Charles!' His mother stared at him in distress. 'Are you saying that what happened to Sarah was your fault?'

'Yes, I had dreaded that it might be,' he admitted. 'And Sarah has just confirmed it.' His regretful eyes dwelled on his sister. 'Forgive me, Sarah. I never meant that you should pay such a price. It was just a careless hand of cards that I gave no more than a thought to at the time or afterwards. Only when Daniel told me that he suspected Forsythe did I realise that you might have been taken to spite me.'

'It was because of you—' Sarah suddenly burst into tears and went rushing from the room.

'Sarah…' Charles said, his face going white.

'Excuse me,' Arabella said. 'I must go to Sarah. I shall hear the rest of your story later, Charles. Please tell Mr Elworthy that I am very grateful for what he did this evening.'

She left the room quickly and ran up the small flight of stairs at the end of the landing to the wing where the best guestrooms were situated. She was in time to see Sarah disappear into her room. Following swiftly, she knocked and asked if she might enter. After a moment she heard a sobbing affirmative. She went in cautiously and saw Sarah lying on the bed, crying. She approached softly and sat on the edge of the bed, reaching out to touch her shoulder.

'Do not blame Charles, Sarah. He had no idea that winning a hand of cards would result in your abduction, dearest.'

'I am not crying because I blame him,' Sarah said in a muffled voice. She raised her tear-stained face and looked at Arabella. 'I am relieved that it was not something I did, Belle.

I have been so afraid that I was a bad girl—that I must have done something wicked. Now I understand that it was not because of me. It was done out of spite because Charles had beaten them at the card table. It wasn't my fault.'

She sat up and Arabella gathered her into her arms, holding her as she sobbed out her relief and her distress. At last Sarah stopped crying and sat back, looking at her steadily.

'I remember it all now,' she said. 'They took me to a house somewhere. It was a long way and I was lying on the floor of the carriage, for they had bound my wrists and my feet, but I was awake and knew what was happening. I was very frightened. I thought they meant to kill me. It was late in the afternoon when we reached the house, and they carried me inside. I was thrown on to a bed and left for an hour or two...' Sarah paused, her eyes dark with fear. 'It was night when someone came back. He was carrying a candle. I felt very frightened, for the way he looked at me made me shudder. He told me that I was to be privileged that night and he untied my hands. He gave me a glass of wine and told me I must drink it. At first I resisted, but then he said that I would be forced if I would not do it willingly—and I was too scared to withstand him. I drank some of it, but it made me choke and I spat half of it out again.'

'Oh, my poor Sarah,' Arabella cried, shocked. 'What a wicked man he must have been!'

'He started to laugh then and said that he was looking forward to seeing me sacrificed to his deity. I did not know what he meant. I thought he was going to kill me. I had begun to feel sleepy and I fell. I think he caught me and then—' She stopped, her eyes wide and terrified.

'Go on, Sarah,' Arabella urged. 'Tell it all, my dear. Once you have faced the worst it can never be as bad again.'

Sarah went on and it was clear that she was reliving her nightmare. 'I do not know what happened next—but when I woke we were in some woods. There was a fire and I think three or perhaps four figures…men, I suppose they were, though at first I could not see properly for it was as if a mist was in my eyes. I know that one had a devil mask and horns on his head, but another was unmasked and he was naked…' She shivered as her eyes sought Arabella's. 'He was bending over me. I think he must have been drunk for his eyes looked wild. I am not sure, but I believe he meant to ravish me. I screamed and jumped to my feet and then I ran away.'

'Charles told me this part, Sarah. Someone—a man called Mr Palmer—was the one who was about to ravish you. Forsythe had given him an evil drug and he did not know what he did. Afterwards, he regretted his part in the affair and he confessed it to the Earl of Cavendish.'

'I ran and ran for a long time,' Sarah went on. It was as if she could not stop now that she had begun. 'At first they came after me, but I managed to hide and after a while they went away.' She closed her eyes and shuddered. 'I was cold and my head ached. I was afraid to move, but eventually I did. I began walking in a daze, not knowing where I was or what I was doing. I remember that someone spoke to me and I think he meant to help me. He took me to a cottage and left me there. I was in such a state that I did not know what was going on—but after a while my mind cleared a little and I knew that I must run away again. I left the cottage and I kept walking. I think I walked for several days. I had no money and I did not dare to ask anyone for food. I just kept walking and walking. It rained hard one night and after that I was ill….' She sighed and looked at Arabella. 'I do not know what happened next, except that I woke up in Nana's bed and could not recall my own name.'

'I dare say there is not much more to remember,' Arabella said and stroked her cheek. 'You have been through a terrible ordeal, my love, but it is over now. You must rest and try to forget the things that hurt you, Sarah.' She stood up. 'I shall ask Mrs Bristol to prepare you a tisane to help you sleep. Would you like to see your mama before you sleep?'

'Yes, please,' Sarah said and the tears began to trickle down her cheeks. 'Poor Mama. How she must have suffered all this time—and then I did not know her…'

'Your mama loves you,' Arabella told her. 'She cares only that you are safe again.' Hearing a knock at the door at that moment, she turned to see Mrs Hunter standing in the doorway. 'Please come in now,' she said. 'I was just about to ask you if you would come to Sarah. I shall leave you together.'

She stood up, leaving Mrs Hunter to comfort her daughter and going back downstairs. Seeing Mrs Bristol in the hall, she requested that a tisane be sent up to Sarah.

'Not for a few minutes. She wishes to be private with her mother—but one of your soothing tisanes will help her to sleep, Mrs Bristol.'

'I expect it has been an ordeal for her,' the kindly woman said. 'I've been seeing to Mr Elworthy, ma'am. He has a little wound to his arm. Nothing very much. I've bathed it and put a poultice on for him, but he says he doesn't need the doctor.'

'We shall ask him to call, none the less,' Arabella said. 'I prefer that everything is done that ought to be, Mrs Bristol. We owe a debt to Mr Elworthy, and he must not be neglected.'

'That's what I thought, ma'am,' Mrs Bristol said. 'I've already sent one of the grooms to ask for him.'

'Thank you.' Arabella returned to the drawing room, where Charles and Lady Tate were still discussing what had taken place that night. 'Sarah has remembered everything,' she told them. 'She is feeling a little weepy, but her mother is with her and Mrs Bristol is making her a tisane. I am sure she will be better in the morning.'

'How strange that it should all come back to her so suddenly,' Lady Tate said. Charles turned to stare out of the window, his shoulders tight with tension. Clearly he was under a strain, blaming himself for his sister's distress.

'I dare say it has been happening for a little while. I think it may have been Tilda's abduction which finally released her memory.' She went over to where Charles was standing and touched his arm. 'You did not tell us that Mr Elworthy was wounded.'

'It was merely a scratch. He asked me not to say anything in front of Sarah.'

'That was thoughtful of him,' Arabella said, looking pensive. 'I am glad that Sarah has remembered everything, Charles. I believe she will begin to get over it soon now. It seems that she was not...' She saw the hope in his eyes. 'Forsythe told her what was to happen when he had forced her to take drugged wine, but she spat out much of it. It made her sleepy, but it did not put her into the deep trance he had expected. She woke up before anything happened and ran away. Someone tried to help her, but she was in such a state that she became frightened when he left her to get help and she ran away again. After that she just kept on walking until she became ill. She still does not remember what happened then, until she woke up in Nana's bed—but I doubt there is much to remember. She was soaked through by the rain, near to starving, and her feet were bleeding. I think that was enough to make her lose her senses, do you not agree?'

'Yes, it would be enough for anyone,' he said and gave a sigh of relief. 'It seems that my worst fears have come to nothing—thanks to the kindness of your nurse.'

'Nana was happy to help her. She was a dear good woman. I wish you could have known her, Charles. She would have approved of you—and you would have liked her.'

'I am sure that I should,' he said. A look of near-despair came into his blue eyes. 'Do you think that Sarah will ever forgive me, Arabella? What can I do to make it up to her?'

'I do not think she would ask anything of you, other than that you continue to love her as you always have. Sarah was afraid that she had done something to deserve her kidnap. I think she imagined she might have brought it on herself by flirting with a gentleman.'

'No, how could she? She was an innocent child,' Charles said. 'All our friends adored her. She had not yet gone out into society, for Mama wished to wait until she was older. I think she did not want her little girl to grow up too soon—but she has, and in the worst possible way.'

'Sarah is still an innocent,' Arabella said. 'Yes, she has suffered, but not as much as she might. You must not continue to blame yourself as you do, Charles.'

'Whom else should I blame?' he asked and his eyes had taken

on a wintry shade that made them more grey than blue. 'I know that nothing I can do will ever make up to her for what happened—but I am determined to do whatever she asks of me.'

'Charles…' Arabella felt helpless as she saw that look in his eyes. Was there no way that she could reach him, release him from this self-torture?

'Excuse me, I must speak to John,' he said and gave her a curt nod. 'This business is not yet over. I think Welch will have bolted for his hideaway, wherever that may be, but we cannot afford to relax our vigil. If he would help Forsythe plan Sarah's kidnap for a lost hand of cards, goodness knows how he is feeling now. I do not imagine that he will be content to let things lie. He must hate us all. My only prayer is that he will try to take his revenge on me, rather than you or my family.'

Arabella watched as he walked from the room. Her heart ached to see him go. She knew that he was hurting terribly, his guilt beating at him like an iron bar. He blamed himself for Sarah's kidnap, and he was probably blaming himself because Sir Courtney had escaped that evening. He was such an intense, passionate man. He took everything on his own shoulders and believed that he must be responsible for everything ill that befell his family. Quick to fire up, impatient and proud, she knew that he was the man she loved—and she always would.

But how was she to get him to admit that he loved her? She sensed it, believed that it was true, but the doubts would not let her be. Charles might care for her, might want her in his bed, but was his feeling for her strong enough to overcome his guilt over what had happened to Sarah?

'Charles is a very conscientious man,' Lady Tate observed

as he left them alone together. 'His attachment to his sister is creditable—but I am not sure that it is wise. I think that Sarah might become irritated by too much devotion from her brother. Of course, it might be another thing if it were Mr Elworthy.'

'Oh, Aunt, have you seen that too?' Arabella smiled at her. 'I think he likes her and I believe she may like him—though it may be a while before she is ready to trust any man again.'

'Yes, I suppose,' Lady Tate said thoughtfully. 'Was Ralph mixed up in this business, Arabella? Please tell me the truth. I know that he wished to be rid of me when I would not give him what he wanted—but if he planned to harm you, he must be punished.'

'Let us see how he is when the doctor has finished with him,' Arabella suggested. 'If he was involved with Sir Courtney—and I am not saying that it was so—why was he shot? Perhaps he merely pretended to go along with him until the last and was preparing to betray him to us.'

'Do you think it might be the case?' Lady Tate looked hopeful. 'Ralph was always a coward at heart. I think that is the only reason I am still alive. He hoped to make me unwell so that I might die—but had not the courage to carry it through to the end.'

'Oh, Aunt Hester,' Arabella said. 'I hate to admit it, but I think you are right. I am so sorry.'

'I think that I shall go down to the village tomorrow and see Ralph,' Lady Tate said. 'He may be a rogue, but he is still my son.'

'I shall come with you,' Arabella said. 'We shall take an escort with us, but I doubt that we need it for the moment. Sir Courtney must have left the district by now. If Mr Henderson puts out an order for his arrest, he will not dare to come this way again.'

'Thank you, I hoped that you might,' Lady Tate said. 'I think that I shall go up now…' She stood up just as Mrs Bristol tapped the door and then looked in on them.

'Doctor James has been up to see Mr Elworthy, my lady,' she said. 'And he has asked if he may speak to either you or Lady Tate.'

'Ask him to come in,' Arabella said. 'Stay for a moment, Aunt. He may have news of Ralph.'

The doctor entered a moment or two later. 'This is a sorry business, Lady Arabella,' he said. 'I believe I have recently attended your cousin—and your son, of course, Lady Tate. I thought I should tell you that he has nothing worse than a nasty cut to the back of his head. He did suffer a slight concussion, but soon came to himself. I have given him something to help him sleep this evening for he would try to get out of bed and I was afraid he might harm himself.'

'Ralph was very lucky that the shot did not kill him,' Arabella said.

'Yes, indeed he was. His good angel was a silver card case, I understand. I saw the ball lodged in it. The case was of good quality and on the back it had your family motto inscribed, Lady Arabella—that is what made me think I would tell you what had happened. Your cousin was fortunate that you had given him such a gift, for it saved his life.'

'Yes, very fortunate,' Arabella said. 'Thank you for telling us, sir. Lady Tate was concerned for her son, but she may rest easier now.'

'Yes, that is what I thought,' Dr James replied. 'Goodnight

then, ladies. I must get home—I am expecting to be called to the bedside of a dying woman this night. Annie is ninety years of age, and she has had many narrow escapes from death, but I think she will not this time.' He nodded to them and went out, closing the door behind him.

'Well…' Lady Tate said, 'fancy that, Arabella…' She made a sound of disapproval. 'And where did Ralph get your card case? I do not believe that you gave it to him as a gift.'

'No, I do not recall it,' Arabella said. 'I believe I may have left it somewhere—perhaps downstairs. I had some new cards printed in London and the carrier delivered them, with other things, the morning that Ralph called here. I remember opening the package and placing some of the cards in the case. I may have left the case lying in the parlour downstairs. Yes, now I think about it, I am certain that I did.'

'The parlour where I took him when he asked to speak to me alone.' Lady Tate frowned. 'So now he has become a thief as well. Did you know that the case was missing, Arabella?'

'I had not thought of it,' Arabella said. 'It is no great matter, Aunt—though Mrs Bristol did mention that an engraved silver music box was missing from one of the display cabinets. It was a present from Ben on our wedding day.'

'Oh, how could he?' Lady Tate shook her head. 'I do not know what has become of him.'

'It does not signify,' Arabella said. 'I thought I must have moved the music box—but if Ralph took it that solves the mystery. At least I do not need to search for it and we may dismiss it from our minds. I am glad that Mrs Bristol will not now have to question the servants, for that would have been grossly unfair.'

'You are too forgiving!'

'I care for you, Aunt. I would gladly have given Ralph money to see you safe. In fact, I may do so now…providing he agrees to leave England.'

'You would do that?' Lady Tate's eyes filled with tears. 'He does not deserve it, Arabella. He ought by rights to be in prison.'

'But that would make you unhappy,' Arabella said. 'If Ralph will agree to be put on a ship for the West Indies, I shall have my bank send money out there for him. I think ten thousand pounds should be enough.'

'Oh, Arabella, you are too good…' Lady Tate sniffed and reached for her kerchief.

'Please do not cry or I shall change my mind,' Arabella said, teasing her. 'I think I shall go up now, dearest. I believe we could all do with some sleep. It has been an exhausting day…

# Chapter Ten

Lady Tate came down much earlier than usual the next morning and Arabella ordered the carriage brought round. She slipped her pistol into the pocket of her elegant gown in case she should need it, though they had an escort of four armed men, which made her feel protected, but also slightly uncomfortable. It was not pleasant to think that every time she left the house she must be guarded, but for the moment she must accept it.

When they reached the inn, Ralph was still in the parlour having his breakfast. He had slept late, but was preparing to leave immediately after he had eaten, and he seemed startled to see his mother and cousin walk in. He stared at Arabella, registering surprise, disbelief and then, finally, relief. He stood up to greet them.

'Arabella! How did…I mean, I thought…' He floundered as he realised that he could be convicting himself of collusion in the attempt at abduction.

'I am very fortunate,' Arabella said. 'I owe it to my good

friends that I am not a prisoner and on my way to a forced marriage in Scotland.'

'You know…I mean, did something happen?' Ralph looked slightly green. 'Oh, damn it, cousin! I am glad to see you—and you, Mama.'

'You seem no worse for your accident,' Arabella said drily. 'I am happy that my card case was of use to you, Ralph.'

He had the grace to look ashamed. 'Yes, I took it, and the silver music box from your display cabinet. I shall return that to you at once. I know that I have behaved badly, Arabella—but believe me when I say that I am glad to see you here and well this morning.'

'You plotted with that wicked man to abduct Arabella,' his mother said, giving him a look of reproach. 'That was a terrible thing to do, Ralph—and after I had told you that I would sell the house and give you half of the money. How could you contemplate such an act?' She stared at him reproachfully.

'I owed Welch far more than I could ever pay, even had you given me all of the money from your house,' Ralph said and there was a flash of fear in his eyes. 'You don't know him, Mama. He is a devil. It was his plan to abduct Arabella and I was foolish enough to go along with it. He wanted Arabella's money, but more than that—he wanted revenge on her because she refused his offer of marriage.'

'It is as we thought,' Arabella said, accepting it calmly. 'But why did he shoot you, cousin?'

'Because I refused to help him at the last,' Ralph said. 'I had done my part in it and I thought he might let me go, but he tried to kill me. I do admit that if I had not carried your silver case in my breast pocket I should probably be dead, cousin. In a way, I owe my life to you.'

'Then you may thank me by agreeing to my proposition,' Arabella said. 'If you will sign a statement telling how Sir Courtney planned to abduct me and force me into marriage, and then agree to go and live abroad, I shall instruct my bank to send ten thousand pounds to your new country. I have been told that the West Indies is a good prospect for men wishing to make their fortunes.'

'I would prefer America,' Ralph said, looking at her thoughtfully. 'You did not need to bribe me to leave the country, cousin. I dare not stay in England—Welch will kill me if he finds me still here. However, I shall take your money as I would be a fool not to—but Mama need not sell her house. Ten thousand pounds will see me settled. I have learned my lesson. I think I shall not lightly gamble beyond my means again.'

'You would be well advised not to gamble at all,' his mother said severely. 'You are fortunate that neither Arabella nor I wish to see you in prison. Let this be a lesson to you, Ralph!'

'I regret that I did certain things…' A red flush crept up his neck. 'I was desperate. I can say no more than that I am sorry.'

'Very well. We shall none of us mention your part in this affair again,' Arabella said. 'Ride back to the house with us. You may write your statement there and someone will witness it—and I shall keep my promise, Ralph. You may present the draft on my bank wherever you choose, as long as it is not in this country, and it shall be honoured.'

'You are more generous than I deserve,' Ralph said uncomfortably. 'I admit that I had thought of arranging an accident for you so that Mama would inherit everything, cousin—but I have discovered that I do not have the stomach for it after all. I must beg for your forgiveness—and Mama's. All that is at an end. You may rest easy as far as I am concerned.'

'Thank you,' Arabella said, unmoved by his apology. He was feeling chastened at the moment, aware that he had narrowly escaped death, but she did not trust him, which was why the money would not be paid until he was living in his new country. She would be happier when the matter was settled and Ralph was out of England. However, she gave no sign of her feelings, maintaining a cool reserve.

'Come, we shall return to the house and you will write your statement. I have friends who will ride with you to the ship and see you safe on board, cousin. You shall have an extra two hundred guineas in your pocket to see you on your way.'

'You mean that you do not trust me to keep my word?' Ralph looked angry, but he did not protest. Arabella thought that he was too terrified of Sir Courtney to do anything but agree to her terms.

'You took a risk going to the inn,' Charles said when he saw Arabella return to the house a short time later. He met her in the hall, for he had seen the carriage approaching from an upper window. His eyes moved to Ralph, narrowing in anger.

'Ralph, come into the study with me,' Lady Tate said. 'I wish to speak to you alone.' After one brief, rather nervous glance at Charles, Ralph followed her, looking slightly sick.

Arabella looked at Charles as she took off her bonnet and gloves. 'Please come into the parlour, sir. We may speak in private there.'

'You have brought him here—why?' Charles demanded once they were alone.

'My aunt wished to visit her son and naturally I went with her. We were well protected. I have business with my cousin and thought it best to bring him back here.'

'Why did you not tell me what you planned? I could have gone in your stead. We do not know for sure that Sir Courtney has left the district.' Charles said when he had listened to her story.

Arabella had removed her bonnet and pelisse. Turning to him with a smile, she said, 'I was well protected, and I do not care to be a prisoner in my own home.' She took out the small pistol she carried and showed him. 'I had this with me. It is ready to fire and I would do so if need be.'

A wry smile touched his mouth. 'You are courageous, Arabella, if a little reckless. You will face the future whatever comes, I think.'

'Yes,' she replied 'I have told Ralph that on receipt of his signed statement naming Sir Courtney and accusing him of attempted murder and the plot to kidnap me, I shall give him a draft on my bank, which will be paid in the country of his choice. He prefers to go to America rather than the West Indies. I agreed and he is prepared to be escorted to the ship.'

'It was my intention to have him brought here under escort when he attempted to leave the inn this morning,' Charles said. 'My men were waiting for him, but you have done the thing yourself, Arabella. He has narrowly escaped death and that must have its effect. I believe your cousin will cause you no more trouble—but there is still Sir Courtney Welch. This statement from your cousin and the testimony of Mr Henderson should be enough to have Welch arrested, but we have to discover his whereabouts first. I do not think you are truly safe at this moment. And I think I should speak to your cousin quite soon.'

'Yes, of course. I know I must be careful. Oh, do not go yet, I pray you,' she said, as he seemed about to leave. 'I have something I wish to say to you.' She lifted her head, a proud look in her eyes. 'You say that I shall not be safe until Sir Courtney has been caught and punished—but I do not think I shall be safe even then, Charles. I am in the fortunate position of being very wealthy—but unhappily there are men who covet that fortune. Until I have a husband to protect me I shall be at the mercy of fortune hunters.'

'If you were to make a will…'

'I do not think that will serve,' she said, 'for wills and even trusts can be overturned. I must be married, Charles.' She took a deep breath, steadying her nerves. 'And I am hoping that you will do me the great favour of becoming my husband.'

'Arabella?' Charles was momentarily stunned, for he had not expected it. No other lady of his acquaintance would dare to make such a proposal. 'You know that I admire you, care for you…'

'I believe that we like each other well enough,' Arabella said in a calm, flat tone. 'And perhaps there is a physical attraction between us that would make a true marriage possible. I should like children, but I am not a demanding woman— I should not be a clinging wife, I promise you.'

'Arabella…' Charles was torn between wanting to sweep her into his arms and confess his love, and the doubts that haunted him. How could he make her happy when he was possessed by guilt? 'You know that I have sworn to devote myself to making Sarah happy…'

'I do not see that your intention to give Sarah anything she desires need necessarily prevent a marriage between us.' Arabella raised her head proudly. 'I should not expect you to live in my pocket, Charles. Obviously, this is not a love match on either side, but we are friends and many marriages are built on less. Once we were married, I should no longer be in danger and we should both be free to carry on our own lives.'

'A marriage of convenience?' Charles stared at her uncertainly. 'Are you sure that is what you want, Arabella?'

She crossed her fingers behind her back. It was not in the least what she wanted. She wanted him to love her, to spend all his nights in her bed, and most of his days with her, but she would take what she could for now and hope that he would come to love her one day.

'It would be a true marriage in that I should hope for children,' Arabella said carefully. 'But if you wished to live elsewhere I should look forward to your visits, when you could spare the time.'

'That is hardly a good bargain for you, Arabella.'

'I should be only too happy to chaperon Sarah sometimes if she wished for it,' Arabella said. 'You know that I love her as dearly as if she were my own sister.'

'When we first met, you told me that you had no wish to marry.' His eyes were intent on her face.

'Perhaps I should not had this unfortunate affair not happened,' Arabella lied. She had fallen in love with him almost from the first, but she could not admit it—would not admit it until she was sure of his feelings for her. 'It is a business arrangement, Charles. You will have the charge of my estates and I am told that they amount to more than half a million pounds.'

'That is a great deal of money,' Charles said, an odd look in his eyes. 'If I agreed to your proposal, I should insist that most of the capital be invested in a trust for your children. I shall make a settlement on you from my own funds and we shall use that part of the income necessary for the upkeep of the estate. My estate is not worth the half of yours, Arabella, perhaps no more than a quarter—but I have sufficient income for our needs. I should not wish to benefit financially from this arrangement.'

'Are you saying that you will marry me?' Arabella held her breath. She had hardly dared to believe that her bold move would secure his agreement.

'I have been thinking about your situation for some time,' Charles said, his expression serious and unsmiling. 'It seems to me that you must marry. If you are content with the arrangement we have discussed, then I shall be happy to wed you, Arabella.'

'Thank you…' She blinked back the tears that stung behind her eyes. It was her true wish to be his wife, but she was not sure that she had done the right thing in asking him. It was going to be very hard to keep up this reserved manner, especially once they were wed. But she had made her bed, as Nana would have told her, and she must lie on it, even if she shed private tears.

Charles moved towards her, a smile on his lips. 'You know that I have a deep and true regard for you, Arabella. Will you do me the honour of becoming my wife?'

'Yes. Yes, I shall, thank you,' Arabella said. She forced

herself to smile. 'It is very good of you to ask me. You need not fear that I shall be a complaining wife, Charles.'

'I do not think it,' he said. 'We shall divide our time between our estates and the London house, unless Sarah wishes to travel abroad—and now I think I should kiss you.'

Arabella nodded, standing quite still as he moved closer. He leaned forward, his lips soft and sweet on hers. She felt a hot, liquid flame flare within her, leaping through her whole body as she swayed towards him, wanting to feel herself pressed hard against his body.

'We shall do very nicely together,' Charles said and there was a little smile on his lips now. 'I have been talking to Mama and Sarah, Arabella. Mama was saying that perhaps we should go home now that Sarah has recovered her memory, but I shall suggest that we all stay here a little longer. You were planning a trip into York. I think you might purchase a gown for the wedding while you are there. I shall see my lawyers and have the marriage contracts drawn up, and I shall ask your local vicar to call the banns for the first time this Sunday. We can be married in three weeks, and then we shall all go to my estate. After that we shall see. It might be that we wish to take a trip abroad and that Mama and Sarah may wish to accompany us.'

'I think that is a very good plan,' Arabella said. 'I shall ask Sarah if she would still like to visit York with me; if she is happy to do so, we may go tomorrow. I shall also visit my lawyers and make all the necessary arrangements.'

Charles nodded at her, his brows raised. 'Shall I tell Mama and Sarah the news—and you may wish to tell your aunt?'

'Yes, of course,' Arabella agreed. 'And now I must go to

the study and inquire if my cousin has finished writing his statement.'

'Oh, I think you may leave that to me,' Charles said. 'Now that we are engaged, it will be my pleasure to deal with Sir Ralph…'

Arabella saw the determination in his eyes and smiled inwardly. 'Yes, Charles. I shall be very glad to leave that affair in your hands. It will be much more comfortable having a husband to take care of such things.'

She walked from the room, her back straight, head held high. For the moment she had managed to hide her true feelings from Charles. She thought that it would not take him long to discover them once they were married. She must hope that he would not be angry at her subterfuge. She had made a bargain with him and she meant to keep it. Charles would give her his protection and she would give him his freedom in return. It was not to be a love match and she must make no demands on him.

'Oh, Arabella, that is wonderful news,' Lady Tate said when she was told of the understanding between her niece and Charles Hunter. 'I am so happy for you, dearest. Charles may be a little intense at times, but he is a man you can trust—and you know that I have been anxious for your sake. I could not like the idea of you living alone for the rest of your life, my dear.'

'Yes, I know,' Arabella said and smiled at her. 'For ages I believed that I could not bear to put anyone in Ben's place. We had such a short time together, but it was wonderful and I thought it was enough to last me for a lifetime. However, this business with Sir Courtney has made me realise that I must marry.'

'You will certainly be safe from fortune hunters,' Lady Tate said. 'But you should not marry for such a reason, Arabella. I hope that you have thought this through, my dear?'

'Yes, I have,' Arabella told her. 'It is not a love match, but we are good friends and we have respect and liking for one another.'

Lady Tate looked at her uncertainly, as if she wished to say more on the subject. However, Tilda came into the room at that moment and she burst into warm congratulations.

'Sarah has just told me the news, Arabella,' she said. 'I am delighted for you. I have always thought that you should marry again.'

'It does not mean that you must leave here,' Arabella said. 'Charles and I will not live in each other's pockets. There will always be a home for you here, even if I am not always resident myself.'

'You are always so kind and generous,' Tilda said. 'However, I must tell you that it is my intention to travel for a while. I have always wanted to go to Italy, Arabella, and now that I have the means I shall do so—though if you needed me, I should come to you at once.'

'Tilda!' Arabella laughed, her face alight with pleasure. 'I think that is wonderful—but are you certain you wish to travel abroad? You have never cared much for travelling.'

'It is true that I am an indifferent traveller,' Tilda said and smiled. 'But one must put up with much if one wishes to see the world. Years ago I made so many plans, but time passed and I was unable to do the things I had wanted to do as a young girl. However, when I was tied up and left alone in that cottage, I realised that I still have years left to me—and that I wanted to make the most of them.'

'That is so brave of you,' Lady Tate said. 'I have sometimes thought that I should like to travel somewhere warm, but I should not have the courage to go alone…' She looked thoughtful, but before she could continue Mrs Bristol came in to announce a visitor.

'Captain Hernshaw has called to see you, my lady,' she said. 'He is waiting in the downstairs parlour.'

'Please ask him to come up,' Arabella said. She turned to her aunt and Tilda. 'This is a surprise. I do hope that he has not brought bad news. Melinda was in good health when I last saw her.'

'He has certainly come out of his way to call on you,' Lady Tate said. 'I hope Lady Hernshaw is not ill.'

'Excuse me,' Tilda said. 'Sarah asked if I would walk with her in the garden. I said I would ask you if it was safe to do so now.'

'Yes, as long as you stay close to the house,' Arabella said. 'I believe the grounds are still being patrolled day and night. Tell Sarah that I shall see her when you return.'

Tilda nodded and went out, stopping to pass a few words with Captain Hernshaw as he entered.

'Lady Arabella…Lady Tate,' Captain Hernshaw said, inclining his head to both ladies. 'I hope you will forgive this intrusion…'

'It is no intrusion,' Arabella said and went to greet him, offering her hand. He kissed it, holding it perhaps a moment longer than necessary. 'Pray tell me at once, is Melinda well?'

'Yes, very well when I left her,' Captain Hernshaw said. 'It was on her behalf that I came. She has been concerned since you left town in a hurry and she asked me to call on you as I came this way, to discover if all is well with you?'

'I am very well,' Arabella said. She did not think it right or proper to burden her friends with the story of the abduction attempt.

'And she has asked if you will join her at her home.'

'I am not sure that I shall be able to get away,' Arabella said. 'But I shall write to Melinda and tell her my news. Perhaps you would care to stay for nuncheon, which will be served very soon? My letter may go from the receiving office, unless you intend to see Melinda on your return.'

'Thank you, I shall stay and you may give me your letter,' he said and glanced at Lady Tate. 'I wonder if I might have a few minutes in private with you, Lady Arabella?'

'Yes, of course. I was about to go and find Mrs Hunter,' Lady Tate said, getting to her feet. 'I am glad to hear that Lady Hernshaw is well, sir.'

She left the room, closing the door softly behind her. Arabella was a little puzzled, and then she saw that Captain Hernshaw was nervous and intuition told her what he was about to say. She walked away from him, standing by the window to glance out at the gardens. Sarah and Tilda were walking arm in arm, apparently enjoying each other's company.

'I shall write to Melinda of my news,' Arabella said as she sensed him close behind her. 'But there is no reason why I should not tell you, sir. Mr Hunter has asked me to marry him and I have agreed. We are to be married quite soon.'

'Ah, I see…' Captain Hernshaw expelled a low breath. 'I

have left it too late. There is nothing for me now but to wish you all the happiness in the world.'

Arabella turned to face him, lifting her gaze to his face. She saw strong regret and a flicker of pain in his eyes, and realised that his feelings for her had been deeper than she'd guessed. Always charming, a light-hearted, teasing man, she had mistaken his gallantry for merely that and perhaps misjudged him.

'Forgive me,' she said and reached out to touch his hand. 'We have been good friends, I think. And I would not grieve you for the world, sir.'

'Arabella…' He took her hand and held it tightly. 'I must tell you that I love you. I did not think you were ready to marry again or I should have spoken when you were in town. You left so suddenly…but it is too late…'

'Yes. I am sorry…'

She might have said more for she had always liked him, but at that moment the door opened and Charles entered. Captain Hernshaw let go of her hand and moved away at once.

'My apologies,' Charles said and frowned. 'I did not know that you had company, Arabella.'

'Captain Hernshaw came to bring me a message from Melinda,' Arabella said in a calm voice that belied the frantic beating of her heart. 'She has asked me to stay with her at her home for a while, but I have been telling Captain Hernshaw our news, Charles. I shall write and invite Melinda and Sir Harry to our wedding instead.'

'Yes, of course,' Charles said and came forward, offering his hand to Hernshaw. 'Good to see you, sir. I do hope that you will come and wish us happy. The wedding is to be in three weeks. I have not yet settled the date, but it will not be much longer.'

'Thank you,' Captain Hernshaw replied and took his hand. 'It depends on my circumstances, for I may be going overseas on a diplomatic mission—but I wish you both happiness.'

A gong sounded in the hall below, summoning them to luncheon. Arabella was glad of the interruption—she sensed that Charles had seen that moment of intimacy between her and Captain Hernshaw, and that perhaps he had misunderstood it.

'Shall we go down, gentlemen?' she said, looking from one to the other. She could sense the atmosphere between them and wished that she had not given way to a moment of sentiment. There was no question of her regretting the bargain she had made. She liked Captain Hernshaw, but would never have married him. 'We must not keep the others waiting.'

She led the way from the room, aware that the gentlemen were making polite conversation as they followed. She had thought them friendly in London, but at the moment they might have been perfect strangers.

John Elworthy had come down to join them for the midday meal. He was holding his left arm a little stiffly but otherwise made nothing of the injury he had received. He smiled at Arabella and congratulated her.

'Charles tells me that there is good news at last,' he said. 'I am very glad to hear it, Lady Arabella. Charles is very lucky and I have told him so.'

'I am aware of my good fortune,' Charles said and his expression could only be described as grim. 'I trust you are well enough to be up and about so soon?'

'Yes, thank you,' John said. 'It was a mere scratch, as you know.'

He was clearly in a good humour; perhaps a little amused

at his own thoughts. Arabella was glad of his presence at the table, for it might otherwise have been awkward. Charles had lapsed into what appeared to be a moody silence and she felt that he was angry about something. And Captain Hernshaw looked very serious, smiling only when one of the ladies spoke to him.

After lunch she and the other ladies left the gentlemen to talk and smoke a cigar if they wished. Arabella went to her study where she wrote a long letter to Melinda. She met Sarah as she was leaving the room and they discussed their visit to York the following day.

Sarah was clearly feeling much better and looking forward to the outing.

'Shall we go into the garden?' she asked as Arabella deposited her letter on a silver salver on the hall table. 'It is quite warm out, Arabella, and we have been cooped up for days. I want to tell you that I think Tilda has come out of her ordeal remarkably well. She has been telling Mama that she intends to travel. We have been talking of it and Mama has decided to ask if she would likc to accompany us, at least as far as Italy. We could take a villa together and spend the winter in the sunshine.'

'That would be wonderful for her,' Arabella said. They stopped to take shawls from the hall cabinet, draping their shoulders as they went out. 'She told me that she wished to visit Italy, and it would be so much nicer if you went as a group.'

'Yes. We hardly need Charles to escort us,' Sarah said. 'I know he means well, Belle, but he is so…intense. He makes me feel guilty, because he used not to be that way. I know that he is desperate to make up to me for what happened—and it was not his fault, though he believes it was because of that card

game. I think that if the three of us went together—and
Mama's coachman and grooms, and perhaps her secretary to
take care of all the official things…' She laughed at the picture
of their entourage this conjured up. 'There will be so many of
us—besides, you will not want us on your honeymoon, Belle.'

'I should not mind at all,' Arabella assured her as they
linked arms and went outside. 'You must know that I'm
always pleased to be in your company, Sarah.' She smiled and
lifted her face towards the sky. In a tree nearby a thrush was
singing and the scent of flowers drifted on the air. 'It is beautifully warm, is it not? We have had some cool days, but now
it is almost like summer again.'

'Yes, lovely,' Sarah agreed. 'I think the weather is much like
this all the time in Italy. I am really looking forward to our trip.'
They strolled across the lawns towards the rose arbour. 'Mama
asked me if I felt ready to meet our friends. She said we might
go home or to Bath for a while—but I think I prefer Italy, at
least for the moment.'

'It might be easier to go into company with strangers at
first,' Arabella agreed. 'You would be able to adjust without
your friends asking uncomfortable questions—and there is
plenty of time for a London Season when you come home.'

'I am not sure that I shall want a Season at all,' Sarah said,
wrinkling her forehead. 'Perhaps I may change my mind in a
few months, but at the moment I do not feel that I could trust
any man enough to give myself to him.'

Sarah's face clouded with doubt. She stopped walking just
short of the rose arbour, looking at Arabella with wide,
anxious eyes.

'You will learn to trust again,' Arabella told her. 'Believe me, dearest. Sometimes, when one has been hurt, it feels as if you are bleeding inside. You think that you can never be happy again—that you will never be able to love again.'

'Is that how you felt after Ben died?' Sarah's eyes were on her, appealing and sad, soft with sympathy.

'Yes.' Arabella reached out to touch her hand. They were so close in that moment, such good friends. 'I was not sure that I would ever wish to marry again. Everyone said that I ought, but I felt that my heart was dead.'

'But you are going to marry Charles.' Sarah gave her an odd look. 'Do you love him, Belle? I mean, really love him—as much as you loved Ben?'

Arabella hesitated, then, 'Yes, I do love Charles. In a slightly different way. Ben was my hero. I adored him as a child and as a young girl. We were very happy in the short time we had, but when he died that girl died too. I became a woman, a different woman—and it is that woman who loves Charles.'

'He loves you,' Sarah said. 'I am not sure that he understands it himself yet—but I have seen it in his eyes. There is a kind of hunger…a longing that he cannot hide.'

'I know that he feels something for me,' Arabella agreed. 'I pray that he will let himself love—'

She broke off suddenly, for she had seen someone in the rose arbour. He was half-hidden by the overhanging trailing roses that cascaded down the wooden poles, but she had caught sight of him as he moved. She did not know why, but instinctively, she pushed Sarah behind her, sheltering her as the man stepped forward into full view. A thrill of fear shot through her as she saw that he was holding a pistol and it was directed straight at her.

'So we meet at last,' Sir Courtney said and gave a high-pitched titter. 'Did you imagine that I would allow you to make a fool of me?'

'There is an order out for your arrest, sir,' Arabella said. She moved back a few steps, keeping her own body in front of Sarah, and intimating with her hand behind her back that the girl should go. As she moved back, the man came forward, emerging from the shelter of the rose arbour where he had been hiding. 'You are wanted for the attempted murder of my cousin. He has signed a statement and you were seen at the crossroads by a magistrate.'

'So the fool survived, did he?' Sir Courtney snarled. 'I'll deal with him later. But first there is you, my proud lady. I wasn't good enough for you, was I? Well, I shall teach you your manners. You will be on your knees begging for scraps before I've done with you.'

'I shall never beg for anything from you,' Arabella said, raising her head proudly. She moved back a few more steps. 'I would rather die than let you touch me—and I shall never be your wife.'

Behind her, Arabella heard Sarah gasp. She screamed out her brother's name and began to run towards the house. Sir Courtney's attention was diverted. His eyes narrowed as they followed her fleeing form. He swore and raised his arm, taking aim at her back. In that instant, Arabella, who had not taken her eyes from him, threw herself at him. She caught at his arm, causing him to fire wide.

He swore at her as they struggled. 'You deserve to be taught a lesson.' He thrust her back. She stumbled and he pointed his pistol at her, trying to fire again. The hammer came down, but nothing happened; as happened with so many pistols of its kind, it had jammed on the second shot and was useless. With a scream of fury, he brought the pistol crashing down against her temple.

Arabella gave a cry of pain and fell to the ground, losing consciousness as everything went black. She did not hear the shouts of anger as three men ran from the house and one fired, his ball finding its mark. A small round hole appeared in Sir Courtney's forehead. His face wore an expression of startled surprise as he swayed from the force of the shot, and then he buckled at the knees, falling forwards to the ground.

'Arabella!' Charles cried. He was the first to reach her. He went down on his knees, gathering her still form in his arms, cradling her to his breast. 'Arabella, my love…my love.'

John Elworthy turned Welch over onto his back with his foot and looked down at his face. 'That was a damned good shot, Hernshaw. Remind me never to challenge you to a duel.'

Captain Hernshaw smiled bleakly. He had learned his trade on the battlefields of Europe and was known to be the best marksman in his regiment. He watched as Charles lifted Arabella in his arms and began to stride back towards the house. Some of the men from the estate had come running after hearing the shot.

'Lady Arabella has been hurt. One of you must go immediately for the doctor,' Hernshaw said. 'And the magistrate must be informed about what has happened here.'

'I'll go for the doctor, sir,' one of the men volunteered and set off at a run towards the stables.

'There is a warrant out for Welch's arrest,' John said. 'You did what you had to do, Hernshaw. Had it not been you, it would have been Charles or I—and we all thank you for it. Arabella could never have been truly safe while that madman lived.'

Something flickered in Hernshaw's eyes. He inclined his head, a grim line to his mouth. 'I shall wait at the house until the doctor has been—unless you wish me to accompany you to see the magistrate?'

'No, I shall do well enough alone,' John said. 'But he may wish to speak to you, hear your own account of what happened. I suggest you prepare to stay in the district for a day or so longer.'

'Yes, of course. I should feel disinclined to leave until I know how Arabella goes on.'

John looked at him, nodding as he saw more than Hernshaw meant to show. 'I understand. Go up to the house, then.' He glanced at Arabella's bailiff. 'Someone should move the body and keep a watch on it until the magistrate returns with me. This business must be done properly.'

'I saw it all,' Mr Grant said. 'I was too far away to do anything, sir. I am sorry that he managed to get into the grounds. We've been patrolling the bounds since first light, but he must have sneaked in during the night—came over the wall, I shouldn't wonder.'

'It can always be done if someone is determined on it,' John said. 'I believe the danger is over now, but Mr Hunter will speak to you later.'

He set off almost immediately for the stables. Captain Hernshaw walked back to the house.

As he entered, he saw that a small group had gathered in the hall, including Mrs Hunter and the housekeeper.

'How is she?' he asked. 'I believe she was rendered senseless by the blow from his pistol. Would that I had shot a moment sooner.'

'Oh, sir, you were wonderful quick,' Mrs Bristol said. 'It was lucky that you had your pistol with you.'

'I was about to leave and I never travel without it,' Hernshaw said, a grim light in his eyes. 'It has seen off many a highwayman—but Arabella, how is she?'

'My son carried her upstairs,' Mrs Hunter said. 'She was still unconscious when he rushed past me. I can tell you no more than that, I'm afraid.'

'Captain Hernshaw—' Lady Tate spoke from the top of the stairs '—will you please come up and sit with us in the drawing room? Mrs Bristol, please bring tea and coffee. Selina, please come and join me. Sarah and Tilda are with Arabella. They will come and tell us when they know what is happening.'

'Yes, Hester, of course,' Mrs Hunter said. She smiled at Captain Hernshaw. 'I believe we all owe you a debt of gratitude, sir. Arabella is hurt, but, had you not acted so promptly, she might have been dead.'

'Will she recover?' Charles pounced on the doctor when he left Arabella's room. He had waited outside while an examination was made, pacing up and down the hallway in anxiety. 'How badly is she hurt?'

'She has had a nasty blow to her temple,' Dr James said. 'But she was stirring a little as I examined her just now. I believe she will be better soon, though she may have a headache. There is a small cut to the side of her head, which I have dressed. However, I am fairly certain that no serious damage has been done.'

'Thank God!' Charles felt the relief sweep over him. 'I thought for a moment that he had killed her.'

'No, no, I think it is more the shock than anything. She should rest for a few days, take things quietly. In a week or so she will be back on her feet again—though it may take longer for her to recover from the distress. It was a terrible thing to happen, Mr Hunter.'

'Yes, it was,' Charles agreed. 'She was so brave. All the time he was pointing that pistol at her, she kept her body between him and Sarah—and then when Sarah ran and he tried to fire at her, she wrestled with him. He might have killed Sarah had she not prevented it.'

'You do not surprise me,' the doctor said and smiled. 'Lady Arabella is a great lady, Mr Hunter, and much admired in the district. I believe you are to be congratulated. I must say that I thought she would never marry again. She was devastated when Ben Marshall died—but I am very glad to hear that she has found happiness with you, sir.'

'Thank you.' Charles offered his hand. 'You will come again tomorrow?'

'Yes, I shall look in on my rounds,' Dr James agreed. 'But if you should need me, I am only in the village and I shall come at once. Lady Arabella would be a great loss to the community—but I do not fear it and nor should you.'

'Thank you again. Will you see yourself out, sir?'

'Yes, yes, no need to worry. I shall have a word with Lady Tate before I go. She was looking a little pale when I arrived. She may need something from me.'

Charles turned away, knocking softly at the door of Arabella's bedchamber. Sarah came to open it, inviting him in with a smile. 'She spoke to me just a few moments ago, Charles, and I think she is sleeping now. I gave her a sip of the doctor's mixture and she smiled before she closed her eyes.'

'She saved your life, Sarah. That devil meant to shoot you in the back.'

'Yes, I know,' Sarah said. 'I love her so dearly, Charles. She is like my own sister. Had it not been for Belle, I might never have found the will to live. Nana took me in and nursed me, but Belle gave me reason to hope. She visited every day and brought me things…presents, clothes, delicious trifles to eat. She gave me books to read and asked me to live with her…' Sarah smothered a sob. 'She saved my life not once but twice. You are very lucky to have won her, Charles.'

'I am not sure that I have,' he said, looking at Arabella as she slept. For a moment she stirred, her eyelids flickering as she murmured something. 'She agreed to marry me because it would make her safe from Courtney and other fortune hunters. We are friends, but…'

'Of course she loves you,' Sarah said. 'She told me so just before that man came out of the bushes and started abusing her. I was terrified, but Belle stood up to him. She told him that she would rather die than let him touch her and would never marry him. I do not think that she would marry you unless she cared for you.'

'I know that she feels something…' Charles moved closer to the bed. He leaned over, kissing Arabella's forehead as she slept. 'She might come to love me in time, perhaps.'

Sarah laughed. 'That is what Belle said of you. If she has not confessed her love to you, Charles, it is your own fault. You have been obsessed by your guilt over what happened to me. Arabella thinks that you are denying your love for her—and she is right.' She smiled as he turned to look at her. 'I do not want you to devote your life to me, Charles. I shall do well enough with Mama and Tilda—and Lady Tate is considering whether she too may come with us to Italy. We shall be a large party with all our servants to care for us. We do not need you, Charles. I do not need you—and I do not blame you for what happened to me. You could not have known what those wicked men would do; besides, it is over.'

Charles straightened up, leaving Arabella's side to come to her, looking into her eyes. 'Is it truly over for you, Sarah?'

'The nightmares have gone,' Sarah said. 'I am happy now that I know Mama and can remember what I was before it happened—but I am not ready to be the girl I was. I must become someone else, the way Arabella did after her husband died. I was an innocent girl when I was abducted. I do not know what I am just now—but travelling abroad with Mama and our friends, I shall learn to become someone different.'

'And what of John Elworthy?'

'John…' Sarah's eyes clouded for a moment. 'I like John very much, but for the moment that is all it can be. I have told him how I feel and he understands. I do not know if I shall ever wish to marry.'

'I pray that you will find happiness one day,' Charles said and reached forward to touch her hand. 'I love you very much as my sister, Sarah, but you are right. You must move on and perhaps you will do that better without me.'

'It is not that I do not love you,' Sarah said, tears in her eyes. 'But it is what I want for now.'

'Yes, I understand,' Charles said. 'Go and join the others now, Sarah. I want to sit by her bed alone for a little.'

'Yes, very well,' Sarah said and smiled at him. She moved towards him, kissing his cheek and moving back quickly before he could return the gesture. 'I love Arabella. Take care of her and love her, Charles. She needs you even if her pride will not let her admit it.'

Charles nodded. He drew a chair up to the bed and sat down, watching Arabella as she slept. She was so beautiful, so lovely in every way. He had known that he was in love with her before this, but only when he feared that he might lose her had he realised what it would mean.

She was the woman he had waited for all his life. All his other affairs had been light-hearted flirtations. This time it was the kind of love that hurts, the kind that gives as well as takes, and the kind that would last throughout his life. He hoped that it was not too late. She had asked him to marry her, telling him that it was not to be a love match. He suspected that she had done so out of pride. He prayed it was so, for he wanted her to love him, wanted it, needed it more than he had ever realised he could need anything.

'I love you, my dearest Arabella,' he murmured softly. He reached out to touch her face, his heart aching to see her lying there so still and pale. She had always been so full of life, so confident and caring for others. If he lost her now…but he could not bear to think of it. Without her he would once again become the empty shell of a man he had been until she came into his life and forced him to feel again. 'Please be well, my darling—and please forgive me…' He smothered a sob. 'I need you so, my love. Please do not leave me.'

# *Chapter Eleven*

Arabella opened her eyes. Her curtains had been partially drawn and the sun was streaming in, warming the room. She stretched, becoming aware of a sore place at the side of her head. She put her hand up to touch it and encountered a sticky ointment, remembering as she did so what had caused the injury.

'Sarah!' she cried and sat up. Then she breathed a sigh of relief. Sarah was all right. She had prevented Sir Courtney's shot from finding its mark and then he had hit her when his pistol jammed. She thought she vaguely recalled Sarah smoothing her forehead before she took the doctor's mixture the previous day. She must have slept a long time! Looking about her, she saw that one of the maids was at the washstand, pouring water into a bowl. 'Maisie—what time is it?'

'Oh, you are awake, my lady,' Maisie said and looked regretful. 'It is nearly ten o'clock. Did I disturb you, ma'am? I was just getting some water ready to wash your hands and face.'

'Thank you, but I shall get up in a few minutes and do that

myself,' Arabella said and frowned. 'I am late and I promised Sarah that we should go to York today.'

'The doctor said as you were to rest for a few days, ma'am,' the maid said. 'You should not think of getting up today, let alone going to York.'

'Nonsense,' Arabella said and swung her legs from the bed. However, as she attempted to stand up her head began to spin and she sat down again with a bump. 'Perhaps I shall not go to York until tomorrow, but I shall get up soon. I think I will have some tea and bread and butter, and then you can help me dress, Maisie.'

'Yes, ma'am,' the girl said. 'I'll go down and fetch it now.'

Even as she walked to the door it opened and Tilda came in. She was looking anxious, but when she saw that Arabella was awake she smiled.

'Ah, you are better, dearest. Mr Hunter forbade us to come too soon, for he said that you were resting peacefully—but I thought I would just look in to see how you go on. How is your poor head?'

'A little sore,' Arabella said. 'It does not signify. Sarah is all right, isn't she? I remember that his shot went wide and I think she was here in this room before I slept.'

'She stayed until after the doctor had been,' Tilda said. 'We have all taken our turn to sit beside you for a little, though Mr Hunter was here for hours.'

'That was kind of him,' Arabella said. 'I would expect no less of Charles. He is always thoughtful. Tell me, what happened after that man hit me?'

'Captain Hernshaw shot him,' Tilda said. 'I have never seen anything like it in my life. Just one shot… He was magnificent, Arabella. Not that I approve of violence as a general rule, but if anyone deserved to die it was that wicked man! I have no sympathy for him, none at all!'

'Yes, perhaps it was best,' Arabella said. 'I must write and thank Captain Hernshaw.'

'Oh, you may do that in person,' Tilda told her cheerfully. 'He stayed here last night. Mr Elworthy brought the magistrate to take everyone's statements. He seemed to think that Captain Hernshaw had done exactly the right thing in the circumstances and so that is the end of the business. Captain Hernshaw will not be arrested or charged with any crime.'

'Captain Hernshaw stayed here—in the house?'

'Yes, Mr Hunter invited him. He was concerned about you—everyone was. Mr Elworthy is leaving later today, but he waited to hear how you were. We have had a stream of people from the estate and the village asking after you—and one of your neighbours rode over to see how you were.'

'Everyone has been so kind.'

'You deserve that they should be,' Tilda said. 'You saved Sarah's life.'

'I only did what anyone would have done.'

'Of course you would say that,' Tilda said. 'Is there anything I may do for you—or shall I just go and leave you in peace?'

'Maisie is bringing my breakfast. I shall get up in an hour or so.'

'Are you sure that you ought?' Tilda shook her head and straightened the silken coverlet. 'Well, I dare say you know best. I shall go down now. I am sure that Lady Tate and Sarah wish to see you.'

'I shall see them both when I come down,' Arabella said.

'And please ask Captain Hernshaw not to leave before I have spoken to him.'

'Yes, of course.' Tilda walked to the door and turned to look back. 'I am so glad that you were not killed, Arabella.'

'Thank you,' Arabella said. 'I think that we shall all rest easier now that that man has been dealt with.'

She sat back against her pillows, closing her eyes. Her head was aching a little but the dizziness had passed. She would eat her breakfast and then she would get up.

She frowned as she realised that circumstances had altered now that Sir Courtney was dead. She had asked Charles to marry her to keep her safe from fortune hunters, and in a way that still held good—but the immediate danger was over. Most of the men who had asked her to marry them after Ben was killed had taken her refusal with dignity. Some had undoubtedly been more interested in her money, but some had genuinely had at least a warm affection for her.

She recalled the expression in Captain Hernshaw's eyes when she had told him that she was to marry Charles. He had looked devastated—and it was due to his prompt action that she had not been more badly hurt, for Sir Courtney could have inflicted more damage had he not been stopped. The least that she could do was to thank Captain Hernshaw in person.

Would Charles wish to withdraw from their arrangement now that she was no longer in such dire need of protection? He was too much the gentleman to jilt her—but ought she to offer him the chance to stand back? Their engagement was not generally known, though the news would have spread to their neighbours, as had the news of her injury. However, the engagement had not yet been officially announced in the papers. She could tell Charles that she had changed her mind.

It was too painful to think of for the moment, Arabella decided. She would have her breakfast, get up and then, later, she would talk to Charles.

'I do hope I am not intruding?' Tilda asked as she put her head round the door of the back parlour, where Charles, John and Captain Hernshaw were talking over a glass of wine. 'I just wanted to tell you that Arabella is going to get up in about an hour. She is having some breakfast and she says that she is well enough to come down. She particularly asked that you stay, Mr Hernshaw. She wishes to speak to you. I thought I would tell you at once in case you left in the meantime. I shall leave you to your talk now, gentlemen. I must tell Lady Tate and Sarah that Arabella is quite herself again.'

She went out, closing the door carefully behind her and walking upstairs to the larger parlour where the ladies were sitting, quite unaware of the false hopes and doubts she had left behind her.

Arabella came downstairs a little more than an hour later. Mrs Bristol had told her that the gentlemen were in the back parlour, but when she entered she discovered that only Captain Hernshaw was there, lounging in a chair by the window. He had been glancing through a news-sheet, but put it aside as she entered.

'Good morning,' he said, springing to his feet at once. 'You look lovely, Arabella. I hope that you are feeling better?'

'Yes, much better,' she replied with a smile. 'I believe I

have to thank you for what you did, sir. Had your shot not been as true, I might not have escaped with my life.'

'I am glad that my shot went home as it was intended,' Captain Hernshaw replied. 'I should have been devastated if he had killed you.'

'Thank you,' she said. 'I am glad that you waited, sir. I wanted to see you to tell you how grateful I am. A letter would not suffice in the circumstances.'

He came towards her, taking the hand she offered and lifting it to kiss the back. 'It was my pleasure and my privilege,' he said. 'Mr Hunter is a fortunate man.'

'Thank you,' Arabella said and her cheeks were a little pink. 'Please tell Melinda that I look forward to seeing her soon. She might care to arrive a little before the wedding and stay for a while. I hope that you will attend our wedding too, sir?'

'I shall if I am permitted,' he replied. 'I have been asked by the Government to conduct a diplomatic mission to Rome, but I shall certainly come if I can. And now I must leave you. I dare say you have much to do.'

'Yes, thank you. I shall never forget you—or what you did for me, Captain Hernshaw.'

He bowed his head and walked to the door. Arabella moved to the French windows. She looked out and saw that Charles was standing with Mr Elworthy in the drive. Opening the window, she went out to join them, walking proudly, her head high, her smile warm but a little reserved.

'Were you about to leave, Mr Elworthy? I had hoped to see you first, though I know you must be anxious to go home. You have been here some days longer than you expected. I wanted to thank you so much for all that you have done for me.'

'It was Captain Hernshaw who fired that shot,' John said. 'Neither Charles or I had a pistol about us.'

'But you have done so much more,' Arabella said. 'You and Charles prevented the first kidnap attempt and I am so grateful. I have spoken to Captain Hernshaw, thanking him for his prompt action. I believe that he may have prevented more harm, for Sir Courtney had lost all semblance of reason. He would have killed me where I lay if he could.'

John moved towards her, hesitating before kissing her cheek. 'I am happy to have been of service to you, Arabella. You are a good person. Sarah owes her life to you—and that makes me for ever in your debt.'

'You care for her a great deal, I believe?'

'I love her,' John said. 'I cared for her before she was abducted, but she was still a child and I…did not know my own heart for sure until I saw her again. Perhaps it was merely friendship then, but it is more now. I would give anything to spend my life making her happy, but she does not want my devotion.'

'At the moment Sarah does not quite know what she wants,' Arabella told him. 'Do not give up, sir. A few months in Italy may bring about changes for the better.'

'Thank you. I shall hope that it may,' John said. He turned towards Charles, offering his hand. 'I shall see you at the wedding, my friend. I think I must be on my way. There are things at home needing my attention.'

Charles was silent as he watched John walked away. Arabella moved to stand by his side.

'I think Sarah likes him very well,' she said. 'She just needs time. She could not think of marriage until she has come to terms with what happened to her.'

'You are right, as always,' Charles said and looked at her. 'You knew Sarah's heart long before I did, did you not?'

'We had become close over the time that she stayed at Nana's cottage,' Arabella said. 'Will you walk with me for a little, Charles? I should like to be private with you, for I need to talk to you.'

'Is Hernshaw still here?'

'He was about to leave when I came out to you,' Arabella said. 'He has been a good friend to me, Charles. I wanted to thank him personally.'

'He is in love with you.'

'Yes, I think perhaps he is,' Arabella agreed. 'In London I imagined that it was merely flirtation, but I believe I wronged him. I am sorry to have given him grief, but it could not be avoided.'

'Did he ask you to marry him yesterday?'

'It was his intention, but I told him that I was to marry you and he offered me his best wishes.'

Charles nodded, his eyes dark and brooding as he looked at her. 'Would your answer have been different if we had not already come to an understanding?'

'No, it would not,' Arabella said. 'I like Captain Hernshaw as a friend. He is good company and can be amusing—but I do not wish to be married to him.'

'You do not love him?'

'No, I do not love him.'

'Sarah said that you would not marry without love.'

'Did she?' Arabella glanced away. She was trembling inwardly. 'I am safe from Sir Courtney now, Charles. It is still true that I should be better married, for I have received too many offers since Ben died—some before he was cold in his grave. Most of the gentlemen were more enamoured of my fortune than me, though some may have been genuine in their regard. I did not wish to marry any of them.'

'Do you wish to marry me?'

She took a deep breath, turning to face him. 'Yes, Charles. I still wish to marry you—but I shall allow you to withdraw if you prefer. We can wait for a while and then tell our friends that we were not suited.'

'You would do that?' Charles frowned. 'But only if I wish it?'

'Yes, of course. I appreciate that I asked you and that you agreed out of concern for my well being, Charles. I know that you are too much of a gentleman to withdraw unless I agree, but—'

Arabella got no further, for he moved towards her, taking her into his arms, his lips on hers, kissing her in a way that stole her breath. His kiss was hungry, needy, demanding a response, which she gave with all her heart, melting into his body, pliant and giving in his embrace. When he drew away at last and smiled at her, she swayed towards him and might have fallen had he not steadied her.

'You are still unwell. I am a brute.'

'No,' she said and laughed huskily. 'It was what I wanted—what I have wanted for such a long time. I did not wish you to stop.'

Charles looked into her eyes and then a big grin spread over his face, his eyes dancing with laughter. 'I have been such a fool, have I not? Almost from the first I felt the attraction between us, Arabella. When I touched your face that day in the park I wanted to sweep you up in my arms and carry you off somewhere so that we could make love—but I knew that I had no right. I had to find Sarah, and having found her—safe in your house—I thought that I must spend my life making up to her for what I had done. I was consumed with guilt…'

Arabella leaned forward, closing off the words with a sweet brush of her lips. He responded by crushing her hard against him. It was a while before either of them were able to speak again, but when they did it was Arabella who began.

'Sarah does not blame you, Charles. She is relieved that she had not done anything to merit the abduction.'

'I know. She told me—in no uncertain terms.' Charles looked rueful. 'She made it quite clear that she neither needed nor wanted my devotion. My sister has changed, become stronger, determined—and I believe I have you to thank for that, Arabella.'

'I think Sarah would have changed as she grew older anyway,' Arabella said. 'She was petted, spoiled and protected by her family and so she remained an innocent child. When she was thrust into a hostile world she was frightened and her mind could not cope with what had happened to her. Once she was safe with her family she began to remember— but it was Tilda's abduction that unlocked her memory. I may have helped her to regain her confidence a little, but in time she will become a woman you will be proud of.'

'Not as proud as I was of you, my dearest love,' Charles told her, his eyes tender as he reached out to touch her cheek. 'You faced that devil so courageously, and you saved Sarah's life. When I thought he had killed you…' His voice broke with emotion. 'Had you died, I should have had nothing more to live for, Arabella. I love you so very much

'Oh, Charles,' she whispered tears in her eyes. 'I prayed that you would come to love me in time. When I asked you to marry me I tried to hide my feelings for you, believing that you would not marry me unless you believed it a marriage of convenience.'

'And I accepted, knowing that I loved you, hoping that we might learn to love each other when we were married—that I could deserve you. I know that I am fortunate beyond my deserts to have secured your affection, Arabella.'

'Foolish man,' she chided. 'You try to take the world on your shoulders, Charles. No one man can do that, my love. But you will not be alone now. In future we shall face the world and its challenges together.'

'Yes,' he said, and took her hand in his. 'I cannot wait for the day that you become mine, Arabella. And now, I think we should go in, for your aunt and my mother have been watching us from an upstairs window for the past several minutes.'

Arabella laughed and pressed his hand to her cheek. 'I am so happy that I do not mind if we have an audience,' she told him. 'Tomorrow we shall go into York and I shall buy my wedding gown.'

'Are you sure you feel well enough?'

'Yes, perfectly sure,' Arabella replied. 'And as for our wedding day, that cannot come soon enough for me!'

Arabella was dressed in the ivory gown of satin with a dusky pink lace overskirt that she had ordered for her wedding. In her hair she wore a confection of silk flowers twined with ribbon to match her overskirt, and diamond earrings hung from the lobes of her ears. The past three weeks had flown and much that had happened in the past seemed almost unreal, a bad dream that had passed away.

'Oh, you do look beautiful,' Sarah said as she fastened the necklace of large pearls that had been Charles's wedding gift to his bride around Arabella's throat. 'My brother does not know how fortunate he is to have you, dearest Belle.'

'She is always beautiful,' Lady Tate said and sniffed, dabbing at her eyes with a lace kerchief.

'Do not cry, Aunt,' Arabella said. 'Or I shall cry too and that would be foolish. I am too happy to cry. It is my wedding day and I am marrying the man I love.'

'Charles was so nervous last night,' Sarah said, a teasing light in her eyes. 'He kept telling me things. I think he was afraid that you might change your mind and run off, Belle.'

'Oh, no, he could not think it,' Arabella said, laughing. She had taken a reluctant farewell of him the previous afternoon, just before he went to the inn, because she had not wanted to part from him even for a few hours; but the tradition was that he should not see his bride on the morning of their wedding day, before they met at church. 'He knows that I would never do that, Sarah.'

'Well, perhaps not run off,' Sarah admitted with a smile. 'But he was nervous. It isn't at all like him. He was always my confident big brother, lording it over me—but so protective and kind.' She gave Arabella a hug. 'I am so glad that you are marrying Charles, Belle. Two of my favourite people making each other happy.'

Arabella smiled, but before she could answer the door opened and Tilda entered, carrying a posy of wild roses.

'Oh, Tilda, wherever did you get them?' Arabella cried.

'There were a few left in the woods,' Tilda said, looking smug because Arabella was obviously so pleased. 'You look lovely, Arabella. I came to tell you that the carriages are starting to take everyone to church. Lady Hernshaw is just finishing her *toilette* and will join you in a moment…'

Even as she spoke, the door opened again and Melinda came in. She handed Arabella a white leather prayer book tied with blue ribbons.

'Something old, something blue,' she said and kissed Arabella's cheek. 'You look wonderful, dearest Belle. Charles Hunter is very lucky and so I shall tell him later.'

'Thank you, Mel, but I think he knows. We both know how lucky we are to have found one another.' Her eyes were misty as she smiled at her friend. 'I am so very happy.'

Her announcement was greeted with kisses and laughter from the other ladies, and, since Arabella was ready, they all left the room and walked along the landing together. Tilda and Sarah lifted the short train of her gown to stop it getting dirty or snagging as she walked.

Below in the hall the whole household had gathered to watch and there was a little burst of applause as Arabella seemed to float elegantly down the stairs in her gorgeous gown. She was greeted by Mrs Bristol, who gave a little speech about how happy they all were to see her going to be married. She thanked them and then went out to the waiting carriages.

Several workers from the estate had gathered outside to watch her leave and there was more cheering and clapping. As her only near relative, Lady Tate had claimed the right to assume the privilege of giving her away, and they got into the front carriage. Sarah, Mrs Hunter and Tilda followed in the second, and a third took up Mrs Bristol and some of the other servants. Mrs Bristol would see them married and then return to the house to prepare for the guests. It was not to be a huge reception, merely a few neighbours and close friends, but it would be all the happier for that and everything had been arranged exactly the same as if they had invited the cream of society.

It was but a short drive to the church. Arabella was soon entering the beautiful old building with her aunt and friends. It was filled to capacity with her guests and people from the estate and the village, who had squeezed in at the back to see her married.

Arabella saw only the man who waited at the end of the long aisle for her to take her place at his side. He turned his head and watched her walk towards him, smiling at her as she reached where he stood with John. Arabella turned and gave her posy to Sarah and her prayer book to Tilda, who were her bridesmaids.

She was aware that sunlight streamed through a high window, shedding a spray of colour on to the stone flags of the church floor, and of the Vicar's voice as he performed the service that made them man and wife. Yet it seemed to be a dream that enfolded her, a little unreal, and she could not quite believe that it was happening until Charles slipped his ring onto her finger, and then, at the Vicar's bidding, lifted the veil of her head-dress to kiss her.

And then, suddenly, it was all very real. They went into the vestry to sign the registry and then she was walking back down the aisle on her husband's arm to the sound of church bells. Outside, the sun was warm on her head as they stood to be showered with rose petals and receive small gifts of flowers and good luck charms from friends and villagers alike.

Arabella was laughing when at last they were allowed to escape to their carriage, which was to drive them back to the house for the wedding reception. Charles had brought in extra cooks so that the villagers and estate workers could enjoy their own feast while the invited guests were entertained to a splendid buffet. The champagne flowed as bride and groom mingled with their friends, and then went outside to hear themselves toasted by all the people who lived and worked on the estate.

'You look so beautiful, my love,' Charles whispered, pulling her into his arms as they returned to the house and were for a moment alone. 'I cannot wait to have you to myself.'

'Soon, my dearest,' Arabella promised as she gave herself up to his kiss. 'Soon we shall be alone together—and we have the rest of our lives to love each other and be happy.'

Arabella woke, stretching as she felt a sense of well being. She was relaxed, content, and, as she felt the hardness of her husband's body lying by her side, she smiled, snuggling up to him. She loved the scent of his warm flesh, the slightly salty taste of his lips as she bent her head and kissed him. It was a light kiss, meant to leave him sleeping, but his arms closed about her suddenly, pulling her down to his chest.

She laughed and reached out to touch her finger to his cheek. 'I thought you were asleep, Charles.'

'I have been awake for some minutes,' he replied, his hand stroking down the smooth, silky arch of her back, pressing her closer to him. 'But you were sleeping and I did not want to wake you. You looked so beautiful. I was afraid to touch you in case you disappeared.'

'Did you think it was all a dream?' she asked and took his hand in hers. 'You have such lovely hands,' she murmured. 'When you touch me I feel so alive.'

'You are alive—the most vibrant, exciting woman I have ever known.'

'I wasn't alive until I met you,' Arabella said. 'Not truly so, Charles. After Ben died, I built a wall around my heart. Oh, I cared for others, but I did not allow myself to think of loving or being loved in this way. I believed that that part of my life was over.'

'Tell me,' he said giving her a wicked, teasing smile, 'when did you fall in love with me? I think for me it was in London, when I found that I was thinking of you every moment—even though I thought that I had no right to happiness.'

'I loved you long before that,' Arabella said. 'It was when you had a fever and I nursed you, bathed your body to cool you when you were so hot…and I saw how beautiful you were. I realised then that I was lonely, but I told myself that I was foolish and that we should never meet again. That day in the park I wanted you to kiss me and…do all the things we did last night.'

'You are a wanton wench, my love,' Charles said and laughed as he rolled her beneath him in the bed. He began to kiss her, taking his time, teasingly, sweetly, his hand stroking and caressing so that the passion flamed between them once more. 'And that, my darling Belle, is exactly how I want you.'

'Oh, Charles,' Arabella protested, but her words were lost in the heat of delight as they came together once more in sweet harmony, their bodies moving together in the slow, intoxicating dance of love.

\* \* \*

Afterwards, Arabella lay luxuriating in the feeling of having been well loved, her limbs relaxed, her mind at peace, knowing that she was happier than she had ever expected to be—perhaps happier than she had ever been. She had been still a child when she married Ben, but now she was a woman, an ardent, caring woman who had known sorrow and was all the stronger for it, a woman who loved and was loved.

'I love you so much,' she said as he lay with his arm still about her, holding her close. 'We are so lucky Charles. I wish…' She sighed and shook her head as if she did not quite know how to go on.'

He leaned up on one elbow to gaze down at her, his eyes serious. 'What do you wish, my love? There are no regrets?'

'None at all,' she told him. 'I could not be better. I was thinking of Sarah, wondering whether she will ever find the happiness we have together, Charles. I love her as my sister and I cannot help but think of her.'

'Sarah will travel to Italy, and perhaps there she will find herself again,' Charles said. 'You know that I would do anything for her, Belle—but she told me that she needs to find her own way. John would have asked her to be his wife, and I think he truly cares for her, but she told him that she does not wish to marry yet—that she may never wish it.'

'Poor John,' Arabella said. 'Love is such a strange thing, Charles. It comes when it chooses and one cannot force it.'

'That is true,' he said. 'To find real love is a blessed thing. I pray that my sister will be blessed as we are one day, but only she can find her way to that special place, Belle. You saved her life and perhaps her sanity. Only Sarah can know what she wants to make of herself.'

'Yes, I know,' Arabella said and smiled as she nestled up to his chest once more. 'I am so glad that she came to us, Charles. Had she not stumbled into Nana's cottage that night, we might never have found each other.'

'That is very possible,' he agreed, a faint echo of remembered grief in his eyes. 'For had I not found her, I must have gone on looking for as long as it took…' He pulled Arabella closer, his throat tight with emotion as he stroked her silky skin. 'I thank God for the gift He gave me in you, my darling— and I pray that He will give happiness to my sister one day.'

'I think perhaps He will,' Arabella said and smiled. 'And now, my love, I think we must get up—unless you wish to stay in bed all day?'

Charles's answer was lost as he kissed her.

# *Afterword*

Sarah stood looking out of the window of her bedchamber at the sea. They were staying at an inn in Portsmouth, and had been for two days while they waited for the weather to settle. At the moment, it looked stormy and black, for it was a wild day, the wind whipping the waves into peaks of foam. She shivered, feeling that the sea was a hostile environment, and glad that they were not due to sail that day.

Restless, and unsure of her own feelings, she moved away from the window, discouraged by the view. Her lovely eyes were sad, her face paler than it should be for one so young and pretty. Being cooped up here was making her feel ill at ease, reminding her of things she would rather forget.

At the moment she was sharing a room with Tilda, and she understood that they were to share a cabin when they went on board. Sarah did not mind—they got on well enough these days, and it would be only a short trip across the Channel to France. From there they would travel on by carriage. Besides, Tilda had changed since her abduction, becoming less timid and more friendly. She found it easier to talk to Tilda about certain things than to her own mother.

Sarah had remembered everything, apart from what had happened between running away from the cottage she had been taken to by someone who had tried to help her and waking up in Nana's bed. She did not have the nightmares now, and Arabella had told her that probably nothing much had happened during that period—but Sarah still felt nervous around men. It was bearable with her brother and John Elworthy, but if other men stared at her she felt uncomfortable, almost frightened. She knew that it was foolish to have this irrational fear, but she could not help herself. It made her reserved, cool in her manner whenever gentlemen were present—and yet even that did nothing to deter them staring at her.

It had happened the previous evening when they were at supper in the parlour downstairs. They had hired the parlour for their exclusive use, but a man had wandered in while they were eating, clearly a little the worse for strong drink. By his clothes he was a gentleman, but his eyes were bold and the look in them as he saw Sarah had sent shivers down her spine. Sir Montague Forsythe had looked at her in that way when he'd forced her to drink the drugged wine. It made her feel vulnerable, afraid, almost as though he was stripping away her clothes with his eyes.

Sarah knew that her mother hoped that she would marry one day, would find happiness with someone. John had wanted to ask her to be his wife, but she had forestalled him, telling him that she did not believe she would ever wish to be any man's wife. The hurt and grief in his eyes had almost made her change her mind. For a moment she had wanted to tell him that she would marry him—if he could be patient. But that would not be fair to him. John was a good man, a truly gentle man. She knew that he deserved more than she could give him at this moment. Perhaps she would never be able to offer him the kind of love he wanted from her.

'I wish…' Sarah smothered a sob. 'I wish that it had never happened.'

If she had never been stolen from her home, never experienced the trauma of abduction…never seen that naked man bending over her and the evidence of his arousal…perhaps she might even now be married to John. A part of her longed for it, for the closeness of sharing, the joy of holding a child in her arms—something that must be for ever denied her if she did not marry.

'Sarah…' She turned at the sound of her mother's voice, forcing herself to smile as if nothing was wrong. 'Are you coming down, dearest? I thought we would go shopping as the voyage has been delayed. They say that the weather will clear tomorrow. I am looking forward to our trip—aren't you, my love?'

'Oh, yes, very much,' Sarah said. 'I do not like these grey skies, Mama. The sea looks angry at the moment, but when the sun shines again it will be different.'

'Everything will be different in Italy,' Mrs Hunter promised. 'You will see, my love. After a few months in the sunshine of Italy all the bad things that happened to you will seem like a distant dream. You will learn to be happy again.'

'Yes, of course I shall,' Sarah said. 'I am sorry to have kept you waiting. I shall put on my pelisse and come down at once.'

She lifted her head, courage returning as she thought of

Belle and Charles. They had found happiness against the odds, and there was no reason why she should not find it too.

'Everything will be better when we get to Italy,' Sarah said, because she knew that her mother was anxious. And, as hope surged in her heart, she believed it was true. She had been hurt, but she was still alive and she would learn to be happy again.

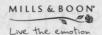

# THE STEEPWOOD

# *Scandals*

### *Regency drama, intrigue, mischief...*
### *and marriage*

### VOLUME FIVE

*Counterfeit Earl* by Anne Herries

Scarred after his experiences in the Peninsular War,
Captain Jack Denning feels unable to love. But caught
in a compromising situation with excitement-seeking
Olivia, a proposal is the only option!

*The Captain's Return* by Elizabeth Bailey

Captain Henry Colton is stunned to find his lost love
living as a widow. Given the way they had parted, in
anger, could he now expect Annabel to let him
back into her life?

## On sale 2nd March 2007

*Available at WHSmith, Tesco, ASDA,*
*and all good bookshops*

*A young woman disappears.*
*A husband is suspected of murder.*
*Stirring times for all the neighbourhood in*

# THE STEEPWOOD
# *Scandals*

### Volume 5 – March 2007
*Counterfeit Earl* by Anne Herries
*The Captain's Return* by Elizabeth Bailey

### Volume 6 – April 2007
*The Guardian's Dilemma* by Gail Whitiker
*Lord Exmouth's Intentions* by Anne Ashley

### Volume 7 – May 2007
*Mr Rushford's Honour* by Meg Alexander
*An Unlikely Suitor* by Nicola Cornick

### Volume 8 – June 2007
*An Inescapable Match* by Sylvia Andrew
*The Missing Marchioness* by Paula Marshall

# FREE

## 2 BOOKS AND A SURPRISE GIFT!

We would like to take this opportunity to thank you for reading this Mills & Boon® book by offering you the chance to take TWO more specially selected titles from the Historical Romance™ series absolutely FREE! We're also making this offer to introduce you to the benefits of the Mills & Boon® Reader Service™—

- ★ **FREE home delivery**
- ★ **FREE gifts and competitions**
- ★ **FREE monthly Newsletter**
- ★ **Books available before they're in the shops**
- ★ **Exclusive Reader Service offers**

Accepting these FREE books and gift places you under no obligation to buy; you may cancel at any time, even after receiving your free shipment. Simply complete your details below and return the entire page to the address below. You don't even need a stamp!

**YES!** Please send me 2 free Historical Romance books and a surprise gift. I understand that unless you hear from me, I will receive 4 superb new titles every month for just £3.69 each, postage and packing free. I am under no obligation to purchase any books and may cancel my subscription at any time. The free books and gift will be mine to keep in any case.

H7ZEE

Ms/Mrs/Miss/Mr......................................Initials ................................................
**BLOCK CAPITALS PLEASE**

Surname ....................................................................................................................

Address ....................................................................................................................

....................................................................................................................................

..............................................................Postcode ................................

Send this whole page to:
The Reader Service, FREEPOST CN81, Croydon, CR9 3WZ